AN AMERICAN
WITCH IN PARIS

MICHELE HAUF

MILLS & BOON

First Published in Great Britain 2018
by Mills & Boon, an imprint of HarperCollins*Publishers*
1 London Bridge Street, London, SE1 9GF

An American Witch In Paris © 2018 Michele Hauf

ISBN: 978-0-263-26675-7

49-0318

MIX
Paper from
responsible sources
FSC™ C007454

This book is produced from independently certified FSC™
paper to ensure responsible forest management.

For more information visit: www.harpercollins.co.uk/green

Printed and bound in Spain
by CPI, Barcelona

This one is for the witch in me.
And it's for the witch in you.
Honor your soul for what it has been,
is now and will be. Namaste.

Chapter 1

Ethan Pierce stood before a steel-barred cage in the Acquisitions department's clean room. He was the director of the department, which was responsible for hunting, collecting and containing objects of magical nature, dangerous curses and talismans, even volatile creatures that may prove harmful to common humans if left unmonitored in the mortal realm. Ethan sent retrievers out on jobs that canvassed the world, and those adventuring professionals returned with the items.

This latest acquisition, brought in hours earlier by the retriever Bron Everhart, was needed to help locate an even more important item. For what Acquisitions ultimately sought was the blood demon Gazariel, who had stolen the code for the Final Days. If that code was to be activated, all the angels from Above would fall and smother the mortal realm with their smoldering wings. Literally. And the only way to find the demon was with the one thing in this world that wore its sigil.

"A witch," Ethan muttered as he paced before the cage.

Behind the steel bars, which were warded to keep in the subject, yet also wired with electricity to keep her docile and hamper any magic she should attempt to use in defense, stood the witch. She was a head shorter than Ethan, thin and dressed in clingy black leggings, fierce-looking black ankle boots with high heels and a silky black shirt that revealed a toned abdomen. Over it all she wore a heavy coat made of what looked like fake gray fur, which was studded with silver and black spangles. Her long white hair spilled forward, concealing one eye, and fell messily over one shoulder to her waist.

The other eye held him intently. It was a blue eye, the iris circled with black as if someone had drawn those eyes to be colored in. And on her eyelids, black shadow granted plenty Gothic melodrama. All together the look was…

Wicked, Ethan thought.

Hatred was too strong a word to apply to his feelings about witches as a species. Not all witches were evil or malicious. Yet he'd never completely get over his dislike for witches. They'd once held a murderous reign over his species, vampires, when their blood had been poisonous. One dip of the fang into a witch's vein could bring an ugly and permanent death. That was no longer. The Great Protection Spell, which had turned all witches' blood poisonous, had been broken decades earlier.

Rationally, Ethan knew not all witches were dangerous. And besides, it was the twenty-first century.

Things had changed. He worked with a few witches here at Acquisitions and the overseeing department, the Archives. For the most part, witches of the light were safe and trustworthy.

But the dark witches, such as the one standing in the cage before him? A shudder traced Ethan's spine.

The witch didn't move, only held his gaze, as if breaking it might arrest her breathing. And he wasn't about to look away. He must show her his dominance. In order to work with the witch to find the demon, she must be kept under control. Subdued. Yet her magic should remain accessible, which would keep the sigil she supposedly wore somewhere on her body open and ready to lure in the demon Gazariel.

Capturing this specific demon would prove a challenge. All perfunctory means of tracking him through Acquisitions' database had turned up nothing, though intel revealed that he was definitely in Paris.

Upon receiving orders to obtain the missing Final Days code—from a highly unprecedented command— Ethan had considered all the dozens of retrievers he had on staff. Who could do the job? Most were currently on assignment. None were stationed in Paris at the moment. But that wasn't the problem; any retriever was available and on call 24/7, able to move about worldwide.

The problem was that blood magic may be required to hold the demon once found. And the best one to deal with such magic? A vampire. Of which Ethan had been since his birth in the 1500s. Of course, he wasn't willing to give his own blood for this mission, but he didn't expect he would have to. He'd learned once that his blood could have a devastating effect on another being.

He never made the same mistake twice.

It had been decades, maybe even close to a century, since Ethan had gone out on a job. He'd become complacent, sitting behind a desk, clacking away at reports on the laptop and ordering others around. He loved his job. He did it well.

And yet, the call to adventure, to get out and actually participate in life again, was too strong to resist. He'd once stood alongside his fellow warrior vampires in the Blood Wars of the sixteenth century, defeating werewolves and slaying random witches who would deign to assist the nasty wolves. Then, he had been undefeatable, powerful and virile. He still was. The urge to exercise his soul beyond the paperwork and office politics was strong.

So Ethan had assigned this job to himself. His knowledge on the various demon breeds was minimal, yet he knew Paris, and more importantly, had the determination to root out the target. And he was the perfect partner for a witch. He wouldn't fall under her spell or forget for one moment who or what he was dealing with.

A dark witch who wore the demon Gazariel's mark.

The deflecting vibrations coming off the steel bars were strong, electronic in nature, but Tuesday didn't allow that to bother her. Yet. What was more disturbing was how she'd just been sitting in a bar, nursing a pink Panty Dropper cocktail, and then the world had gone black. And now she was standing in a cage.

Had someone roofied her? She always wore protective wards to deflect any silly human trick. And a clasp of the obsidian crystal that hung from a leather cord around her neck and above her breasts confirmed they hadn't removed her grounding and protective wards. That could only mean someone with power greater than hers—and was aware of who and what she was—had been able to drug her, kidnap her and cage her.

And while that realization was humiliating she had to remain calm and focused. She wasn't about to let the vampire see her sweat. *No weakness here, buddy.*

She knew the man was vampire because his red, ashy aura gave him away. Very few witches had the Sight— an ability to see vampire auras. Tuesday found it more of a nuisance. There were so many vampires walking the world. Sometimes the frequency of red glows in large, overcrowded cities annoyed her. Seriously. The biters were everywhere.

Not that there was anything wrong with vamps. Every once in a while, she didn't mind the occasional bite with a side of no-strings sex.

The vampire had been observing her for a few minutes. Hadn't said a word. He'd strode into the large, steel-walled, hexagon-shaped room, which only contained the cage and her, and had turned on the lights, which were blue LEDs along the floors and one blindingly white overhead spotlight.

He shoved his hands in the front pockets of his clean black jeans, which fit well, and were tucked into his combat boots. His shirtsleeves were rolled up to the elbows to display muscled forearms dusted with dark hair to match the slicked and cropped hair on his head. From under the shirt, a glimpse of a gray T-shirt hung over his pants. He looked to be strong, a force. And his carriage screamed of discipline, perhaps even military.

A smartly trimmed beard hugged his jaw and a neat mustache framed his solemn mouth. Sprinkled under his lower lip were gray strands amongst the dark brown. His face was expressionless, yet his gray eyes saw everything.

Her unprofessional assessment said that he looked world-weary. Like he'd been doing this far too long and needed a break. Although, what it was that he'd been doing, exactly, she had no clue.

"I'm Ethan Pierce," he finally said. His voice was deep and not unfriendly, and while he used English, he had a noticeable French accent. Tuesday had known a few Frenchmen in her lifetime. She'd visited France a couple times over the centuries.

"And you are Tuesday Knightsbridge," he stated.

He didn't score points for knowing her name. Unless kidnapping random witches was a thing nowadays.

Maintaining her stance, Tuesday held his gaze. But now he swept his eyes back and forth, and his hands slid out of his pockets to clasp before him. Classic villain hand-twist pose? Check, please!

"Do you know where you are?" he asked.

She wasn't ready to speak. Of course she knew where she was. She stood in a frigging cage.

"Not talking? I can deal with that. For now. You are in a holding cell at Acquisitions. We're a division of the Council's Archives."

The Council? That was a supposedly nonviolent ruling board that oversaw the actions of the world's paranormal nations, and was composed of various species to represent most. But they were watchers; they never interfered.

Guess that was a myth.

"In Paris," he said.

Paris? What the—? She'd been flown across the

ocean, from her current residence of Boston, Massachusetts, to France?

Anger rising, Tuesday lunged forward, gripping the steel bars. Vicious electricity zapped at her fingers, and she released them, taking the brunt of the shocking force through her body. She was violently tossed backward to land on her ass in the center of the cage. Legs splayed, she shook off a shiver. Her fur coat slipped down her shoulders to her wrists. She sucked in a gulp of air.

The man smirked. "By the way, those bars are activated."

Tuesday flicked up the sign of the Devil and growled, "Be taken to Beneath!"

"She speaks. And with a curse, of all things. I would expect nothing less from a dark witch. But the cage is warded. As is this clean room. No magic can get in or out. Nice try, though."

Oh, he wanted a curse? Utterly incensed, Tuesday spread out her fingers and focused a stream of magic at the man's crotch. *"Languidulus!"*

While normally invisible, once her magic hit the cage bars, a shot of violet light bounced off and splintered in dying pink embers onto the cage floor.

"What was that?" The vampire's smirk was annoyingly sexy. "Another curse? Did you try to give me a tail?"

Tuesday smiled nicely and tilted her head. "Actually, I cursed your dick to forever remain limp. And my magic is much stronger than you can imagine. I'd invest in Viagra, if I were you." She winked at him.

The slightest flinch moved the corner of one of his eyes. Bull's-eye. She could get under the man's skin. With mere words. This predicament was going to prove an easy escape. She just had to dig under his outer machismo to access the key.

But Paris? That meant she'd been out, at the very least, for eight or nine hours. And moved around according to this bastard's will. Not cool.

"What the hell is the benevolent Council doing sending someone to kidnap me?" she asked. Standing, her heels clicked on the cage floor. She shook out the alpaca fur coat she wore over black leggings and a comfy shirt. The coat was spangled in warding designs. A Tibetan monk had initially made it for her. A glitter sidhe-witch had sewn on the wards a few years ago. "And who the fuck is Ethan Pierce?"

"I'm the director of Acquisitions. We acquire things that need to be locked away. Behind chains and wards."

"And you think *I* need to be locked away?" She flipped him the bird. Yeah, so it wasn't a hex. Some common gestures were much more to the point.

"Actually, Acquisitions needs you to get to what we really want."

"Which is?"

"The blood demon Gazariel."

Tuesday's hand slapped across her chest, below the obsidian crystal. Though rarely spoken, the sound of that demon's name always provoked such an action. She could feel his sigil burn her skin under the silk shirt.

"We know you wear the demon's sigil," Ethan explained. "Got it in the seventeenth century, if our records are accurate. Will you show it to me?"

She wouldn't give him anything. Not until she heard what weird and strange plans he—they; Acquisitions?—had for her.

"The sigil is some kind of blood curse, yes?" He

paced a few steps to the side then turned back to her. "Doesn't matter how you got it. Or what it does. But I've been told, because of your connection to the demon, it makes you one of the darkest of the dark witches. I don't like dark witches, by the way."

"Would have never guessed. Your hosting skills are severely lacking. And I don't care what the hell you are, Pierce, I don't like you."

"I'm vampire."

"I knew that." She sneered. "A flesh pricker. Who is also a Richard."

"A… Richard?" The man narrowed his eyes and shrugged in question.

"Think about it a bit," she offered. He'd get it, sooner or later. "So you think you have the right to pluck any old witch off the streets and force her to do your bidding?"

"I wouldn't use the word *force*. But you are old, aren't you?"

His self-satisfied smirk did not rile her. Too much. Age was relative when a person had immortality; he should know that. She snapped the rubber band she wore about her wrist. The man would not like to see her dark magic in all its wicked glory.

"You have been brought to Paris to assist us in locating Gazariel."

The sigil she'd worn since the seventeenth century burned over her skin. "Quit saying that name," she insisted. "You only grant the demon more power with each utterance. Do you know that?"

Apparently he did not.

The man hung his head for a few seconds, then looked up at her. "I know my demon lore. Basically.

The saying a name three times thing generally only works with Himself. Demons are much more slippery when it comes to summoning them. Which is why you are here in Paris."

Paris! She could not believe this.

"Now, you'll serve to lure the demon to us—me, since I'm in charge of this mission—and then I will obtain from him what we seek to contain."

"The demon has something you want?"

He nodded. "It's dangerous to all. In the demon's hands, the world could be destroyed."

Tuesday scoffed. Always so dramatic with the end-of-the-world crap. It was never a small portion of the world, but the whole thing. What kind of villain would even think to destroy a world he would like to remain on to rule? The demon couldn't rule anything if he didn't have followers to bow down to him. End of the world, her ass.

But then she considered what she knew about Gazariel. He was a trickster. His title was The Beautiful One. Because he was a pretty bit of charm and allure. Vain and self-serving, as well. And deadly. He liked to take advantage of a person when they were at their lowest, defeated. But most importantly, he was an asshole. And she didn't want to get any closer to him than she already was. Wearing his sigil did not make her his bitch—so long as she kept her distance from him.

"So let me get this straight." She walked up to the bars until the shock waves from the wards teased at her skin and lifted the hairs in her pores. Must have been warded by another dark witch with a tech edge. It messed with her personal vibrations, so she took a step back and, with a thought, pulled a white light over herself. All she could manage in this damnable cage was a weak veil, but it gave her some solace. "You want to dangle me before the demon as bait?"

The man tapped a finger against his jaw, then nodded. "Yes, that's about it."

She turned and paced in a half arc, hands to her hips, head down in thought. A glance to the man's face found him stoic, trying to show her he would not back down, no matter what. Tough guy, pushing around a helpless woman. Been there, done that. Never going to let it happen again.

If she should refuse him, he would force her. And enjoy it. Typical male.

But he didn't know Tuesday Knightsbridge at all. Helplessness was not a condition she had ever ascribed to. And that would give her the upper hand.

"Sounds like fun," she said cheerily. "Let's do it."

Chapter 2

Another man entered the clean room and Tuesday immediately felt familiar vibrations flow off of him. Another dark witch. He was tall and lean, and everything about him was black, from his long straight hair and thin mustache to his clothing. Spell tattoos covered his hands and exposed neck. A coil of thin rope was attached to his hip holster à la the Wild West. Weird. Also, he wasn't wearing shoes.

"You've got her in a cage?" he said to the vampire. "What the hell?"

"She's dangerous," Ethan said.

Yeah, and don't forget it, buddy. But Tuesday didn't say that.

Instead she crossed her arms and stood in the cage center, taking in her opponents. The dark one was on alert in his movements as he walked around the cage as if sizing up an animal. Shame threatened to rise up in her. She'd been made to feel like less than dirt many times before. Always by those who claimed witches were foul and evil things, and who would seek to allay their shortcomings and misguided beliefs by harming her. But that had been centuries ago.

Would this world never get a clue and drop the old, ingrained prejudices?

"This is Certainly Jones," Ethan said to her. "He's head of the Archives and our resident dark witch."

"Are you okay? Have you been treated well?" Certainly asked her. A touch of British accented his voice, and his tone felt calming.

"I've been kidnapped. Most likely drugged. I'm hungry. And I have to pee," she offered. "How's tricks with you?"

He stopped before the front of the cage and looked over his shoulder at the militant vampire. "You should feed her. And let her go to the bathroom."

"As soon as we've shackled her, she can do whatever she desires."

"Shackle?" Tuesday closed her eyes, fisting her fingers at her sides. "What the hell is going on?"

"We need you to work for us. You've agreed, saying it would be fun," Ethan said. "But in order to work alongside me you'll have to be out of this cage. And I can't risk you running off or using your magic against me. CJ here has a simple shackle spell that'll keep you subdued."

"You are a—" She lunged, aiming to grasp through the cage bars, but too late, she remembered it was electrified. The jolt sent her flying backward again to land on her back in a sprawl. "I hate you!"

"I don't need you to like me. I just need you to help me find Gazariel."

"Stop saying that bastard's name," she said from her position on the floor. Humiliated and utterly exhausted, she wasn't about to pull herself up until he gave her a good reason to do so.

"Saying the demon's name won't invoke him," Certainly said.

"I know that. I just hate his name. You think the two of us were friends? That's why I'm wearing his sigil?" Letting her head fall back, she flipped them both the bird from the floor.

"She's definitely going to be a handful," Certainly commented. "Open the cage and let me in. I've got this rope bespelled to shackle her."

The dark witch was coming inside with her? Well… she wasn't in the mood to fight him. And he thought to shackle her with a rope spell? That wasn't going to go as successfully for him as he expected. Tuesday decided to play along. Just for giggles.

The bars suddenly flickered with static and then Tuesday felt the electric energy shut off. The cage door swung open with a creak. She remained splayed on the floor as the dark witch stepped up into the cage and padded over and stood above her. The door closed and she heard the vampire twist the lock then tap in a digital code.

"I'm sorry about this," Certainly said. "I know you didn't ask for this, but sometimes things have to be done to ensure worse things don't happen."

"Now you're going to tell me not to blame you and that we can all get along, right? Peace, love and 'Kum-

baya'? Get it done with, witch. I do need to use the fa-
cilities."

"Will you stand, please?"

Tuesday held up her hand and gestured for him to
grab it to help her stand. As he did so, she felt his magic
jolt against her own. He was strong, but not as powerful
as her. But he was cute, and she had a plan, so she was
going to let him off easy. Mostly. And hell, she wasn't
sure she could even invoke her magic inside this crazy
warded cage. But she wouldn't be Tuesday Knightsbridge if she didn't give it a go.

She slapped her palms to his temples and fixed her
gaze onto his intense jade eyes. Before he knew to look
away she fixed onto his soul. It was a witch's skill, to
hold a soul fix on another witch. She felt his inner struggle, his need to close his eyes and lock her out. But she
had been doing this far too long to allow anyone escape
from her delving soul gaze.

The witch's soul was dark to the core. Less than two
centuries old, he'd walked a free and defiant path. He
was…connected closely to another. A twin? Yes, he
had a twin brother for whom he held great love and respect. He'd once carried dozens of demons within him
after a trip to Daemonia. Some of those demons had
made him hurt himself. Others had taught him to care
more deeply than he could have fathomed. And…the
man loved deeply. Another witch, who was mother to
his one-year-old twin sons.

That feeling, the emotion of unconditional love that
flooded the man's system, pricked at Tuesday's will-
power. She winced, fearing what may happen should
she allow herself to linger in his eyes. To fall into the
deep and devastating emotion of love.

Tuesday released the man and he stumbled backward, catching himself before he hit the bars.

"What did she do to you?" Ethan asked from outside the cage.

"I'm…fine," Certainly said, catching his hands on his knees and huffing. It took a lot out of a person to have his soul tapped. "She just…"

"I looked into his soul," Tuesday explained to Ethan. "I like this one. He's strong." She pointed at the vampire. "You. I do not like."

"We've already discussed our mutual lack of admiration for one another. *Like* isn't a requirement to work together. You going to be okay, CJ?"

The dark witch nodded. "Yep. Just gathering back my wits." He straightened and snapped the simple rope before him in warning. "You going to behave?"

Tuesday nodded. "I saw your wife. You love her very much."

"I would die for her," Certainly said with an ease that tugged at Tuesday's hardened heart. Because she believed that he would. What a lucky woman.

Romantics and silly sops would have a person believe love was the be-all and end-all. Whatever.

"Get on with it."

She held her hands before her, wrists together, waiting to be bound. The rope wouldn't impact her movement or physical health. It would keep her from performing any sort of magic, hex, spell or charm. But if the rope was damaged after the spell had been cast…

"On second thought," she said, "it'll work better if you drape it across my chest."

"Across your heart," Certainly said. "Good idea. And you will need the use of your hands." He lowered the lariat over her head and rested it on a shoulder, then draped it across her heart to fall between her breasts. "You're going to have to remove the crystal."

"I never take it off."

"The spell won't fix otherwise."

She shook her head and clasped the cool obsidian.

"Do you want to get out of here?" Certainly asked.

"Did they drug me?" she asked quietly. "Just tell me what they used to incapacitate me."

"I don't know for sure. Henbane, possibly?"

Tuesday nodded. Henbane, when mixed with a vile adjuvant, could take out a witch for the better part of a day. Damn it! Her wards should have caught that.

Certainly Jones could prove an ally if she played her cards right. But for now she must submit in order to gain freedom. She pulled the leather cord from around her neck and handed it to him. "That must be returned to me immediately."

"It will. You'll be able to wear it after I've cast the spell." He tucked the crystal in his front pocket, then jumped a little in reaction.

"It's not yours to possess," Tuesday warned. "It will come back to me quickly."

"I get that." He tapped the rope. "This will shackle your magic only against Ethan Pierce. You will still be able to wield magic in all other instances. It may be necessary to protect yourself against the demon."

"I appreciate that. What the hell is that guy?"

Certainly looked over a shoulder. Ethan paced, arms across his chest.

"Vampire."

"I know that. I mean, what's his deal? He's so…angry."

"Really? This coming from the angriest witch I've ever met?"

"You guys *did* kidnap me."

"Point taken. Don't give Pierce such a hard time. He generally works behind the desk telling others what to do. But I think this time it's personal."

"How so?"

Certainly shrugged. "Not sure. And even if I did have a clue? That's for him to give to you, not me. Close your eyes."

Tuesday did so because she was tired and wanted to get out of this stupid cage. Much as shackling her magic against anyone would piss her off, at the very least he wasn't completely disabling her.

The witch chanted a spell that caused the rope to suddenly squeeze about her. She felt the sigil beneath her shirt warm and reach out for the rope. It didn't like being controlled. Which was a good thing. And she counted on its retaliation.

In a matter of moments the witch said, "So mote it be."

And the rope fell slack again, as if an ill-hung necklace. Tuesday let out a breath. Her skin tingled, but otherwise, she didn't feel any different. In the next instant, the obsidian on the cord flew out from the witch's pocket and landed smartly in Tuesday's grasp.

The cage door opened and Ethan asked, "How will we know it worked?"

"It worked." CJ stepped out of the cage. "My magic always works." He winked at Tuesday. "I'm sorry, but the rope is the shackle. You'll have to figure out your own style for that." He turned to Ethan. "You going to take her upstairs for a bit, then…off to adventure?"

The men shared a look that was a few seconds too long for Tuesday not to wonder what had gone unspoken.

"Right," Ethan suddenly said. "I've got some things to finish up in the office. Come on, witch."

"Really? You're going to let your new pet out on a leash?" She flopped the lariat around before her. "Aren't you the kindest master ever."

"Good luck," CJ said and wandered out of the room.

"Get out of the cage, witch."

She stepped up to the threshold. "My name is Tuesday. Treat me well and I will return the kindness."

Ethan nodded. "Lead me to the demon and I'll be more than grateful."

"I'm not going to lead you anywhere without cold hard cash."

"What?"

"You think I'm going to do this for nothing? Slavery went out last century. If you want me to cooperate we need to talk money." She jumped down onto the concrete floor, blessedly relieved to have left the smothering confines of that magic-busting cage. With a shiver and a flip of her hair over her shoulder, she walked up to the man.

He stood a head higher than her, but she was accustomed to looking up to people, mostly men. Her stance spoke louder than her lacking height.

"How much do you want?" he asked, surprising her that he hadn't argued.

"A million. US dollars, not your freaky French euros."

He broke out into throaty laughter that, in any other circumstance, might have grasped her by the lusting heart and teased her to flutter her lashes at him. But this was not any other time. With a flick of her forefinger, Tuesday tossed a beam of pain at the vampire.

The magic burst into a spray of violet sparks just inches from his face and dispersed.

Damn shackle.

"Good to see CJ's spell works," he said. "Tough luck, witch. I'm impervious to your magic now."

Only so long as the shackle stayed in place. And her sigil was so hot that it could burn through pretty much anything right now…

"Half a million then," she said.

"Ten grand."

Tuesday spun and jumped up into the cage opening. "I think I'll stay here then. Apparently, I'm the only one who can do what you need done. I'm worth more than a few bucks. You think about it, then get back to me."

"I've got a budget, witch."

"And I've got all the time in the world. Do you?"

He rubbed his stubble-shadowed jaw. Tuesday rather liked it when a man tickled his stubble over her skin, as his gaze journeyed down her stomach and lower. And his beard was frosted with a touch of grey in the dark brown, which added a delicious seasoning to his appearance. If the man wasn't so obstinate he'd actually be sexy.

"A hundred thousand," he offered. "That's as high as I can go."

"Deal." Tuesday jumped down again and marched past him toward the door. She would have taken the ten grand. "Let's get out of this dungeon. Did you forget I need to pee?"

The witch had gone into the private bathroom attached to the office Ethan occupied in headquarters. There were no windows in the small washroom for her to escape through, so he trusted her to shut the door.

Meanwhile, he checked his email. No new orders waiting for retrieval assignment. And he'd sent details regarding his taking this particular mission to the Council. No reply, so far, was good news.

He glanced to the maple-wood bathroom door. He and CJ had only planned things so far. And that plan hadn't quite come to complete fruition. It would, soon enough. He wasn't sure how he was going to work with the witch.

She was obstinate. A smart-ass. And he hadn't expected her to be gorgeous. Utterly beautiful. In a weird, silver Goth sort of way. Behind her defensive, smart mouth and angry rubber band-snapping machinations he felt sure a sensual goddess inhabited the irresistible curves and gemstone blue eyes.

He raked fingers through his hair and shook his head. What was he thinking? He needed to do this right. He was the boss. And he wasn't about to show weakness or failure to his employees by letting his thoughts stray from the task at hand.

He'd handle the witch with a strong hand and command. He had to stay on guard with her. To set an example for others. But it would prove a challenge, not only because of her odd appeal, but also because it had been so long since he'd actually worked a mission. If she learned that he was questioning his own abilities—and thus had taken the job to prove he wasn't washed up and was physically capable of handling such a mission—he'd never succeed.

They headed out, Tuesday following Ethan's sure gait. It was a confident walk. A sexy walk. After many turns and an elevator ride down four floors, the sight of a door up ahead gave her great glee. Soon.

She pressed her hand over the shackle rope, which she'd been holding snug against the sigil. The rope fibers were hot and smoldering. It was working.

"I don't live far from here. We'll walk," Ethan said.

He'd mentioned they would discuss a plan for capturing the demon. Why they didn't simply do it in his office was beyond her, but she appreciated the opportunity to get out of the building. And away.

He opened a heavy steel door. Bright daylight filtered in, making Tuesday blink. She had lost all concept of time, and even though her muscles were dragging her downward from exhaustion, the crisp winter air, inhaled deeply, worked to lighten her. And keep her focused. Tugging her coat closed, but keeping one hand inside on the shackling rope, she followed the vampire outside.

They exited into a narrow, cobblestone alleyway. Ethan turned left.

Tuesday turned right and started to run. She made it ten feet, pulling away the rope that had burned apart thanks to the demon sigil, and dropped it behind her. But as her speed increased and she began to pump her arms, her body collided with an invisible wall, slamming her backward to land in the arms of Ethan Pierce.

"I expected as much," he said. A flash of his bright smile did not give her any mirth. "So did CJ. The rope was merely a distraction until CJ had time to work up a stronger spell."

"Bastard," she muttered, and collapsed in his arms.

Chapter 3

The steel door through which they'd exited opened and the dark witch swung out with urgency. He lifted his hand, exposing the glowing spell tattoos that covered his palm. As he approached, he asked Ethan, "You sure about this, man?"

"Nope. But someone's got to do it. So do your darkest."

"Oh, no." Not knowing what was coming, but not stupid, either, Tuesday struggled out of Ethan's grasp.

The vampire stretched back an arm toward his approaching cohort while he managed to hold her by the coat with his other hand. She wasn't going to let whatever might happen…happen.

She began to speak a deflection spell, but a slash of Certainly's hand caused Tuesday's words to suddenly jumble and drop in the air. He'd deflected her deflection. He was stronger than she'd anticipated.

With his full body, the vampire crushed her against the brick wall. She kicked, unwilling to be contained. Suddenly, she smelled blood. What the—? The dark witch grabbed her wrist and an icy pain seared the center of her palm. A coppery scent filled the air. He was invoking blood magic?

"No!"

Kicking, Tuesday hit Ethan's gut, but the vampire lunged forward and slapped his hand into hers. Heat from his blood mingled with hers. The dark witch held their hands together and recited a simple incantation that she recognized as a binder.

Tuesday growled, but the exhaustion from what she'd been through since sitting in the bar—back in the United States—had depleted her magic. The blood spell coursed through her system, and she felt it bite at her neck from the inside. Certainly Jones's dark and masterful magic bound her to the vampire. They would not be able to leave one another's side, nor would they be able to harm one another.

"This is the only blood you'll ever get from me," the vampire said on a low, accusing tone.

With a shout for survival, Tuesday pushed away from her captor with a shove of her free hand to his chest. The dark witch stepped away, allowing her to stumble against the wall. She caught her hands flat on the rough brick behind her, cursed, then watched as the knife wound sealed in a glow of violet on her palm.

"Had to be done," Certainly commented.

"How close do we have to stay to one another now?" Ethan asked, as if he'd only been given a simple handshake.

"Not sure. Try it out."

"Try running off," Ethan said to her. "See how far you get."

"Try fucking yourself, vampire."

"Like I said, she's going to be a challenge," Certainly said.

"Challenge accepted. I'll start walking home," Ethan said. "We'll see how far I get before you have no choice but to follow." He slapped a hand into the dark witch's. "Thanks, CJ."

Ethan strolled off down the alley. And Tuesday tugged her coat up and adjusted her hair. She pointed an accusing finger at Certainly. "You, Jones, are on my shit list."

He shrugged. "I honor your power, Tuesday Knightsbridge. You are an old and strong witch. But I can feel your darkness is even greater than mine."

"Yeah? Warlock's looking pretty good right about now." If she grievously harmed another witch the warlock title would be slapped on her. "That would really put you in your place."

"As well, it would put you in a place you don't want to stand. Don't let it overwhelm you, Tuesday. Remember what you once were."

Really? The man was trying the New Age-y bullshit on her? "You know nothing about me."

"No, but I saw into your soul when you were looking into mine." He bowed his head toward her. "I am sorry for the things you have suffered because of what we are."

Yeah, so witches had been a favorite cat's-paw over the centuries. She'd survived, and she would continue to so do thanks to her hardened heart.

Suddenly, Tuesday's body jerked forward. Certainly stepped aside and they both looked down the alley. Ethan stood about fifty yards off. He gave them a thumbs-up.

And when he started walking again, Tuesday was pulled after him.

"Shit list!" she called back to Certainly, who had the decency to place his palms together and bow to her in reverence.

Ethan chuckled to himself as the witch reluctantly followed him down the street to his place in the eleventh arrondissement. He lived in a third-floor loft close to Père Lachaise cemetery, which boasted an excellent view of Sacré Coeur up on the hill.

He left the front door open behind him, not feeling the need to wait on the witch. She'd stand back just to piss him off, surely. He tossed his keys onto the gray granite kitchen counter and kicked off his shoes, then wandered through the living area. With a few words to the electronic house butler—"Stuart, modify for sun"—the electrochromic shades fixed between the double windowpanes that looked out over the city adjusted to a soft white that would allow in light but not the UV rays that gave him the most caution.

The layout of the loft was open—no walls, save the ones enclosing the bathroom. Strolling through the living room, around a corner and through the bedroom, he went into the bathroom but left the door open behind him. "Stuart, warm water." Ethan splashed water on his face, then manually twisted off the faucet and took a few deep breaths.

He opened his palm. The cut CJ had given him had already healed. Sharing blood with the witch hadn't been as horrible as he'd expected. Remnants of fear over the once-poisonous witch blood remained. He'd have to get over it. And fast. If the demon was a blood demon, surely much blood would be spilled in the coming days. The witch's. And the demon's. Ethan wasn't willing to give any more than the few drops he'd provided today.

He liked blood. As sustenance. But he never drank witch's blood, even since the Great Protection Spell had been broken. It couldn't harm him now. And there were even some vampires who liked drinking from witches. If you added in sex and a specific spell for bloodsex-magic, the vampire could steal some of that witch's magic for himself.

He had no desire to own magic. But to taste the witch's blood? He couldn't shake the scent of her blood as it had trickled into the air in the alley outside head-quarters. It had roused him so much in that moment that he'd used violence and had shoved her roughly to hide his burgeoning desires. He hoped she wouldn't bleed near him again.

That would prove a challenge.

"Honey, I'm home!"

He shook his head, but no reflection in the mirror showed his exasperation. CJ had warned she would be a struggle. But that was a challenge he welcomed. Now, to work with the witch.

Tuesday had shucked off her coat and now reclined on the leather sofa that sat against a rough brick wall. She'd kicked off her shoes and waggled her bare toes—the nails were painted bright blue—as she stretched out her arms and yawned. The black shirt had a but-ton below her breasts and was open from there down, revealing abs. And much more skin than he wanted to notice right now.

"Tired?" he asked.

"Unlike vampires, we witches do need a little shut-eye now and then. And after all the torments I've endured?"

"Why don't you take twenty minutes to rest? Stuart, close the shades completely."

As the windows darkened, Tuesday sat up and glanced over a shoulder. "Who the hell is Stuart? A house brownie?"

Ethan chuckled. "A bit similar. That's the name of the electronic house butler. This place is high-tech. If you need something, Stuart can usually get it."

"Stuart, book me a flight back to Boston, STAT," Tuesday said.

As the butler began to confirm, Ethan canceled that request. "And ignore all requests from any voice but my own," he ordered.

"Of course," Stuart replied.

"That's creepy." Tuesday lay back down and crossed her arms over chest. "And so not fair."

"While you rest I'm going to make a few calls. Plan our first move."

"You don't have a plan?"

"Of course I do," he lied. Sitting before the kitchen counter with his back to her, he pushed aside her spangled coat. A pad of paper and a pen waited near the phone. He was all about the high-tech, but he'd never give up the landline. "You want a blanket or something?"

"Fuck you, Richard." And she turned over on the sofa and snuggled up in a ball.

Again with the Richard? He thought about it a few seconds. Ah. Richard shortened was... All righty then. He shouldn't expect her to think very highly of him after having one of his retrievers kidnap her and fly her across the ocean. And then forcibly bind her to him.

He may have to find a means to cozy up to her in order to get her to trust him or he'd never get anywhere with her. At the very least, he needed her to want to trust him.

Pulling out his cell phone, he scrolled through the contacts. He knew the person he had to speak to first to learn anything about any demon in Paris.

Edamite Thrash was a sort of demon overlord with a penchant for niceness. But Ethan didn't tell anyone that, or Thrash would scratch you with the poison thorns that grew from his knuckles. The man was a corax demon, which meant he could shift into an unkindness of ravens and take to the skies. He also made it his job to oversee the demons of Paris, knowing who was where, and when and why. He kept a loose rein on his species, and enforced punishment only when one of them threatened to expose their kind with their foolish actions.

Ethan knew most of the major players in the paranormal realm who inhabited Paris. That was his job, to know whom he could trust and with whom he had best watch his back. Ed was trustworthy.

The dark feather tattoo on Ed's neck always drew Ethan's eye. He wore many sigils tattooed on his skin, and combined with his standard dark business suit and smartly parted and slicked black hair, he looked dangerous yet disturbingly *GQ* stylish.

He shook the man's hand, noting he always wore

black leather half gloves that exposed his fingers. He needed only cover the thorns on his knuckles to prevent an accident.

"Good to see you, man." Ed nodded over Ethan's shoulder. "Who is this pretty?"

Tuesday, who had followed Ethan into the building at a distance, was acting petulant, yet she strolled forward and offered her hand to shake. "Tuesday Knightsbridge."

Ed clasped her hand. "The witch. I've heard about you."

"You have? From who?"

"My girlfriend, Tamatha Bellerose."

"Bellerose? Oh, yes, her mother is Petrina. I know that witch." And the quickness with which Tuesday pulled her hand from the demon's clasp clued Ethan she probably didn't have a good relationship with the family. "Just in Paris for a visit," she added. "Forced, as it is."

Ed looked to Ethan for explanation.

"Tuesday is helping me to locate a demon. That's why I wanted to check in with you. See if you've any information that may lead us to him."

Ed leaned against the desk behind him and crossed his arms over his chest. "Which demon?"

"The Beautiful One," Tuesday said before Ethan could say the name.

"Ah. Gazariel." Ed winced and rubbed his jaw. "I do know he's in town. But haven't a clue where. He hasn't been making much noise so he's not on my give-a-fuck radar. Why is she helping? You only require a witch when you need to summon a demon from Beneath or Daemonia."

"I'm bait," Tuesday said, tossing out the words at the same time Ethan said, "She's my lure for the demon."

"You two don't get along very well, do you?"

Ethan kept an eye on Tuesday as she walked about the demon's office, looked over the marble conference table and then wandered to the wall where various artifacts were displayed on small individual shelves.

"We had to take her away from her home to get her to work with us," Ethan offered.

"Kidnapped me," Tuesday called over her shoulder as she peered into a glass container that likely held faery dust. The contents sparkled in all colors from the afternoon sun beaming in through the windows.

"Sounds on par for Acquisitions," Ed said. "So, a lure, eh? Why would Gazariel be interested in that witch?"

"She wears his sigil. Or that is the information we have."

Ed stood and now he gave Tuesday his full attention. She turned from her curious seeking and splayed her hands. "Yep, I'm the demon's bitch. I carry his curse. And Einstein here thinks that'll draw him to me. Idiot."

"He'll come to you. We just have to get you close enough he puts up his head and notices," Ethan said. "Give him a sniff of the witch's scent."

"He's not going to be attracted to the one who wears his curse," Ed said. "Why would he? I know a bit about The Beautiful One. He put an unwanted curse in her many centuries ago when he had the opportunity. And now he's done with it. I'm not sure of the nature of the curse, but if the demon wants it gone from him, there's not a thing in this world that would incline him to set one foot near her now. She's useless."

"Hey! I can hear you," Tuesday called. The blue glass sphere she had touched wobbled and rolled off the shelf.

She caught it just before it hit the floor. "Oops. Good save, though, yeah?"

"Don't touch the breakables," Ethan said, chastising the overly curious witch. And to Ed he said, "Are you serious? But we need her to open that curse and hold Gazariel so he will submit."

"Why do you need him to submit?"

"He's got something that Acquisitions wants."

Ed lifted an eyebrow.

"It's a book of angel names and sigils. A muse wrote it. It holds the code for the Final Days."

"Is that thing back in circulation? I thought the angel Raphael had taken it underwing, so to speak?"

"It made a series of exchanges before Raphael secured it from a vampire intent on populating the world with nephilim. Let's just say it's been in so many hands, even the Archives' records are confused as to where it was last seen before landing in the demon's hands. But I have good intel that The Beautiful One currently has it."

"Doesn't sound like a party."

"It's not. The list of angel names, when ordered correctly, holds an ancient coded word, or words, that when spoken, will send all angels plummeting to earth to smother mankind with their multitudes. Their wings will burn human flesh, young and old. Paranormals are not exempt, either. The earth will become an ashy cemetery of the mortal, the paranormal and the divine."

"Whew!" Ed ran a gloved hand through his slick hair. "That's something you want to stop. But your challenge will be getting the demon to come to you, *without* knowing you've got the witch, and then surprising him with her at just the right moment."

Ethan's temples had begun to pulse. He hadn't expected this particular complication. If he would have known before the demon didn't want anything to do with the witch, he wouldn't have bound himself to her until after they'd secured Gazariel. Of course, he needed Tuesday to bring the demon to him. This was a mess. Had she known as much?

Her self-satisfied grin answered that one for him.

"Keep her out of sight until you need her," Ed suggested.

"Too late. I bound myself to her to keep her close and protect myself from any retaliatory magic."

"Then you've got a problem, Pierce."

No need to state that one out loud. Tuesday's soft tsking sounds riled him and Ethan fisted his hands. Yet when he saw her smile beam at sight of his anger, he relented the knuckle-whitening clutch. The witch would not get under his skin. He was smarter than this. And he didn't need to snap a rubber band to remind him of that.

He turned to Ed. "Can you help by telling me where Gazariel might be?"

"I haven't a clue."

"But you keep tabs on all the demons—how can you know he's in the city and not have a location on him?"

"It's a feeling, Pierce, not an exact science or even a map. Believe me, I would help you if I could. The Beautiful One is from Beneath, so you might start at l'Enfer."

The Devil Himself's nightclub. It was frequented by demons, vamps, werewolves and most any sort looking for dark and devious indulgences. Just the place Ethan wanted to visit. Not.

"Hey, how much you want for this?" Tuesday waggled a pearlescent alicorn she'd found on a shelf.

Ed shrugged. "You can take it."

"What? Are you serious?" The witch actually tittered with glee. "You do know how valuable this is?"

"It's…" Ed winced. "I should have never obtained that thing. It was taken from innocence. It's not something I have a right to own. I've been meaning to get rid of it for a while now. You'd be doing me a favor by taking it."

"Nice!" Tuesday stabbed the air with the thing. "I can so use this."

Ethan could but shake his head and wish the day would get better.

"I guess you'll be clubbing then?" Ed offered as he extended his hand to shake.

"Sounds like it." Ethan thanked the man and started out of the room, knowing Tuesday would have to follow. Sooner or later.

As he got on the elevator, the witch entered, twirling the alicorn gaily. "I got a prize," she teased.

"What the hell can you do with that thing?"

"You'll find out soon enough. By the way, I'm going to need some magical supplies. You whisked me away from home and cauldron. I need certain items to work magic, put up wards and generally survive."

"Like what?"

She shrugged and tapped the alicorn against her jaw. "This is a start. There's got to be magic shops in the city. And you'll have to pay, sweetie, since my kidnapper decided against bringing along my purse. And I'll be needing some clothes as well. Can't go clubbing looking like this, can I?"

"You like fine. All black and perfectly witchy? You'll fit right in at l'Enfer." Ethan checked his watch. It was around six in the evening. A few more hours before the club opened.

"Can a chick get pizza in this town?"

Rolling his eyes, he strolled out as the elevator doors opened. The witch had no taste whatsoever.

Chapter 4

At the plain black metal doors to the club l'Enfer, they stopped before the bouncer with red eyes. A sign over his high left shoulder stated, in Latin, what basically translated as "no funny stuff" and "you take your own chances entering." Tuesday boldly met the bouncer's gaze and focused her intent toward him. The demon looked down, chastised by her audacity. Served him right. He was young and needed to learn to show respect for his elders.

Blowing him a kiss laced with pizza sauce and some kind of cheese that had not been mozzarella—the French really liked their weird cheeses—she then glided down the dark hallway. The music thudded in her heart and veins. Not worrying whether Ethan gained access, she picked up the beat and danced as she walked.

She sensed the brooding vampire was behind her, and

felt his hand go to her hip, as if to guide her through the darkness, but he quickly removed it. Tuesday smiled. Had he forgotten himself for a moment? Thought of her as an actual desirable female he might get close to? She could work with that.

Much as she had developed a liking for clubbing over the last several decades, Tuesday preferred less crowded venues, and with more upbeat tunes. L'Enfer had not invested any expense in color. Everything was black, with hematite and silver metallic bits and trim here and there. The lighting was red, and flashed across the inhabitants and dancers, who also wore mostly black.

Tuesday was dressed for the part, right down to her matte black nail polish and eye shadow. Yet she felt naked without some lip gloss; a deep violet would be perfect for this Gothic milieu. As it was, she felt virtually exposed without any magical accoutrements to hand, and bound to a freaking vampire. Yet she wasn't powerless. Her simple mastery over the bouncer had proven that. And she did have the alicorn stuck in her waistband. She felt it tremble. This was not a place for such a thing. The demon hadn't wanted to possess innocence? Interesting.

She wouldn't test the alicorn's power here. The place was owned by the Devil Himself, and the sign on the door had clearly stated no funny stuff. The bouncer should have frisked her for weapons. Idiot.

On the other hand, a place like this probably thrived on the illicit use of weapons and how much damage could be done before a person was kicked out. If that would even happen. Again, the sign mentioned taking one's own chances.

"You see him?" Ethan shouted next to her ear.

Tuesday leaned away from him. "I can hear well enough over the noise, vampire. And I just got here. Let me look around, will you? You want to dance?"

"I'm not a dancer. And I'm on a job."

"Right, all work and no play. Should I call you Jack?"

"Just keep your mind on business."

"Can I at least have a drink? We should try to blend in. Look like we're here to party and not jack up some asshole demon, yeah?"

Ethan sighed then reluctantly nodded. "What do you want?"

"Anything that doesn't contain a live entity. I suspect that's on the menu here. And I prefer vodka."

"Live entities," he muttered. With a frown, he headed toward the long, black quartz bar that was edged with a cut-in of red crystals that seemed to glow like LEDs.

Tuesday allowed her body to inhale the beat. Despite the fact this club was owned by the rather dour Dark Prince, the music wasn't too terribly dirge-like. The Goth singer with a string of spikes embedded down the sides of each bare arm sang about his friends being heathens and suggested she should take it slow. All righty, then.

Tuesday swayed to the beat as a crimson-haired faery with violet eyes matched her with a smile and a shimmy. If she was going to be forced to work for some rogue organization to capture a pompous, yet also vicious demon she had no wish to ever see again, at the very least, she could enjoy herself. Lifting her arms, she spun onto the dance floor.

Below her, the Plexiglas floor flashed red and black and then segued into flames. It was a realistic effect, and she almost fancied to feel the heat. A brush of fur tickled her right hand, and with a spin she eyed the tattooed back of a thin person who moved a little too jerkily not to be demon.

A guitar solo screamed and coaxed the crowd to pump their fists and jump in a pounding stomp of fraternity to whatever dark gods were the current rage. Tuesday preferred Loki. The one portrayed in the movies by the handsome dark-haired actor, most specifically. As she spun, arms swaying above her head and hips shifting, she spied Ethan standing at the edge of the dance floor, holding a red glowing drink. His grim look spoke much louder than the music.

"Spoilsport." She wandered over and took the drink, then tilted back a healthy swallow. Instead of the expected burn, she felt a distinct icy grab at the back of her throat, which then melted into a blaze of heat down her esophagus. And it tasted of cinnamon and chocolate. "Whew! That is some good stuff."

"I thought it would be the drink for you. It's called The Devil's Bitch."

"Oh, Ethan, you can hate me all you need to." She fluttered her lashes at him. "I'm not going to crack under all that loathing. You know your emotions only reflect back onto you? Also makes it easy for a witch to use against you. That is, if the witch could drop some magic on your vampire ass. Ditch the frowny face and let's agree to disagree, and then get on with things, shall we?"

"So you've decided to stop pouting and work with me?"

Yeah, she was being as much of a problem child as he was. And if she didn't get to work now, she'd never be free of the man and his brooding grey eyes. And could his teeth be any whiter? She wanted to see his fangs.

To touch them and feel them pierce her neck…but no. She would not bone up this task by falling all puppy-eyed over the vamp. She was better than that. Because she had no choice.

"We're partners." She held out a hand and he shook it, holding it for a few seconds longer than was proper. She could feel his heartbeats in that hold, and they were sure and confident. Powerful. And, yes, controlling. The man would not relent. "Good then. I'll take a look around. You probably wouldn't recognize the demon if he was choking you, so you just…"

His eyes took in their surroundings. He put off a very militant, I'm-ready vibe. "I'll stay close to you."

"Sure, keep close. I'll protect the big bad vampire from a suggestive side glance or a dance-off. Ha!"

She strolled off into the clove-scented shadows that edged the dance floor, knowing the man would follow. It wasn't as if she could get any farther away from him than fifty yards. Nothing like having a puppy dog on her tail. Of course, she liked puppies. Had once owned one, until the local troll had stolen it and— She tried never to imagine what had become of her sweet Nugget after that. Long time ago. Always avoid trolls, had been the lesson.

Noting every face she passed, Tuesday pulled on her Sherlock cloak. It was easy to tell the demons, as their eyes were generally red, although some demon-possessed humans' eyes gave off a dull blue glow. Most natural demons who did not require a human meat suit could disguise their irises, but when out at the club they apparently let their freak flags fly. Red irises everywhere!

Thinking of freaks…

She strolled toward a tall sliver of a demon who looked like a walking skeleton, yet he wore thin, clear muscle over those bones. A wraith? They were usually dangerous and she was surprised one would put himself in a social situation. But when the creature turned to cast her a violet gaze she realized it was faery. And faeries could be even more vicious than demons.

Propping her palm over the alicorn at her waist, Tuesday detoured from her approach, wisely dismissing the oddity. With a flick of her fingers she could reduce them all to gibbering sycophants. But she would not because she didn't want to call attention to herself.

Finishing off the drink, which still cooled then burned, she set the empty goblet on a table and eyed the flashing red-and-silver staircase leading up to the balcony. She skipped up the steps, edging past a couple who made out carefully, for the woman's spiked bra looked quite deadly. Blood tinted the air. Hmm... Perhaps the bra served the exact purpose its wearer desired.

Tuesday glanced back to see Ethan following and noticed his expression when he neared the couple. He winced and shook his head. The man was discerning. Points for him.

Stepping up into the dark and smoky balcony, Tuesday was immediately surrounded by three tall men, all of them demons. The one before her flashed a silver-toothed grin, punctuated by curved fangs, and his nostrils flared and put out little wisps of black smoke. It wasn't cigarettes or weed producing the smoke, but rather the thickness of demons here above the crowd. "A tasty witch has dared to broach our private balcony?"

"I wasn't aware it was private." She lifted her hand, prepared to repel the demon, when suddenly Ethan gripped her wrist and eased himself around to stand before her.

"She didn't know, gentlemen," he offered. "Demons only up here?"

"You got it, vampire. But if she wants to stay—" Silver Tooth let his gaze creep over Tuesday's skin "—we want to play."

"Oh, yeah?" Tuesday reached around Ethan with her free hand and he turned to clasp both her wrists. "Don't restrain me before them," she said. "I can stand up for myself."

"Hear that, vampire? She can take care of herself. Why don't you leave the tasty little witch to us?"

Now Tuesday did feel a shiver of caution, and the touch of someone's fingers from behind, sliding across her ass, made her jump. Right against Ethan's arm, which slid across her shoulder and directed her back toward the stairs.

"We're leaving," he said more to her than the randy demons. "But before we do…" He cocked a look over his shoulder at the silver-toothed leader. "Any of you familiar with Gazariel?"

"He means The Beautiful One," Tuesday quickly amended. It was not cool to call demons by their names, especially around others.

"Get that witch out of here," Silver Tooth said.

"But the demon I'm looking for—" Ethan began.

"No pretty demons in this club, vampire. And if you don't take your pet witch and leave we'll make sure no one ever calls her pretty, either."

Ethan clasped Tuesday's hand and led her down the stairs. The couple was still making out. Blood beaded in various spots on the man's chest and neck. Ethan quickened their pace.

When they landed on the main floor, he directed her toward a wall, where a private moment could be found behind it, as it was set off from the frenzy of dancers.

"I had no idea that was a demons-only area," she said. "But you don't score points for rescuing me. I was fine."

"I know that. But no funny stuff, remember? And I like to take care of my assets. Make sure they survive the length of the job."

"I'm an asset to you? I don't know if that's a good or a bad thing. I'm guessing not especially good."

"You are valuable. What's so bad about that?"

"My value, as determined by what I can do for you, is a very bad thing. Any man who tries to put a—" she made air quotes "—'value' on a woman is not a man at all."

Feminism was her right, and she would never stop to point out the patriarchy's misguided beliefs and lacking empathy for those who were their equals. She strode off toward the front hallway, where they had entered. "He's not here. Let's blow this joint."

Once outside on the street, she walked swiftly away from the nondescript doors, but abruptly hit an invisible wall and couldn't press onward. Curse that vampire! She cast a glance over her shoulder. Ethan stood a good distance away, unmoving, giving her a sly wave.

"Such a Richard," she muttered. "Well? What are you waiting for?"

"I'm going this way." He pointed over his shoulder, then turned and walked off.

And the pull of the binding dragged Tuesday along after him.

* * *

"It was a stupid thing to do anyway," Tuesday muttered as she followed Ethan down the quiet, dark Parisian street toward wherever he was headed. She hadn't a choice in the matter. "Going to that club? Why would The Beautiful One hang out at that depressing place? Do you even know who you're after? That demon likes to shine. To see and be seen. He's vain and all about pleasure and self-gratification. He thrives on attention. Adoration. Love. He's not for darkness and murk. That's why he pawned off his curse on me."

Ethan cast a glance over his shoulder at her, then resumed his pace.

"What kind of sorry adventuring detective vampire are you?" she called. "Don't you know how to do this stuff? I mean, let's go to the least likely place the dude is going to be and feed the witch to the demons, why don't we?"

She smirked to think about getting hit on by those nasty demons. The one with the silver teeth had to have doused himself in body spray for the young and bepimpled. Ugh. And then Ethan had felt the need to intervene. Like some kind of rescuing hero? She could have taken care of herself. But how often did a man step in to try and help her? So rarely, she couldn't think back that far.

"I'm hungry!" she announced in frustration. "That pizza was terrible. Who sells pizza slices out of a freezer? That's like 7-Eleven stuff. So wrong. I thought Paris was classier? Let's get something to eat. Do you have to walk so fast? It's not as if we're going to find the demon now. I'd guess he's more of a day kind of demon. All the better to allow others to admire his beaming gorgeousness. Are you even listening to me, Pierce? Bueller?"

With that, the vampire swung round, marched up to her, bracketed her face with his hands and…

…kissed her.

For no reason. And with no grace. He planted a firm, seconds-long kiss on her mouth. And for those few seconds Tuesday's heart thundered and a tickle-thrill shimmied up the back of her neck. She didn't mind the kiss. In fact, it proved a scintillating connection. The vibrations between them shivered haphazardly, but then quickly started to harmonize. To actually blend—as if they were meant to come together. How weird was that?

But the kiss ended as quickly as it had landed on her mouth. And she hadn't time to determine why it had felt so right.

Ethan stepped back, hands splaying outward. With a sexy wink, he then said, "I knew that would work."

Tuesday touched her lips, stunned that he'd taken her by surprise, but even more stunned that she wasn't upset about the attack kiss.

"I figured a kiss would get you to shut up," he said. Turning, he marched onward.

Really? He'd employed the kiss to make her stop talking? Of all the nerve! She was not one of his victims he could subdue with persuasion or a plunge of fang into vein. And so what if she had been talking? It wasn't as if he'd shown an eagerness to converse with her. She was alone in a strange, foreign city, being led around by a bossy vampire who held her captive with a magical bond. Damn right she was going to chatter away nervously when the mood struck!

On the other hand, she wasn't about to let some cocky vampire feel he had gotten the upper hand with her.

Tuesday raced up behind Ethan. "You want to use kisses as weapons?" She shoved him and he spun to face her with a questioning gape. "One thing you need to know about me—I'm always cocked and loaded."

Grabbing his coat lapel, she pulled him in and planted a kiss on his mouth. This one was as unwarranted and desperately seeking as his had been. The man stumbled backward and his shoulders hit a brick wall, and it gave her the opportunity to move in and deepen the kiss.

His hand caught at the base of her spine under her coat, and he pressed her closer to his hard abs and hugged hip-to-hip. And Tuesday forgot that she was angry and let the lust and want rise and play out.

The man's mouth was incredible. His lips were warm and firm, and when their tongues danced she couldn't imagine doing such a tango with anyone else. And she had tangoed with many in her lifetime. Cinnamon mingled with his clean taste, brewing a cocktail more heady than any weird concoction served in a demonic dance club.

But she was kissing him to make a point. And she'd hate to let him think she actually *wanted* this kiss. She did not. Mostly. Yes, she did!

But that was not how she intended to play her hand.

Shoving away from him, Tuesday swept her hair over her shoulder and assumed a cocky stance. "I won that one, vampire."

If a smirk could get any sexier, she didn't know. A few fine wrinkles creased the corners of his eyes, and she even noticed glints of gray strands silvering the hair at his temples. So sexy. Urm, in a completely uninteresting way, of course.

"Sounds fine by me," Ethan said. "You can have the win, partner."

"Right. Partner." She wrinkled her nose at that one. She *had* suggested they could be partners, hadn't she? "About that food?"

"Just up the street, there's a cheesy little bar that might still be open. It's owned by a couple of expats. They serve American food."

Intrigued beyond what she wanted to convey, Tuesday muttered, "Lead the way."

An hour later, Tuesday was full from pulled-pork tacos with pickled jalapeños, and a fruity drink that had a lot of alcohol and even more sugar in it. She would not even require magic to fly now. And Ethan had watched her gobble the food with little more than that constant smirk and a gleam in his eyes.

They were pretty gray eyes, and added a touch of niceness to his usual dour expression. While he was a handsome man, she could tell he dared not show too much. He had been honed and hardened over the centuries. Much as she had been. And she well knew it was never wise to let life play out on her face for others to interpret and use to their advantage.

"How long have you been walking this seriously whacked planet?" she asked as she noisily sucked the last bits of the red slushy drink through the straw. She wasn't drunk, but she was feeling fine.

"Conversation now?"

"Yes. I'm finished stuffing my face. I'm feeling relaxed for the first time since my captivity—" She caught his scoff. "I was in a freakin' cage."

"Fine. I'm sorry, okay? It had to be done. But now you're out, so get over it."

It took a snap of the rubber band not to flip him off.

"What did you ask?" he said. "How old am I?" He lifted his feet and propped them on a nearby wicker chair, leaning back against the wall in the stuffy bar that had announced last call ten minutes after they'd arrived. "I was born in…the 1500s."

"Can't remember the exact year?"

He shrugged. "Early part of the century. We weren't known for marking our birth dates back then."

"Yeah. I was born in the 1640s, give or take a few years. Or decades. I remember at the time it was the great Puritan migration. They sailed to the New World by boatloads from England. All kinds of religious rabble, preaching and condemning. Fur traders and fishers, too. I dated a fisherman once. He smelled. So! That makes you the old man and me the sexy young thang."

"Which should grant me wisdom and you…?"

Tuesday shimmied confidently on the chair. "A chick with a whole lot of experience on every single thing you can imagine."

"It is interesting walking through the ages, isn't it?"

"It is." She teased a finger around the rim of her glass. "You ever get tired of it?"

"Not yet. Immortality suits me."

"Save for the part about drinking all that blood?"

"Coming from a witch who must have consumed how many vampire hearts to keep her immortality over the centuries?"

"Five," she said proudly. In order to maintain immortality, a witch had to consume a beating vampire heart once a century. Split the rib cage. Reach in. Feast.

And try not to wretch. "Each one of those bastards deserved to die, too."

"And what qualifies as deserving in your book?"

"Assholes. Murderers. And general idiots."

Ethan quirked an eyebrow. "I shall endeavor not to be an asshole or an idiot. At least, not too often."

Tuesday yawned. "You've had a pitiful showing in the trying department. But I won't hold that against you."

"I thought you intended to hold everything that made you uncomfortable against me?"

"Pretty much. But you're lucky I'm tired now. I only got about two winks on your couch. Can we go back to your place? I need to seriously crash and recharge. If I can get some good sleep then I'll be able to think clearly and maybe even stir up a demon-tracking spell."

"Then here's to a well-rested witch."

The witch nodded off within five minutes. Ethan had offered her his bed. It was around the corner in the loft. None of the rooms had separating walls, save bathroom, and he could see the end of the bed from the kitchen. The city lights beamed in through the floor-to-ceiling windows that lined the bedroom area. He'd bought this place for those windows. The view was incredible. He'd wanted to point out Sacré Coeur to her, but she had literally dropped onto the bed and rolled into a snore.

Now, he wondered what their next move should be. And if more kisses would be required to make her comply with his wishes. She hadn't needed provoking to kiss him back after he'd initially kissed her. A retaliatory kiss? Bring them on.

And in his next thought, he frowned. He'd kissed a witch. And…he'd liked it.

Chapter 5

A shower had never felt more welcome. Tuesday dried off in the steamy room. The floor and walls were grey marble that was deeply streaked with clear quartz. Gorgeous stonework. And she could feel some of the earth's energies remaining in the stone when she pressed a palm to it, though they were weak. The manufacturing process tended to rape natural stone of most of its essence, but if she took her time, and had the inclination, she could restore its vital energy with an earthing spell.

It was a hell of a lot more than Stuart could do, that was for sure.

"Take that, Stuart."

It was weird to think that an inanimate object was listening in, all the time, waiting for a cue to turn on ~~me~~ function in the apartment. Electronic witchcraft ~~s~~ not her thing. But apparently Ethan was one of those spoiled rich bachelors who could afford life's luxuries. But he didn't seem to flaunt it, with million-dollar wristwatches or fancy suits, so he earned credit for that.

The bathroom was attached to the bedroom, which was open to the rest of the loft. A nice setup, and she suspected the view out the picture window was awesome, were the shades not blocking the bright sunlight now. She hadn't realized how dead tired she had been last night. Her face had hit the pillow. Snores had commenced.

Now she didn't hear Ethan puttering about in the kitchen, but then, why should she? The guy was a vampire. He didn't eat food. But she certainly hoped he played the charming host and either ordered in or found something for her to nosh on.

Fingering her black silk shirt, which revealed a nicely toned tummy, she sighed. She'd worn it for two days straight *and* a long flight across the Atlantic Ocean. She needed clean things to wear. And at the very least, some basic magical accoutrements.

Combing out her hair with Ethan's comb, she then snapped her fingers and whispered, "Dry," and a whoosh of air fluffed up and through the wet strands, instantly drying them. Sometimes Latin wasn't necessary to kick in the magic. Keep it Simple, Stupid was a motto she followed with her spellcraft. She wove her thick hair into a loose side plait and left some in the back hanging free.

Without makeup or a toothbrush she felt out of her element. Not quite in top form. She scanned the insides of the medicine cabinet and spied the wood-handled toothbrush. Nah. She wasn't going to use a vampire's toothbrush. She squirted a blob of toothpaste on her finger and scrubbed the old-fashioned way. Centuries ago, this had been her only option to dental health. That, or use a bit of twig or the corner of some rough suede. It worked. But her kingdom for a dash of dark eye shadow and lip gloss.

"Ugh. Nature witch," she muttered to her reflection. "I should concoct a makeup spell." She tapped her fingernails against the mirror, thinking it odd that a vampire even had one in his home. "Yeah, I'll worry about the lacking glamour later. I've got bigger problems to solve."

Putting the obsidian crystal around her neck, she held it a few moments. Grounding herself. Finding a calm tone for her personal vibration.

Now ready to face whatever adventure the vampire with the attack kisses had in mind for her, she wandered out into the living area. Seated on the leather sofa, Ethan was focused on an iPad, but he nodded over his shoulder and said, "Ran down to the creperie an hour ago when you were still sleeping. Got you some croissants and *pain au chocolat*. Fresh juice, too."

Points for the vampire. But she wouldn't tell him that.

"You mean Stuart is incapable of such errands? Not sure you got your money's worth with that guy," she said gaily.

Sliding onto a bar stool and tearing into the paper bag, Tuesday bit into a still-warm pastry loaded with gooey chocolate. Crisp, thin layers of pastry engulfing sweet, dark chocolate? By the seven sacred witches, it was amazing.

"What are the plans for today?" she asked around chews.

"Thought you could summon the demon. Witches can do that, right?"

"Right, but I can't summon a demon who has marked me. Just doesn't work that way. I can track him, perhaps even locate him, but he's not going to come when I call like a little bitch."

Ethan's sigh echoed across the room. "I thought you'd be more useful."

"Way to boost a chick's confidence. Besides, Edamite Thrash confirmed The Beautiful One wasn't going to come when I call. So get over it, will you? I know what is first on today's list of adventures."

"What's that?"

"Shopping! I can't wander around in this same getup. I mean, I can work it, but I seriously prefer clean clothes. And I need some lip gloss and eye liner. I feel naked without the black stuff."

"Is that going to help you to locate the demon?"

"It will." She turned and fluttered her lashes at him. "Don't you know a woman's power is all in how she feels about herself? When I look good, I do my best."

"I think you look great."

"You're a guy. Guys always say dismissive things like that."

He shook his head and set aside the iPad. "Shopping it is. And then?"

"And then, I also need to pick up some spell supplies. Outfit myself with a makeshift hex-and-spell armory. Then I should be able to set up a grid to map the city of demons. And hopefully, by incorporating the sigil's power, The Beautiful One will stand out on that map."

"Hopefully? I'm going to need more than that. I require assurance."

Tuesday shrugged and bit off another piece of chocolaty pastry. "You get hope from me for now, vamp. Say, do you mind that I used your comb?"

"As long as you didn't use my toothbrush, I don't care."

"What if I did use your toothbrush?"

"We're stopping at a pharmacy, first thing."

The witch could work the tight black jeans and floaty flowered shirt. Her vibe was definitely bohemian, with her thick white hair braided down one side and the furred spangled coat topping it all off. In the pharmacy, she tore open the makeup packaging and performed a quick makeover on herself, fluttering her newly blackened lashes at him and pursing her deep violet lips.

Ethan nodded approval because the sooner she served her personal needs, the quicker he could be done with this stupid stuff and get on to the important work. But he had to admit the deep color she wore on her lips stirred his desires. The violet lipstick emphasized her plump, heart-shaped mouth. He couldn't take his eyes from them. They might taste like sweet grapes warmed under the Tuscan sun.

Yikes. Ethan checked himself. What was he thinking? He was not attracted to a witch. Yes, he was. And what the fuck was that about?

"Come on!" Tuesday skipped ahead, obviously on some kind of spending high.

Ethan kept his credit card handy. Whatever made the witch happy.

Now, she had managed to find a dusty candle shop that opened to a private room in the back that was filled with all the witchy accoutrements he imagined she'd ever need. And while he suspected the shop owner was one of those kitchen witches who spoke incantations from books she'd bought on the internet and thought she was casting spells, she wasn't a real born witch like Tuesday Knightsbridge. And if she knew that the woman buying smudge sticks and candles from her really did possess natural magic, she would be in awe.

Tuesday popped her head out from the back room with a bag full of goodies and winked at Ethan as she wandered by. "Homeward! Stuart waits for us!"

At the very least, he'd gotten a new toothbrush.

Back at his place, Tuesday dropped her shopping booty on the floor by the sofa, tossed her coat on the chair and beelined to the bathroom while he picked up the mess.

Setting her heeled boots on the rug by the door, he then placed the bags neatly on the kitchen counter. He liked a clean, organized home. Which was probably why his few attempts at living with women over the years had failed. Also, the lack of privacy was jarring. Sharing a home with another person was hard work. And since he could have a relationship without moving in with the woman, he chose to stick with what worked.

Although a few relationships here and there, over the centuries, had worked for him. Most had been so long ago he'd forgotten what it felt like or how it had lasted. That wasn't exactly true. A man never forgot the women who had passed through his life. And the current one was moving through like a hurricane intent on settling and spinning about for a while.

"Stuart, be sure to send the vacuum through when next I leave."

The home butler confirmed with a blip on the wall panel and a solid green light. Ethan had programmed it not to return voice reply unless necessary. It wasn't like he needed to talk to the artificial intelligence to make conversation. He used it merely as the maid he liked to have available at all hours of the day, yet didn't want a human stumbling around in his life discovering that he didn't need to sleep and eat. And he'd bitten a maid once. Early nineteenth century? It was best not to drink from the help.

Tuesday returned, flipping her hair over a shoulder, and stretched out on the sofa. "Where's my stuff?"

"On the kitchen counter. You can't leave a trail of bread crumbs wherever you walk."

"I don't need to. We're attached at the hip. If you should lose sight of me, you'll find me soon enough. Bring me my bags."

"Get them yourself." He settled onto the big leather chair with the wide wooden arms. The wood was worn from decades of use and connection to life. And more than a few frenzied bang sessions. "Dazzle me with your witchy magic and this demon map you said you could conjure."

"I don't dazzle on command." She wandered over to the counter and pulled out things from the bags.

"Then how do I get you to dazzle me?" Ethan asked. "Is there a magic word?"

"*Please* seems to work most of the time."

He pressed his fingers to his forehead. He should have left the witch in the cage.

On the other hand, she couldn't hex him and he did need help with this case. He had absolutely no clue how to lure in the demon otherwise, so he would take her sassy mouth and... Well, he'd kiss her again if need be. Heh. That kiss had set her off-kilter.

But the return kiss had surprised him. And then he'd

accepted it for the retaliation it had been. *Now* a kiss from those grape-stained lips would give him what he wanted from her. Another taste. A teasing test of his abilities to remain completely unaffected by her charms and attraction.

She had some. Somewhere in that scatter of spangles, sass and black eye shadow.

"Black salt and raven's ash." She waggled between them two vials of a dark substance that she'd purchased from the candle shop. "This will do the trick."

She wandered over and pushed the narrow coffee table up against the sofa. The wide dark-stained plank flooring was the original from when the building had once been a millinery factory. Ethan liked it because he'd known a man who had worked here in the 1920s. He'd taken immense pride in the cut of a woman's hat, or even the specific froth of a silk flower adorning a sweeping brim. He'd also asked Ethan for vampirism after learning that the mercury used to cure the felt for his creations was driving him insane. Ethan had convinced him an insane vampire would be worse than a human prematurely dead from bleeding out.

In all his centuries, Ethan had never created another vampire. And he didn't intend to do so anytime soon. It was too much power to simply give away as if a holiday gift. And besides, he was blood-born, not a created vampire. His breed were superior to those who had been transformed in a back alley or at a lover's lusty request. And he wasn't about to tarnish the line. If he ever desired to procreate, he would have a child, who, depending on its mother's lineage and paranormal species, would very likely be born vampire. He preferred to mate with another vampire, but he wasn't rigid in that stance. Love was actually his key requirement to a happy, lasting relationship.

But love was fickle and…well, he'd take it if it came his way, but he wasn't on a quest to track it down.

Ethan leaned forward to rest his elbows on his knees and watched as Tuesday sprinkled black salt in a pattern before her on the floor. He was curious about witchcraft, and knew it was powerful. No man should mess with a witch. But he was feeling cocky with the protective bind against her. So long as it lasted until they found the demon.

Leaning over the scattered salt, which designed a pentagram inside a circle, Tuesday closed her eyes and spread her arms wide. She chanted words that Ethan would never try to decipher. Witch words. Dangerous words. Yet he could feel them forming sentences in his veins, warning that she could take him out if he dropped his guard.

With a snap of her fingers, the salt suddenly illuminated and jittered on the floor, moving, ordering and aligning. The tiny grains jumped and crackled. The scent of salt tinged the air. And when it settled and continued to glow, Tuesday sat back on her heels, hands propped on each thigh.

"A map of Paris," she said with a gesture over the salt. "What do you think?"

Ethan leaned over to inspect the map. It included both the right and left bank, and the Seine and the main island. It even showed faint demarcations for the twenty arrondissements. "You've dazzled me, witch. Now where are all the demons? Or just the one in particular?"

"That requires more intense chanting. And an elemental callout. You stay there. Don't move, because I don't want the bond between us to tug me out of concentration. Deal?"

"I am a captive audience."

She looked at him a moment, and he couldn't decide if she thought she was peering into an idiot's eyes or, in fact, seeing beyond his irises and into his very soul. He'd witnessed it when she'd peered into Certainly Jones's soul. Was it a skill they could only perform on other witches? Or need he worry, too?

"What?" he finally asked.

"There's something about you, Ethan Pierce. Something that keeps me from stabbing you through the heart with this athame." She twirled the knife she'd bought from the store. The hilt looked to be carved from opal. That was why the bill had registered in the hundreds of euros. "I'm not sure what that is, though, so I'm going to keep the blade close."

"Whatever works for you. You couldn't harm me if you tried."

"Probably not. But you are racking up the points against you for when the bond is lifted. Know that."

"I'm not afraid of a witch."

Her head tilted and her gaze narrowed as she said simply, "You should be."

And Ethan realized she was right. But he wouldn't show his anxiety.

Casting her focus over the salt map, she moved up on her knees, spread out her arms and began to chant.

Tuesday felt the presence of every demon inhabiting the city prick at her skin. It wasn't pleasant, but it wasn't painful, either. Rather a sort of vehement and

inner knowing. The elemental spell had been success-
ful. She opened her eyes and looked over the map.

Ethan kneeled on the opposite side of the map and
scanned the results as well. "What are all the glowing
red salt crystals?"

"Demons," she said.

"There's so many. Thousands."

"Are you surprised?"

"No. But how is this going to help our search?"

"Hold your horses, big boy. The real magic comes
next."

Tugging loose the ribbon ties at the bodice of her
new shirt, Tuesday tossed the obsidian crystal over her
shoulder and then pressed her fingers against the sigil
between her breasts. She lowered her other hand over
the map, moving methodically as she silently thought
Gazariel's name. The sigil warmed and she could feel
the tendrils of it creep through her chest and toward her
extremities. It noticed her.

And that was not a good thing.

Wanting to abruptly end the spell, she suddenly noted
the violet glow at one edge of the map. "There! Where
is that?"

Ethan turned his head to assess the map. "Looks
like the Bois de Boulogne. A big, forested park at the
edge of the city. Is that purple spot The Beautiful One?"

"It is. And now I'm cutting the connection before he
catches on."

"Wait!"

Tuesday pulled her fingers from the sigil. The violet
light snuffed out.

"If you would have held on longer, I could have
marked the exact location," Ethan protested. "That

would have made our job easier. Are you helping me or hindering me, witch?"

"What do you think I'm doing? You think I enjoy being your captive? I want this over as quickly as possible. But I will not call the demon directly to me. He could manifest within me. And then what will you do?"

"That can happen?"

"It's likely. But remember what Edamite said. If he's smart he's not going to come near me. And he is."

"Sorry. I, uh… I don't intend to place you in harm's way. I just want to utilize your expertise."

"And this, eh?" She tapped the sigil.

"Can I take a look at that?"

She studied his curious gaze. He wasn't aware that a childlike wonder could overtake his normally serious expression. Nor could he be aware how much that relaxation of his outer shield attracted her. Because it made him everything he probably didn't want to be— soft, kind, accepting.

Tuesday nodded her consent.

Ethan reached over and pressed two fingers to the sigil. It was an intimate touch and her skin warmed. Her breasts hugged his knuckles. He flicked his wondrous gaze onto hers.

"I can feel your fear," he said. "I don't want you to be afraid. I will protect you."

Tuesday wrapped her fingers about his wrist, holding him there at her breast. "There's nothing a vampire can do to protect me that I can't already do myself. You're going to have to make a better plea for my continuing to work with you than that."

"All right. How about this?"

And with that, he slid over the salt map, smearing

the left bank of Paris, and cupped the back of her head as he pulled her in for another sudden kiss.

His mouth warmed against hers and demanded she not ignore him. That she allow him to protect her. And at the same time, it teased her to submit in a way she generally didn't care to with a man. It was the surprise of their connection, their easy manner of locking lips, that excited her, and made her want to not break it.

On her knees, Tuesday scooched closer. He slipped one hand down her hair and clasped his fingers into it, easing her forward, into his arms. Into his interesting acceptance. She'd thought he didn't like witches. So why was he kissing her?

Did it matter? Not in this moment. She wanted to taste every sensual, hot bit of him. Inhale his cool, fresh-air scent, and every breath that he greedily gave and took from her. Moaning into his mouth, she grabbed at his shirt and straddled his legs with hers. They kneeled there on the scattered remains of the city map, a strange fusion of opposites who couldn't resist the pull to experience one another.

And when he put his hand again on the sigil, she moved his fingers to cup her breast. She hugged up against him, giving him permission to touch her, wanting to own the vampire's desire… To control him as he sought to control her.

Ethan broke the kiss and pulled his hand abruptly from her skin. "Uh…"

Appearing befuddled, he probably wasn't sure why he'd kissed her. And had manhandled her boob. So she wouldn't let him consider it too long. Because if she had to use normal skills instead of magic to control him, it was best to keep him unsure and wondering.

"Feel like a walk in the park?" she asked.

"Sure. I um…"

She stood and knotted the ties of her shirt into a bow. "Then let's get to it before I shove you down and have some hex with you."

She'd let him ponder the use of that word for what she really wanted to do to him. The man had ignited something within her. And she had never been a witch to deny herself the pleasures life offered.

Chapter 6

Parked at the curb, Ethan waited for Tuesday while she purchased food from a stand. He didn't use the BMW often because he walked to work even in the winter. Vampires could easily regulate their body temperature. But the trip to the park would prove long on foot, and he didn't want the witch to suffer the cold, especially walking in those high-heeled boots.

Tuesday slid in and closed the door and settled back to chomp on a savory-smelling crepe.

"You want a bite? It's got weird French cheese and ham in it. This is amazing."

"I'd rather suck dead blood," he muttered.

"Oh, yeah? What's wrong with a little taste once in a while? I know vampires can eat small amounts of food."

"I don't have a taste for meat. I get enough of the flavor when I drink blood. And you just dripped fontina onto the leather seat. Would you be careful?"

"Fontina, eh? Don't tell me you don't steal a taste every now and then." She swiped a napkin over the seat and then leaned forward, pointing. "That's the— What is it?"

"The Louvre," he pronounced carefully.

"Louv-ra, with the ra-ra shout at the end," she mocked. "You're not French, are you?"

"I'm English. Born in London, actually, but I didn't stay there more than a decade. I've lived everywhere. Spent some time in the Americas in the 1700s. Right around the time Massachusetts became a state."

"Good times," she said, sitting back. "Puritanical shame, Indian genocide and witch hunts. Go, witch hunters! Not."

Ethan shouldn't have brought that up. If she knew about the travesties he'd committed against witches when he had been a young vampire only set on impressing his tribe leaders? He'd be very thankful for the binding spell that prevented her from using magic against him.

"Have you been in Paris before?" he asked.

"Once or twice. Never for longer than a month or two. And never in a mood to do any touristing. Once I was here looking for a bastard imp who stole my voice. Little creep isn't singing or snickering anymore. What's that?"

"The Luxor Obelisk." Ethan drove by the seventy-five-foot-high yellow granite obelisk placed in the center of the Place de la Concorde at the end of the Tuileries Garden. "Originally located at the Luxor Temple in Egypt—a gift from Muhammad Ali Pasha, the ruler of Egypt at the time."

"You know the city's history."

"I've lived it. Of all my centuries, I've spent the most time in Paris. And up ahead is the Champs-Élysées."

"Oh, I know that's a good shopping street. Should

have waited to get my togs up ahead." She scanned the signs screaming for customers to come in and spend their precious euros. They passed luxury-car dealers and high-end clothing retailers. And… "There's a Mc-Donalds on the classy upscale shopping street?"

"And movie rental stores," Ethan said. "Go figure. It's all a big tourist trap. But then, this street has been ever since Napoleonic times."

"More good times," Tuesday offered. "The Inquisition was still around then. You gotta love a self-righteous maniac intent on destroying that which he does not understand. And if it's a woman, then even more reason to put her in her place."

"Do you remember any good times that were actually good?"

"Oh, sure. I loved the late nineteenth century. So bohemian. We witches really got to shine then. The seventies and the hippies also welcomed us with open arms. What's that? Wait! I know this one."

Ethan stopped the car at a light before he would enter the roundabout before the monument.

"The arch of triumph, right?"

"Right." He wouldn't correct her too harshly. "Napoleon's Arc d'Triomphe, erected to honor those who served in the Revolutionary and Napoleonic wars. There's a tomb of an unknown soldier beneath it. If you go to the top it offers a great view of the whole city."

"Then let's do it. Yeah?"

"After the demon is found you can take all the time you like for sightseeing."

"Because then you'll cut my leash and set me free?"

He didn't like hearing it put that way, but it was the truth. "Exactly."

Ten minutes later they pulled in to the park, which was massive and filled with sports areas, a zoo and playgrounds, housing and entertainment complexes. And yet there was still a preserved forested area, an oasis set at the border of the big, cosmopolitan city. A light dusting of snow clung to the trees, giving the forest a faery-tale touch as sun twinkled on the snow.

Ethan parked in a lot before a hiking trail. He kept the car running because the witch would probably appreciate the heat. He pulled on his blue-lensed sunglasses. He could walk in direct sunlight a few minutes without feeling the burn, and much longer in the winter sun. And these lenses were also charmed to view wards, which served as more than a means to protection from sizzling retinas.

"What's the plan?" Tuesday asked. "Are we going to tromp about the park and call 'Here, demon, come on, demon!'"

"Won't that sigil you wear lead us to him?"

"Right." She touched her chest and closed her eyes. "Or him to me. Not that he'd come running with arms wide open to embrace me."

Ethan sensed she plummeted to some place very low whenever she touched the sigil. He had to ask. "Tell me how you got the sigil? It could be helpful to know what I'm dealing with here."

"*Now* you decide to ask about the stakes? You are so not a romantic, vampire."

"What does romance have to do with anything?"

"Nothing." She crossed her arms over her chest and averted her gaze out the window. "Kisses don't have any place between us, either."

"I beg to differ. They have proven a useful tool for me."

"Again, not a romantic bone in your body, eh?"

"What? Do you require emotion, some feeling next time I kiss you?"

"You think you're going to kiss me again?"

"Probably."

She turned on the seat to look at him. "Why? Do you like kissing me?"

"It was pleasant." He sounded like an asshole, but what was she angling for right now with that teasing question? The woman was a curiously complex mixture of opposites. One minute she was trying to put a hex on him to make his dick limp, the next she wanted to make out. "Do *you* want to kiss me again?"

She sat up, lifting her chin haughtily. "You haven't been kissed by me yet, vampire. When I kiss you properly? You'll know. And you'll never have to wonder if you want another again. Because you will. You'll crave my kiss, my touch. You'll want to hex me every chance you get."

Ethan offered a shrug. "Have to say, that does sound intriguing."

"Damn right it does. So we heading out on the demon quest?"

"First, I need the details." He pushed back his seat and tilted to face her comfortably. Taking off the sunglasses, he asked, "Tell me how you got Gazariel's sigil."

Boston, MA—1680

Finnister McAdams was going blind. He wore a black strip of sack cloth across his eyes now because he had explained to Tuesday how the light bothered him. Made him blink and gave him headaches. 'Twas as if the devil was prodding his eyes with his mighty pitchfork.

Tuesday knew well the Devil Himself did not wield a pitchfork, but to correct him would only put her in danger. She'd prepared Finn an herbal tincture in his morning tea. Rosemary, black salts and feverfew. Had cast a healing spell…without him knowing. Even laid mustard plasters over his eyes. Nothing proved efficacious.

Now she considered calling up a demon to aid in healing her lover's eyes. Such creatures did possess healing powers. At least, a few of them did so. If only the witch summoning them could find a beneficent demon. And that was the challenge.

Tuesday loved her man, Finn. From the moment he'd settled next to her in the lavender field and compared her eyes to the sky, she had loved him desperately. Three months they had been sharing her tiny cabin at the edge of the village with one another. Finn was strong and proud, and very handsome. His hair was copper, his thick beard as well. His skin was ruddy and pale, so he always wore a wide-brimmed hat when outside. He was fashioned of flame and earth. And when he held her in his arms it wasn't tentative or rough. He knew how to hold a woman. And Tuesday's heart fluttered when he kissed her.

But if he knew she was a witch he would be displeased. The man was Puritan. His family had sailed across the Atlantic Ocean from England six months earlier. His father was seeking a congregation to share and spread the word of God. And Finnister, while a godly man, seemed more inclined to craftwork that involved turning wood into beautiful creations. He even fashioned lovely knife hilts, and had skill with a blade.

With the witch trials and all the heinous accusations running rampant of late, Tuesday did not dare reveal her truth to her lover. Because even if he could accept her, she risked the townsfolk putting him on trial for harboring her secret.

But she could no longer bear to see him stumble about the house, seeking wood for the stove and instead stabbing his fingers into the log pile and yelping as slivers cut through his skin. Or to watch him try to piss in the chamber pot and instead spray the stone floor.

She would care for him. Because she loved him.

But she must try one last thing before giving up on his healing. And that required she summon a demon. She wasn't schooled in demons, didn't know which to summon for the healing of sight, but would take whatever beast she could conjure. Surely, even a lowly demon might have some healing skills. And she had a way of winning a man's trust with her gentle confidence and attentive manner.

Shouldn't be so different with demons.

So just before midnight, on a hot summer's eve, she kissed Finn's forehead as he snoozed before the window, and snuck out with her cotton bag of charms and potions under her arm. Her wood-soled clogs took the soft red earth in quick strides and she was thankful for the fast-growing moss that muffled her steps. She would avoid the gatekeepers, and slip into the forest half a mile from the village. It was a haunted forest, or rumors told, so that kept out most villagers.

All except those who knew better. Like her. The forest was a thin place where the realm of Daemonia overlapped this mortal realm. Summoning a demon would be as simple as snapping her fingers. And having the fortitude to do so.

Tuesday had lived nearly forty years, and had honed her magical skills in privacy and under the tutelage of some powerful aunts and good women. She had eaten a vampire's heart to secure immortality and a youthful appearance—at least, for another century—and had cast down the moon and summoned healings and utilized the natural elements to move through life.

She was not like those women who were being accused in the trials. Women who had knowledge of female anatomy and tried to heal and teach others. They were merely humans who sought to educate and save. But the menfolk would not condone a smart woman living in their midst. Females were to submit and serve. And they used them as cat's-paws and accused them of witchery. Anything to subdue and make them submissive.

Of course, Tuesday could be thankful for the distraction of that wayward and unprofessional witchery. It kept most eyes from her, a true witch. And she was wise enough not to share her skills with anyone who had not been vetted to her by a witch elder. Even when Finn slyly questioned if she would ever attempt witchcraft, she laughed and told him he was silly. It was something she imagined most every woman in the village had been asked. Men were suspicious creatures. Their fear of losing control to what they deemed a *mere* woman made them so.

A woman would do well to learn how to control such irresponsible creatures—men. And she was teaching herself that by learning all that she could about herself, her body, nature and the universe. Strength came with wisdom and knowledge.

But tonight she would reach beyond her own capabilities in a quest to save her lover's sight.

Once deep in the forest, she did not light a candle. She didn't wish discovery by hunters. Drawing out a pentagram with black salt on the leaf-crusted forest floor, she spoke the invocation to summon a demon. The surprise she felt when one appeared made her step back and clutch the smoky quartz she wore from a leather strap about her neck for protection. He stood within the circle, but posed gallantly beside a thick oak, elbow propped high to lean against it.

His eyes glowed red, so she knew he was demon. But otherwise he looked a human, dressed in a fine blue silk frock coat, shot through with silver threading, and with lace dripping around his wrists and at his neck. Such finery belonged only to royalty. She had seen Pandora dolls imported from Europe wearing such elaborate silks. And his hair was long and wavy and black as midnight. He smelled...of lilacs. A pretty man—demon—if she was to size him up. And that notion startled her. Should not demons be more creature-like? Horned and possessed of red or black skin with claws? This demon's handsome appearance was disconcerting, to say the least.

"Who are you?" she asked, a bit too timidly for her comfort. So she set back her shoulders and lifted her chin. Courage hummed in her bones. "Have you come from Daemonia?"

"You don't even know who you've summoned? What a sorry witch you are!" The demon tugged out the lace from the end of one sleeve. "Daemonia is the last place

I should ever tread. I am of this realm. And I am Gazariel, The Beautiful One."

Tuesday knew demons often went by monikers, and that one was right on the nose. Beautiful, indeed. And he seemed to believe it himself, judging by his mannerisms. Primping and preening. Not a wrinkle to the silk, nor a hair out of place. Was that rouge on his pale cheeks?

She tested the binding on the summons and did not feel a weakness in the air. He could not approach her, and if he tried, the circle should keep him in check.

"I need your help," she said. "With a healing."

The demon rolled his eyes and shook his head sadly. "Bother. Always with the sicknesses! And here I thought you might request I attend the next village soiree and impregnate a dozen virgins with my demon babies." He gestured dismissively. "You're boring, witch."

"My lover is going blind. You can kiss his eyes and give him sight."

"Of course I can." He rubbed his fingernails against the embroidery edging his silk lapels. "We demons have such skills. Most of us, anyway. I would not dare to ask a wrath demon for some delicate brain trephination, though, mind you. What is this lover's name?"

"Finnister McAdams. His sight is almost completely gone. He is a kind man. And so young. He is strong and contributes all that he can to the village. If you could see to healing him, I would be ever grateful."

"Release me," the demon said.

Tuesday's spine stiffened. She was no fool. "Not until you give me what I ask."

"I can't go near the man unless you unbind me, now

can I?" He splayed his lace-encircled hand toward the circle on the ground.

That was true. He did need to move about freely. And she could hardly lead Finn here to the forest to receive what healing magic the demon could provide. Such had to be managed with cunning.

"You'll follow me home and attend to him while he sleeps?"

"He doesn't know you're a witch? Of course not. You may be a bore but you are not stupid. Take down the circle. I'll see what I can do. And in turn, I'll ask a favor from you."

"Which is?"

He shrugged and flipped out a hand to display the lace grandly. "I'll decide on that after the task is complete."

A favor to a demon? It was only fair to reciprocate. But she wasn't sure what she could do for him. And she had no intention of having one of his demon babies. Well. She could not. Her womb was barren. She'd known that for decades. A condition she'd been born with, according to a wise witch who had gazed into her soul and seen her birth.

With trepidation, Tuesday slashed a foot through the salt circle. The demon disappeared instantly, leaving her alone in the dark woods. An owl hooted, chastising her with his repeated tones.

"I have been a fool! He will never give me what I want. I should have offered him a gift immediately. Given him reason to want to help me."

And what would the creature demand of her should he serve her wishes? It would never be good, she felt sure.

"It is a sacrifice I am willing to make," she muttered and turned to wander back to the village.

By the time she returned home, she saw the demon standing outside her door. His pale blue frock coat was an unwanted beacon in the darkness, and in a village where the only colors worn were black, brown and gray.

She rushed up to him. "What are you doing here? You can't be seen!"

"Oh, Tuesday Knightsbridge, you sad, pitiful witch." He placed a hand over her chest, right between her breasts, and Tuesday felt a searing pain but she could not step away from the demon. "Your lover lies to you. I came here to find him returning from the forest. He followed you. Watched you and I. He knows. And he is not going blind. His sight is as perfect as yours or mine."

"No, that's—"

"That's a foolish witch for you," the demon said piteously. "And you have fallen in love with a witch hunter. Ha!"

The searing at her chest now burned as if in flames.

Then her front door opened, and Finn spilled out with hell blazing in his eyes. He looked right at her. Saw her for what she was. Finn snarled, "Witch!"

The torture began the next day. The water chair was the one that siphoned all Tuesday's gumption from her. She was tied to a chair on the end of a seesaw and repeatedly dunked into the filthy, muddy river. Each time she was lifted above water, gasping, choking, pleading for Finn to stop, she was commanded to confess to being a witch and consorting with demons.

She would not. She would survive this. Somehow.

Later, the whip that flayed at her skin left deep gashes, and caused Tuesday to pass out more than a few times. Hot pokers to her hips and between her toes almost made her confess. Almost.

After four days of suffering her lover's vicious, hateful punishments, Tuesday was lying on the cold, hard dirt floor on a tiny cell at the edge of the village. No moonlight on this night of the new moon. On the other side of the building, the village pigs snorted and rooted, and filled the air with a nauseating odor that she breathed as if a toxin.

All vitality had been beaten out of her. Even the will to live had been vanquished with a humiliating search of her private body parts in search of devil's marks. Finn had done so before a dozen village elders. All men. All leering. If she'd the strength she would have cast a spell over them all, reducing them to stupid, foul, snorting pigs like those outside her cell. Alas, she'd expelled all her energies with a breathing spell during the dunking.

She would be dead by morning. Her tattered heart told her as much. And she sighed with acceptance.

When the flash of red light flickered in the cell and she scented a brief fragrance of lilacs, she tried to lift her head to look at the demon, but the flay marks along her neck pained her with every subtle movement.

The demon's silk, red-heeled shoes were but inches from her face. "Men are terrible, yes?"

Indeed. And yet, she was not prepared to condemn them all. Her father had been a good man. And the village baker, who she knew was married to a witch whom he protected, was also kind. "Not all of them."

"You're right. It is love that is so vile. Can't be trusted. Merely a means to trick and use innocence. And you have been thoroughly used, my witch."

Indeed. Why had the demon returned? To rub her failures into her open wounds? Or did he still require

she serve him something in return? He hadn't healed
Finn, for the man hadn't required any healing.

The demon bowed low and the tickle of his hair
across her cheek smelled sweet and too luxurious. "I
can give you something that you'll find most useful."

"Leave me to die, demon."

"Do not address me so. It is vulgar. I am The Beautiful One."

She could but close her eyes tightly and wish death
would quicken its pace.

"I carry a curse," Gazariel continued. "But I don't
need it. Or want it. And you can have it if you'll willingly accept it."

A curse? Why ever would she ask for a curse?

By some means, Tuesday managed to roll to her
back. The red light surrounding him illuminated her
cell. Her tormentor looked down over her. Pity from a
demon? She'd thought being held under the river waters
for long minutes had been her lowest. Gazariel's pouting mouth reduced her to less than that low.

"If I am dead," she whispered, "curse or not, it will
not matter."

"Oh, you're going to live, witch. I will make sure of
that. The question is, do you want to walk this earth a
wise, smart, powerful witch who will never again be
defeated by love?"

The demon placed his palm between her breasts. And
Tuesday felt a darkness tickle into her heart.

"What is the curse?" she asked.

He leaned in and whispered in her ear, and his voice
was melodious and warming. "You will never know
true love again. Your soul will repel it, and even should
it occur, the moment your lover realizes he loves you

he will suddenly hate you. Perhaps even suffer a cruel malady or some such," he added offhandedly.

Such a curse actually sounded sweet and tempting. She was lying here, near death, because of love. Fickle, cruel love. And she wanted the demon to save her. No one ever wanted to die. And she wasn't singular for wishing it so. Even for the sacrifice of accepting such a deal. To never again know love? To feel the pain of what love could do to her?

To live so that she could walk away from the bastard Finnister McAdams and all those men who had wounded her soul deep?

With a nod, she said, "I'll take the curse."

The demon lifted her under the chin, dragging her body to sit up. With a forceful shove, Tuesday's back hit the cell wall and she screamed at the pain as the sigil seared into her skin.

Gazariel apported out of the tiny cell. And she did not see him ever again.

Chapter 7

That was a heavy past to carry in one's baggage. Ethan rubbed his jaw and shook his head. "I'm sorry."

A smirk to send away the horrible remembrance of the pain she had endured at her lover's hand was all Tuesday could manage. "Don't be. I took the curse willingly."

"To never have love?"

She shrugged. "It was a means to escape the torture and to live."

"But you can't still want such a thing?"

She shrugged and looked aside. Ethan's heart shivered as it had when she'd described the awful torture she'd endured at the hands of a witch hunter, a man she had loved.

He knew what it felt like to wield the whip. Never against a witch, of course. Their blood could have killed him back in the days when such violence had been acceptable, a means to survival. As a young vampire in his tribe, he'd been tested, asked to prove his alliances, most especially during the Blood Wars that had seen his tribe fighting the werewolves. Never had he regretted those acts more than now. Yet to mention it would not win any trust from the witch.

Could his actions since she'd arrived in Paris be construed as a subtle torture, a form of control? Surely. Hell, he didn't want to think about this too much. It would only stifle the mission. He had to focus on the task at hand. Her tale was sad, but she had survived, and seemed the stronger for it.

She'd been punished for caring about another man. By a seemingly selfish and narcissistic demon, who had cursed her only because he could. And yet, she had willingly taken his dark curse in a moment of such weakness she could not have known the impact it would have on her. No one would wish to never know love. Even he, who was jaded by love, would take it if the time was right and his heart leaped.

"We can't wander about the forest calling out for the demon," she said as a means to indicate she was finished talking about her history.

The demon had taken advantage of her.

Now more than ever Ethan wanted to find that bastard, and once he gave up the book with the code, then Ethan would banish him to Daemonia, never to return. Was there a possibility he could have Gazariel take back the curse from Tuesday? With the forced expulsion to Daemonia, all curses, hexes and otherwise foul doings would be erased in the demon's wake. She could be freed if he found the demon and kicked him the hell out of the mortal realm.

"You're right about wandering around without a clear direction." He started the engine and the car heater roared up again. "Tell me what to do."

With a heavy sigh, she pointed behind her. "I think he's probably living in one of those fancy apartments we passed. I mean, he's not living in a tree. The man can obviously walk and live amongst the mortals without suspicion, like all the other demons that showed up on my map. They hold jobs, they live and love, they pass for human."

"As we all do."

"Exactly. So, I need to cast a GPS spell and that should lead us in the right direction."

"A GPS spell? Like the map you cast at my place?"

"This one is more advanced. A witch has got to evolve with the technology, yeah?"

A witch, a vampire and every other paranormal species. The mortal realm was not designed for their sort. At least regarding being out and vocal about who and what they were. His species did what they had to do to survive.

"What do you need to cast such a spell?"

"Your cell phone, and the demon's sigil. And a couple drops of blood."

About to ask why they couldn't use *her* phone, Ethan remembered she'd been taken from a bar in Massachusetts, with little more than her clothes and shoes. She probably didn't have a phone.

He tugged the phone from his pocket and before he handed it to her, he asked, "Is this going to brick my phone?"

"Nah." She grabbed it and tapped the home button. "Maybe? No. I don't know. I've never tried it before. I'm only just learning tech spells. But you're rich. You can afford another."

"What makes you think I'm rich?"

"You're driving a Bimmer. And that apartment with the stunning view had to set you back a couple million."

So he was well off. That happened when a vampire took care to invest over the centuries and kept a healthy portfolio across various international markets and banks. Tech stocks were a gold mine. His accountant was a vampiress who lived near the Eiffel Tower, and she was a gem.

"Just don't set it on fire," he said.

"I won't. I think. Maybe?" She winked at him. "I do have water magic in case of emergency."

Her mood had lifted since she'd told him her tale, and he was grateful for that. Though he'd never discount anyone's suffering. There had been occasions he'd been hunted over the centuries—by slayers and werewolves—but nothing could compare to being caught and tortured. And to live to tell about it.

Tuesday set the phone on the raised center console between them and opened up her coat to tug free the ribbons at her shirt front. Those full breasts were a sweet tease, and Ethan had to remind himself he was on a mission. His attention swerved from her breasts to her lips, and back again.

Hell yes, he'd kiss her again. But thinking that made him wince as he sensed a swift boner could give him up. And the last thing he wanted to do with this witch was prove to her that he was the Richard she'd accused him of being.

"Got a knife?" she asked and extended her forefinger toward him. "I left my athame at your place."

Ethan stared at the finger and all lusty thoughts were replaced by sudden horror. Maybe that limp-dick spell had a delay set on it because he was no longer hard. Because what she asked…

She needed blood for the magic. Blood magic was wicked and he'd known a lot of it might be needed on this adventure. He knew better than to challenge it, or try to interfere with it. But what should he expect from a dark witch?

"No knife," he said.

"Then take a bite, yeah?" She waggled her finger before him. "I just need a couple drops."

"Take a bite?" Aghast at her moxie, he shook his head in bewilderment. "What the hell?"

"Seriously, vampire? Just prick my finger with one of your fangs. Come on, you want to find this demon or not?"

Tonguing the insides of his upper teeth, he met her assessing stare, which wasn't so much aggressive as impatient. She was trying to cast a spell with the tools she had to work with. Yet a taste of blood could do *things* to him. Things that would bring up his erection again. He shouldn't make a big deal out of it.

Fuck, this woman challenged him on so many levels. He'd not expected this mission to become fraught with…emotion and utter mental challenge.

But he would not reveal his consternation. If he'd learned anything about Tuesday Knightsbridge, seeing him in a quandary would make her too happy.

Fangs lowering, he grabbed her wrist and pierced her finger with the pin-sharp tip of one of them. Blood scent curled into his nostrils. It was more alluring than the usual quick bite's coppery, chemical-laced blood. This blood was deep, thick and steeped with the centuries.

He quickly shoved her hand away so the temptation would not drip onto his tongue.

Tuesday squeezed a couple drops onto the iPhone screen. She glanced at him. "You okay, vamp? Not going to attack me in a raging blood hunger?"

"I am perfectly capable of being around blood without turning into a monster." Turning into a horny flesh-pricker, on the other hand? When had he last smelled such…tempting blood?

"Good for you." She stuck her finger in her mouth and sucked at it. "Holster those fangs then, will you? Makes me nervous."

"Really?" He leaned forward, brandishing his fangs boldly. "You scared I'll attack?"

"No, I just like the bite too much."

Startled by that reply, he sat back. Was she a fang junkie? He'd thought only humans succumbed to such base lust for the bite. It was the orgasmic sensations the bite delivered. Such highs could become a drug. Some humans could not get enough.

She winked at him. Ethan willed his fangs to rise to their normal positions.

"Hey, it's as good for the bite-ee as it is for the biter," she said. "You know that. So! Let's get this spell going, yeah?"

Sure. But it was difficult now *not* to think about clasping her long white hair in his hand as he breathed against her neck, dripping with blood. It would taste like the world and all he had lived through. And such memories were both sweet and sour.

Tuesday drew the demon's S-shaped sigil on the phone screen with the blood. A line was drawn through that, connecting both curves. The GPS app was open, he noticed, and now he found it easier to turn his attention to what she was doing instead of slipping into a lusty fantasy of slurping at her neck and making her come with nothing more than the bite.

Pressing her bloodied finger to the sigil between her breasts, Tuesday bowed her head and began to chant. The air in the car grew throat-clutchingly humid, and then it took on an icy chill that hardened his sinuses before returning to normal. Ethan coughed. The phone jittered. The blood purled and rose in droplets, reaching for the hand Tuesday held but inches from the phone. And the scent swarmed Ethan's senses and pushed him headfirst into the unavoidable fantasy.

She would taste old and ancient, laced with centuries of experience. He could sup at her, drain her of her magic… A vampire could steal a witch's power by enacting bloodsexmagic. It required having sex with the witch while drinking her blood and enacting a spell. He'd never thought to do something so wicked. Until now.

A snap of fingers stirred Ethan back to the now. "What?"

"Where were you, vampire?"

In a heated embrace with a witch who could give him so much more than he'd ever dreamed to have.

"Sorry, got lost for a minute there."

"Oh, yeah? Are you aroused?"

He tilted his head, sneering. "You think a few drops of blood is enough to get me horny?"

She shrugged. "I do. Truth be told, I'm feeling it. I mean, like I said, fangs do it for me. Seriously."

Ethan ran his tongue under the tip of one fang. Oh, the serious action he could show her. But he wasn't a fool. And he was a man on a mission. "Did it work?"

"I got a hit." She tapped the phone. "Looks like he's north about a quarter of a mile."

The twosome got out of the car. Ethan scanned their surroundings. Beyond a copse of ancient oak trees rose a gated community that likely sheltered old money and self-made tech millionaires.

"You ever break and enter?" he asked.

"I don't think I should answer that one." Tuesday shrugged up her coat and then shook her hands out at her sides as if preparing for a gunfight. "But whatever fun you're planning? I'm in!"

Attempting to enter a gated community in full daylight was probably not the wisest move, but Tuesday was in it to win it. Besides, she wanted to see if Ethan had a plan. He didn't have a plan. She knew it. But she'd give him the benefit of the doubt. Until he failed, and she'd have an argument for her release and could be done with him.

Telling him about her past hadn't been a problem. She held no emotion for the stupid witch she'd once been. Smarter, wiser, she now did better because she knew better. And she hadn't been looking for sympathy from the vampire, though she'd felt it rise off him in the car. Whatever.

She'd revealed her curse, but she would never tell him the ridiculous means to break that curse. That was a secret she'd take to her grave. Besides, knowing it would keep it from ever happening.

They'd parked a block down from the black wrought-iron gates and now strolled casually along the hornbeam hedgerow that grew eight feet high. Hands shoved in his coat pockets, the vampire kept a keen eye from behind the sexy blue sunglasses. Not many were out walking because the day was chilly.

One small reason to be thankful—when she'd been kidnapped she'd been wearing her alpaca coat. She loved this thing, and it was warm.

The vampire looked…cold. His coat was short, stopping below his waist, and revealed a nice tight ass that was emphasized perfectly by the dark jeans. If the fangs in the car hadn't started her engine, that view certainly revved it to a wanting purr.

To do the guy or not? Everything about his controlling authority screamed *no, run away!* And everything else, from the fangs to the sexy smile, begged her to give him a chance. One more kiss. One good fuck. A no-strings hex-fest of nudity, fangs and orgasms unending.

Tuesday suddenly bumped right in to Ethan, who had stopped walking for some odd reason.

"Really?" he murmured. "I thought witches had a built-in sixth-sense kind of thing. Were you walking with your eyes closed?"

"My sixth sense isn't tuned to idiots," she responded. Good save. She'd been thinking about his fangs in her neck and how strong of an orgasm that would give her. If her tale of taking the curse wasn't enough to remind her what a fool she could be for a handsome smile then…whew!

The entry gate was twenty feet ahead. Time to pull on her stern witch and focus. "What's the plan?"

"I don't have a plan."

"I knew it."

"Why not just stroll in?" Ethan asked.

"Awesome. The direct approach, it is. Let's see you work your skills, vampire."

"I've got skills." And with that he strode toward the small, freestanding office situated next to the entry gate. He cast her a smirk over his shoulder.

And Tuesday was all in with the tease. She hastened her steps, following him like a witch to the lying witch hunter.

Inside the outhouse-sized office situated before the gate, a man pushing ninety lifted his chin and eyed their approach. He shook his head, obviously not recognizing Ethan, and said, "We don't allow solicitors, monsieur. Move along."

Ethan slid his hand through the small space beneath the protective Plexiglas window and smiled charmingly. "This won't take long."

The old man shoved at Ethan's hand, but then all of a sudden his fingers shook and he dropped them onto Ethan's palm. The vampire clasped his fingers and said calmly, "We're here to visit friends. Won't be long. You won't remember us, nor will you consider anything out of the ordinary. Open the gates, please."

Dropping the old man's hand and stepping back to stand next to Tuesday, Ethan waited while the gates swung inward.

"Nice." She marched forward, giving the gatekeeper a thumbs-up as she did. "Persuasion?"

"I can convince a man to jump into flames," he said

as he passed her by and wandered along the edge of the curbed and curved drive.

The road was bare of snow and Tuesday assumed it had heat coils beneath, for she could sense the electric vibrations as she walked it. Ethan's steps moved faster and all of a sudden she was tugged along against her will.

"Damn binding spell." She picked up her pace.

There had to be a way to crack the bond open. For as intriguing as it was to follow Mr. Tight Pants, she could not abide this humiliation for much longer. This was one curse she had not asked for.

Ethan paused before the garage entrance. To each side of the underground lot stood a massive four-story complex that stretched longer than a football field in each direction.

"Now what?" she asked.

"What's your tracker say?"

She checked the GPS on his phone. One tiny blood drop moved over the screen as they had walked. "He's to the left."

And her heart dropped as she realized she could be so close to the one demon she'd tried to avoid and had done so successfully for centuries. Why was she walking into a grand old reunion now?

"Wait, Ethan."

He turned and waited for her to speak.

"Maybe you can take it from here," she said, hating her sudden rise of worry and weakness. She stood up to demons all the time. She was witch! Hear her cackle!

But Gazariel?

The image of the demon's silk shoes with painted red

heels standing but inches from her face was the most heart-wrenching memory.

"You think he's going to hurt you?" Ethan asked. "I don't know why he would. It sounds like you took the one thing from him he least wanted. He should welcome you with open arms."

"Yeah? I don't think so. He probably thinks I can return the curse back to him."

"Can you?"

"No! The only way to break the curse is…" Yeah, that part about a true love willing to die for her? Ethan didn't need to know about that. "Like it or not, we are connected. He probably knows I'm close right now."

"Which means we should hurry. Whether he's happy or angry to see you, we'll find out soon enough."

She grabbed him by the coat. "Give me a plan, yeah? I mean, when we do find him, what then? Are you going to slap a pair of handcuffs on him and hope the steel doesn't instantly melt, and in turn, the demon melts us?"

He took the phone from her. "I've got a containment crew on speed dial. They'll be here five minutes after my call. Can I, uh…use this now?"

"Yes, sure." She wiped off her blood from the screen and he started to scroll. "But what are we going to do while we wait out those very long and most likely painful five minutes in the demon's presence?"

"Certainly Jones gave me a demon manacle." He patted his pocket. "It'll contain the subject."

"Let me see it."

"Don't you trust me? Do you think I'd walk in on a demon ill-prepared? I've done this before."

"Have you?" She wasn't feeling it. He hadn't seemed

to have a plan yet. Why all of a sudden should he be prepared?

"Don't worry, Tuesday. I've got this one."

She sighed and dropped her shoulders. Wasn't as if she had a right to argue. She was merely the lure. And she did want to get this show on the road. The sooner they found Gazariel, the quicker she would be freed.

Ethan talked to someone on the line, confirming arrival in five minutes.

Time to let the guy show her he was the man and that he had everything under control? In her experience that never seemed to go quite as spectacularly as the man thought it would. And she was always left to sweep up the bloody pieces.

He smiled at her as he conferred with whomever he was talking to.

Why she should let Ethan take the alpha route was beyond her, but she submitted because…that ridiculous charming smile did possess a magic of its own.

As did the wanting, needy witch who had been willing to summon a demon to save her fickle lover's eyesight.

"Let's do this then," she said as Ethan hung up. "But don't say I didn't warn you in advance. This is not going to go well."

Chapter 8

Ethan did not appreciate that the witch had no trust in him. Before taking the cozy seat of director of Acquisitions, he'd been a retriever for a century. He knew this job and had chased every artifact, magical spell and creature in existence. Demons were easy enough to subdue if a man had the proper bind. And CJ had promised the manacle he'd given him would work.

He checked his pocket for the small iron pod, which he need only toss at the demon to bind him. And at his wrist he'd drawn a demon protection spell with a felt-tip marker before leaving his loft. He would be able to approach Gazariel, but it should deflect any demonic magic until the subject was securely bound.

Proceeding onward, he strode toward the elevator in the building lobby. Tuesday followed. He probably didn't need her from this point on. The phone GPS spell had taken them as far as it could. The demon was somewhere in the building. But the fact she wore the demon's sigil, and was feeling the demon's presence now, could not be overlooked.

And as long as she was with him, he could protect her from Gazariel. "Up and to the left," Tuesday reported as they stepped onto the elevator and the doors closed behind them. Barry Manilow's "Mandy" hummed out of the speakers while they slowly rose two floors.

"You're tracking now from a...feeling?" Ethan asked.

"It's the sigil. It senses the demon. As I'm sure he feels me. And that is not a pleasant feeling, let me tell you."

"You can wait outside."

"Don't think so, vampire. I'm not a pussy. I'm in it to win it. Besides, how do you intend to enter a private residence?"

Vampires could not enter a private residence unless invited. It was something that didn't ever cause Ethan concern because he'd developed ways to get around that detour over the years. "I'll call out the demon."

"Not going to happen. He's too smart. You'll have to follow me inside." She looked upward, then closed her eyes. "Must be the top floor. Yep." The doors dinged and she strolled out, heading left down the hallway. "You should probably call in your containment crew right now."

"They should already be on the grounds." Ethan took out his phone. He dialed and gave the team leader directions to the building and floor. Estimated arrival time was less than five minutes.

"I feel like it's...just ahead," Tuesday said as she

pressed her fingers between her breasts. "Must be that door at the end of the hallway."

"Must be?"

The witch stopped and tugged apart her blousy shirt to reveal the glowing sigil. It was faint but glowed red, as if it burned. Definitely working.

Ethan nodded. "All right. It's that suite. I suppose if a demon is going to live it up in the ritzy part of town he should go for the best. Let me take the lead."

"Why? You got magic to keep back the demon?"

"I've got the manacle and demonic wards."

"That's sweet." She stopped before him, hands to her hips. "But what are you going to do when the bastard charges us and then smokes out of sight? You can't manacle smoke. We need to catch him unawares. Which I'm guessing is going to be impossible thanks to your bait."

She suddenly hissed and swore, pressing her hand to her chest. Actual smoke tendriled between her fingers.

"He's close. I gotta ward myself." She stretched out her arms over her head, then swung them down along her body to her feet. A whoosh of cool air prickled across Ethan's skin. "You want in?"

Ethan didn't have to consider it. "Hell yes."

She slapped her hands to the top of his head, then dragged both down along his shoulders and his length to his feet, drawing around him with what he felt as a tightening tingle that briefly squeezed his skin. He'd never submitted to witchcraft before, but this adventure was offering up a slew of new challenges.

"What will this do?" he asked.

"Hopefully, keep the demon from peeling our skin off too terribly quickly." She noticed his gape. "I don't know. Maybe he's not the skin-peeling type."

"I thought you knew this demon?"

"I do, but it's not like we had coffee and got to know one another. Last time I saw him was in the seventeenth century. And he placed his hand on my heart and filled me full of yuck."

"A yuck that you asked for."

"Stating facts isn't going to win you points."

"I know. You were near death. Anyone would have taken what he offered just to stay alive."

"Right, I wasn't thinking with all my faculties. And hey, I'm still alive, so I guess I should be thankful. Now. You take the lead. Knock on his door, why don't you?"

Ethan stepped up and took a moment to consider what he was doing. Casually knocking on a demon's door? Perhaps a team fully armed with semiautomatics and full assault gear? His days of knocking down the door to a werewolf pack's lair with a battering ram were long gone, but he never lost the skill or the caution.

Of course, the witch was right. If entry was required, he'd need to follow her in.

Ethan knocked on the door. The containment crew would be armed to the extent that they could hold the demon and some powerful spells. Where were they?

Tuesday hissed and clutched her chest. The demon had to know she was near. If they didn't act now they might lose him. She stood beside him. And he strangely felt like they were two door-to-door salesmen, hawking their mundane and ridiculous goods to complete strangers. Tuesday winked at him.

Her winks always made him feel a twinge of promise. The job did have some high points, after all.

"He's gone," she said with a gasp.

"What?"

"I don't feel him anymore. The sigil has gone cold. Look."

Indeed, the mark between her breasts was now merely dark gray, as if a faded tattoo.

Ethan reacted. He stepped back and lunged a kick at the door right beside the lock mechanism. The door swung inward and slammed against the wall. Tuesday walked over the threshold and said, "I invite you to enter, vampire."

Didn't matter who offered it, the invite was the key to breeching that nuisance vampire deterrent.

Ethan strode into the apartment, which opened into a vast room, gaudily furnished with a leopard-print sofa and chairs. The entire opposite wall sported floor-to-ceiling windows that looked out over the snow-dusted forest below. He had the option to go left or right. Right was a kitchen, so he turned left and raced down the hallway.

Tuesday stayed behind and began to chant some witchy incantation. It tightened the ward about his skin. *Good call, witch.*

The bedroom was empty, though the bedclothes were rumpled and the sheets pushed to the end. He held a hand over the mattress but didn't sense any warmth. In the bathroom the gleam of silver fixtures advertising ridiculous wealth blinded him, but no one hid in there. He rushed back out to the kitchen, where Tuesday stood surrounded by a glowing violet light.

"What are you doing?"

"He's coming," she said from within the violet aura, and turned toward the kicked-open front door.

Charging down the hallway strode a tall, dark-haired

man—demon—with fire in his eyes and wicked curved blades in each of his hands.

Tuesday felt her violet protective ward crack and fall away as the demon crossed the threshold into his own home. She was the intruder, and she felt a wicked tug at her energies because of it. As well, her initial white light began to shiver. It wouldn't hold for long. Nor would Ethan's.

Yet at the same time her chest lifted, her hands reached as if to caress, and her body wanted to walk toward the man. Demon. The one who had cursed her. Who had tricked her and set her on the path toward a loveless life. But as much as she embraced her choice to take that curse—at the time it had been her only option to survive—she did not want to embrace Gazariel. She had too much fight in her to succumb to anything else he should wish to put upon her.

But did Ethan? The vampire stood before the demon, shoulders back and in a defensive stance. He held the manacle bind in one hand, but had yet to toss it at the demon. Because he could not. The demon's power filled the room.

Gazariel clanked the curved blades together before him. Brilliant sparks scattered to the floor. He then splayed out his arms, not quite ready for battle, more a show of power. "So my curse taker has returned for more? Long time, no see, witch."

His voice was liquid and compelling. And indeed, the man was beautiful beyond compare. Dark hair spilled like diamonds past his shoulders. His face was perfectly symmetrical and his eyes glistened like blue gemstones.

A mouth that any woman would dream to kiss curled in wicked satisfaction.

"Idiot," Tuesday admonished herself as she shook herself out of the stare. That was exactly what the demon wanted. Her adoration. "I didn't return of my free will," she said to Gazariel. "I would never purposely seek you again. Never."

"And yet you have." Gazariel glanced at Ethan. "Vampire. Can't release the manacle?" The demon blew him a kiss. "What do you want from me that you would enter my home without permission?"

"You have the book of angel names and sigils written by the muse. Give it to me and we'll leave without incident."

Gazariel's laughter echoed like dulcet chimes throughout the room, but ended on a deafening snarl that coiled in Tuesday's lungs and tightened her breaths. Her white light wisped away, leaving her vulnerable. And the wanting rose. He was so attractive. And his voice...

"I don't know what you're talking about." The demon strolled casually toward the windows. With a flick of each hand the curved blades apported away from him and disappeared.

Taking his chance, Ethan flung the manacle toward the demon. Gazariel put up a hand, stopping the manacle in midair.

Startled out of the ridiculous pining, Tuesday snapped back into focus. She threw her own magic into the mix and asked the bind to find its victim. The small black hexagon manacle shuddered in midair, struggling against the demon's magic and her own. It cracked, emitting a beam of green light, and then dropped to the floor and shattered.

Ethan spoke into his phone. "Now!"

"The cavalry?" Gazariel glanced out the opened doorway. He shook his shoulders and spread out his arms, great black wings suddenly emerging behind him, wide enough to stretch the width of the room. "I don't think so."

With a bend of his fingers, Gazariel tugged Tuesday across the room, her feet dragging on the marble floor and toes tilting backward. She couldn't stop the movement. And when she landed in the demon's arms, he turned her back against his chest and clamped a hand up under her jaw. The icy prick of his fingernails to her skin pushed her back four centuries to that dreaded night he had touched her heart. And had taken love from her life ever after.

A forward sweep of his wing glanced across her face. It burned yet smelled sweet, as if flowers mingled with the most delectable treats. Lilacs. Oh… He was a wicked beauty.

The sigil on her chest burned brightly and she cried out at the pain of it. And at that moment Gazariel cried out, too, releasing her and shoving her to the floor.

"Damn it!" Wings folding down and dusting the floor, he shook out the hand that must have touched the sigil. "I forget we are inexplicably bound. And that was a curse I did not want to ever feel again. You, witch, are an imposition."

"And you are an asshole. But nothing has changed in four centuries, eh?"

"The containment team is on their way up," Ethan

announced. "Hand over the code now and we won't have to use force."

"Force?" The demon laughed. As his wings assumed full, shiny display behind him, he lifted his head regally. "You don't know what you're dealing with, do you, vampire? You, who would ally yourself with a powerful dark witch, yet are completely unaware of how her connection to me is forged. I might have put the curse inside her, but it will forever be rooted in my bones. It is why I have chosen to avoid Miss Knightsbridge for all this time. I can feel that bedamned curse. It wants back inside me." He clutched the fingers of one hand before him. "And know that for as long as she wears my curse, whatever I feel she will feel when we are in proximity."

Ethan glanced to Tuesday, who pushed up from the floor and backed away from the demon. She wasn't about to use any more magic when she knew it would be ineffective. Expelling such would only drain her.

"I think that means that if you hurt him, you hurt me," she said. "Peachy." Especially since she knew the retrieval of the book probably meant much more to Ethan than protecting her.

"She may carry the one thing I least want in this realm," the demon said. With a discerning tilt of his head, he appeared to sniff the air, perhaps take her in a bit more deeply. "But I must admit, it is attractive the longer I stand in its presence. Love can be so…heart-wrenching." He pursed his lips at them. "Oh. Sorry. You don't know that, do you, my witch? Or at least, you don't know anymore."

"If you're having relationship issues, then take it back," Tuesday said. "The curse is yours for the taking. I've had enough of it."

"Is that so? Does the pitiful witch now desire love? Perhaps you wish to fall head over heels with another witch hunter. You wore the gashes in your skin so beautifully." Gazariel chuckled and shook his head. "I will never have enough of the mortal pleasures I am able to enjoy thanks to not being shackled by that curse. Love and adoration are my oxygen! And I have tired of the two of you."

Out in the hallway a crew of three appeared, approaching cautiously.

Gazariel shook his head. "Too little. Too late." With a jaunty tilt of his head, he winked at Tuesday. "Let's have a little fun."

Spreading his arms out wide, Gazariel recited a demonic incantation. His wings closed about him, circling him, yet still kept a border of four feet around him. His own summoning circle, Tuesday guessed. From within the circle it began to glow blue, and a flurry of blue light wavered and then shot out to disperse into the ceiling, walls and floor.

Suddenly the building began to shudder. Tuesday had never experienced an earthquake but this must be what it felt like. Her body jittered. The floor tremored beneath her feet. A lamp toppled and Ethan stepped before her, as if to protect.

The demon smiled wickedly. In his hand he held a glowing blue light. "I will bring this building down if you do not take your minions and leave, vampire."

"He's serious," Tuesday said through a tight jaw. She could feel the demon's intrusion into her very being. He was using her magic, the darkness that coiled in the sigil, to enhance his own magic and spread it out as wide as the building. "Get out of here!"

"I'm not leaving you." But when Ethan tugged her arm, she felt as if she was planted on the floor. Her legs were leaden. She could not move.

The walls began to crack.

"I can't move. You've got to get everyone out of the building. Save them! Now!"

The containment crew shouted to Ethan for orders. Ethan commanded them to evacuate the building—knock on all doors to get everyone out. He caught Tuesday's gaze and didn't ask her anything, but she understood. He would protect innocent lives first and foremost.

"I'll be fine," she said. "If this bastard takes me out, he might take himself out, too. He won't let that happen. Just hurry. Get the people out of this building!"

Ethan dashed off.

And Tuesday growled at Gazariel. "You dare play with the lives of innocents?"

The demon chuffed. He tossed the blue ball of light through the open doorway and down the hall. "Always."

A painting fell off the wall and the window shattered behind him. Tuesday tried to conjure up the shards and send them back at the demon, but she couldn't focus beyond merely standing upright and not screaming. She felt as if he touched her heart. Again. And then a sudden tug at her entire body, similar to when she'd walked too far away from Ethan, briefly knocked her off balance.

Had the bond been severed? Ethan wouldn't be able to run through the building otherwise.

The demon winked at her. "I did that. You're welcome."

She acknowledged the sudden release, a freedom she'd desired since arriving in Paris. That was a good thing. For more than her. It would allow Ethan to clear out the innocents and escape the shaking building.

"Don't harm anyone," she pleaded. "Please, Gazariel."

"You surprise me, witch. With all the darkness I can feel within you, such an incredible lack of love, and still you plead for the lives of innocents. Something wrong with that. You're but one step away from warlock. Why not let it happen?"

"Is that what you want? Wouldn't that then give me power over you?"

Speaking it made her realize suddenly that maybe it could be so. If she went warlock could she control Gazariel? She'd never had a reason to do so—for centuries—until Ethan had gotten her involved in chasing the demon down. Warlocks were witches who had gone against their own, and often committed terrible acts against humanity. But they were so powerful.

Was it worth the sacrifice of her last remnants of light to subdue this threat? Gazariel held a book that could destroy so many innocents.

All of a sudden Gazariel fisted a hand before him and Tuesday was pulled across the room toward him. She slammed against his chest and he spun, gripping her against his body. The final window smashed out and he soared through it and over the nearby treetops, landing her on the snowy ground with a spine-crimping thump.

Tuesday lay on her back with Gazariel kneeling over her. His wings coved them in a private embrace. The demon pressed a palm over her chest. "You have been such a good girl, keeping this wicked curse from me. But the vampire has drawn up your naughtiness. And... do I sense you really *do* seek love? Poor, pitiful witch."

"I get the feeling you are having love troubles yourself. Did someone jilt you? Why not take back the curse so you won't be bothered by such foolish human emotions? If only for a little while?" Desperation did not suit her, but she'd not been able to stop speaking her hopes.

A curl of his fingers felt as if he was gripping her very heart. Tuesday moaned at the pain.

"Ethan just wants the code," she blurted out. "Give him the book and we'll leave you alone. Why do you want to destroy the world when you're having so much fun in it?"

"The book isn't for me. It's a gift for…a woman."

"What? Did you give it to someone else? Someone you love? No. You're trying to win someone's love? Is that it?"

"Enough talk about a stupid book."

She'd guessed right. "So not everyone loves you, eh?"

The demon was not having it now.

"You, witch, are going to leave me alone. Because I promise…" He bent forward, his hair dusting her face. A dark wanting desire melted over her skin as he whispered against her ear, "If you follow me, I will take out your loveless heart and devour it."

With that, a force whisked Gazariel away from her in a beating of wings and a swirl of snowflakes from the ground.

Gasping and panting, Tuesday rolled to her side and coiled up into a ball on the cold, snowy earth. He'd touched her heart again. And each time it left behind a mark that she would never feel heal over.

The demon had plans to give the code book to a woman? Why? And who was this woman? Had to be a lover, someone he was trying to win, as she had guessed. It made little sense. She couldn't imagine Gazariel stooping so low. Couldn't he have love with but a flutter of his thick, black lashes? And he was not a demon who could condone the ending of the world. Who, then, would remain alive to worship and adore him?

Through the wide-spaced tree trunks Tuesday saw a man's legs running toward her. Ethan plunged to the snow-littered ground and leaned over to embrace her. He'd left her alone with the demon.

She shoved him away. "Don't touch me!"

Ethan reared back and put up his palms. "I'm sorry. Everyone is out of the building. The shaking has stopped. I've called in the fire department and the police. Where's the demon?"

"Gone." For good, if she would only stay away from him. Which, at the moment, felt like the safest and smartest thing to do.

"Let me help you up. Get you to the car so you can warm up. Did he hurt you?"

Only for centuries. And so deeply, even she could not have foreseen the depth of such wounds. Something Ethan could never understand.

Tuesday pushed up and stood, backing away from the vampire. She put up a hand and focused her repulsive energies toward him. She was tattered and weak, but she did manage to topple him backward a few feet.

"The binding between us has been broken," she said. "Time for you to let me go."

"We haven't gotten what we want."

"It's what *you* want, not what I want." She sighed and winced. This whole mess was because some demon who had an abundance of love wanted even more? What the hell? "Just let me go, Ethan. Gazariel is…too strong. I need to be away from…this."

"I still need your help."

"As your prisoner?"

He inhaled through his nose and splayed his hands before him. "I'm sorry, Tuesday. You're right. I've gone about this wrong. You should… Yes, you're free to go. I still need your help, but I won't force you. If you feel the desire to stop Gazariel from harming so many, you know where to find me." He stepped back, but then stopped. "Let me at least get you a ride. A place to stay."

"Leave me," she said. A shiver of cold traced over her skin. A hug would feel welcome. She didn't know how to ask for it, though.

Ethan nodded, then turned to stride off. It was too easy for the vampire to walk away from her.

And Tuesday exhaled and held her breath as she watched him slip between the trees and back into the commotion surrounding the evacuation. Police cars had arrived. Red and blue lights flashed. The building had not collapsed, but she suspected it was so structurally damaged it would have to be condemned.

He was needed there in the midst of that chaos. The man had chosen the correct fight, instead of staying and holding her. Because…she did need someone to hold her right now. Her body felt ready to tumble onto the ground and melt into the snow. To surrender.

The demon had taken so much from her today.

She cast a look up into the sky. She did not know where Gazariel had gone. And she didn't want to know.

Chapter 9

Ethan had paced the loft for hours. He'd not been able to get leaving Tuesday alone in the woods out of his mind. Now as he strode the halls of headquarters, destined for the Archives, he wished he would have tried harder. To make her understand that he needed her help and that she could trust him.

And beyond that, to let her know that his initial feelings for her had changed. They'd shared much in the past few days and he'd developed a real understanding for the witch. He genuinely cared for her.

The binding CJ had conjured between Ethan and Tuesday had been a mistake. It hadn't given her a reason to trust him. And she had been a good sport, going along with every request he made of her.

But he'd felt her terror when they'd stood in the apartment and Gazariel had begun to make the walls shake. The demon had connected with Tuesday. In a terrible and painful way. And then to find her lying in the snow outside, looking so defeated and frail, his heart had cringed.

The witch had been cursed to never know love. What sort of hollow, empty life had she lived? He couldn't fathom such a lack of love.

Yet she deserved more protection and respect than he could give her. So he'd let her go. He'd find another way to track Gazariel. He now knew the demon was in the city. And if he had been in Paris for this long, then what reason had he to leave now? Unless they'd spooked him.

Ethan needed to learn as much as he could about the demon. The knowledge could only enhance his search efforts.

The vast Archives was located many stories below ground. It was a repository of all things, from books and ancient artifacts, to histories of the various paranormal species, and related ephemera. It basically housed all the information about the paranormal nations that could be contained. There were also catalogued weapons, shackled magics, volatile items placed in containment and even a few creatures that were much better off—for the humans' sake—locked up than out running loose in the mortal realm.

As director of Acquisitions, Ethan had seen to placing a good majority of the contents of the Archives there. Acquisitions was often referred to as the Archives' dirty little secret, for their methods were brutal and unforgiving. And if the Archives needed to contain an ancient evil—or merely wanted it to study—they asked Ethan to deploy a retriever.

As well, if a mysterious stranger showed up in his office with information that a certain book of angel sigils and names had gone missing, Ethan was charged to react appropriately. At all costs, the mortal realm must be protected from discovering there were creatures and magics that existed beyond myth and fable.

Secrets. It was always about keeping secrets. He knew too many of them. And some days he wished he could erase them all from memory and start anew. Other days, it was good to know exactly what the world could—and did—deal him.

Entering the Archives' office, Ethan spied Certainly Jones sitting behind an ancient wood desk, his feet propped up on the desk as he sipped tea. The man rarely wore shoes, which always startled Ethan. He liked to maintain a certain business decorum at the office. But the Archives was not his domain. And CJ possessed mysterious ways and a manner that was ever polite but also secretive. However, the man was trustworthy, and that was what mattered most to Ethan.

"How'd the containment go this afternoon?" CJ asked, not bothering to sit up from his relaxed posture.

"Do you have a new demon behind bars?"

"Nope."

"Then you know how it went. I need your help, Jones."

"Where's Tuesday Knightsbridge?"

Ethan gestured with a vague sweep over his shoulder. "I let her go. She'd served her purpose."

"Uh-huh." CJ sat up, giving Ethan that I-know-you-better-than-you-know-yourself look. Witches and their looks. A man had to be cautious around them.

"The demon broke the binding between us," Ethan

said. "It didn't feel right to make her stay unless she wanted to actually help."

"And she did not. Makes sense. You did kidnap her."

"I did not—" Ethan knew an argument over semantics was senseless.

The witch stood. "What help can I offer? I can provide knowledge, but as for hands-on, you know I'm not much for taking on demons. Not anymore, you understand."

CJ had once gone into Daemonia, purposely, and had returned from that despicable, demon-infested realm. Actually, his return had been an orchestrated rescue by his twin brother, Thoroughly Jones. The trip there had changed CJ, made him miserable and dark and... he'd come near to death. But another witch—a pretty red-haired woman named Viktorie Saint-Charles—had helped him to escape the psychological torments of those demonic hosts and now he avoided demons like the proverbial plague.

"I need all the information you have on Gazariel," Ethan said. "Specifically, what you can tell me about the curse he had. The one he gave to Tuesday. And if there's a way to break it."

Because if they could break the curse then he need not fear that Tuesday would be harmed when finally he did capture Gazariel.

"I'll have to search the records." CJ gestured toward the silver service by the wall behind Ethan. "Tea?"

Tuesday sipped the thick hot chocolate and tugged the alpaca coat snugly around her shoulders. She was still cold even though she could feel the heat blast through the nearby vent that was level with her ankles. She sat before the front second-floor window of Angelina, having been drawn to the chic yet touristy café because she'd once heard they served the best hot chocolate ever.

Truth. But it was also rich and so sweet she was already flying high on a sugar rush. Good thing she'd foregone checking out the decadent pastries. With but a clasp of her waitress's hand, she'd assured the bill was paid and that no one would remember her sitting here for two hours, staring out over the snow-frothed horse-chestnut trees that edged the Tuileries Garden across the street. And wondering.

What to do now?

Ethan had released her from duty. Well, she would have walked away from him no matter if he'd given her leave or not. Wasn't as if she'd volunteered for the mission. She'd had no choice. It hadn't been duty, but forced servitude.

But now that she did have a choice, she wasn't sure what came next. Her intention was to hop a flight back home. That was the logical decision. Maybe do a little touristing before hopping on that flight? That option was a little less safe and she risked the vampire deciding he needed her again and finding her.

Or she could walk back into the fray and put up her fists and show the demon her teeth.

All her life she had stood up for her beliefs, ever since she'd been given a renewed chance at life thanks to the dreadful curse the demon had put inside her. But if she couldn't know love then she'd be damned to sit around and pout about it. She had not once felt regretful for her decision made in that dark cell outside the pigpen.

And yet, she wasn't feeling so strong or powerful

at the moment. Her chest ached from Gazariel's touch. He had touched her heart. And should they meet again he wouldn't pause to rip it out. That was a truth she inexplicably knew.

Back in the seventeenth century, the demon hadn't wanted the curse he'd put inside her. But this afternoon, she'd seen the glitter of desire in his eyes as he had recognized the tease of lacking love. He'd wanted it. And he had not.

Something was up with Gazariel and his love life. He'd not been able to hide his reaction to her guessing at that. Of course, it was possible not everyone would love him. Yes? Maybe? Tuesday couldn't fathom being loved by everyone she met. Was The Beautiful One growing weary of unending love and devotion? It did sound tiresome.

And yet, a small taste of love seemed too delicious to Tuesday right now.

Yes, she'd been near death, wishing to die, when she'd accepted the curse. Over the centuries, she'd made it her own, embracing the utter lack of love. How easy it was to never have to worry about love and all its ridiculous predicaments.

And she'd been fine with fleeting romantic relationships over the years. Just when the man started to get all doe-eyed and she suspected he was falling in love, he'd suddenly notice something about her he hated, or he'd simply leave. She had expected those reactions, so they hadn't bothered her. Too much.

But now she wasn't so sure. Gazariel's touch had given the curse new life. Had strengthened it. Ethan had walked away from her with ease. And that was because of the curse, surely.

Suddenly the thought of not having love in her life was

tangible and real. A hole in her heart. And she couldn't be a strong powerful woman if part of her had a hole in it.

Did she want to shuck off the curse and allow love into her life? Could she be so brave? It wasn't as if she was in love with Ethan Pierce or he with her. But she wanted that option. She really did.

"Just leave Paris," she whispered over the cup of chocolate. "You know it's the right choice. The vampire has no interest in you beyond what you can do for him."

And what she could do for him might bring back the demon. And that would see her bloody heart dangling from Gazariel's fingers. One way or another, she would not survive if she didn't leave the city today.

She snapped the rubber band.

Yeah, it was the only choice.

Pulling out the cell phone she'd slipped from Ethan's pocket while lying on the snowy ground, she downloaded an airline app and checked the schedule for flights leaving for the US. There were four this evening. And each one still had remaining seats.

The Archives had a room for virtually every species of paranormal that inhabited the mortal realm. The room on witches was the largest. The unicorn room was the smallest due to a lack of information. But Tuesday did wield an alicorn, Ethan thought, as they passed by that room. Just what sort of trouble could a witch get into with that thing? He wanted to know.

He really did.

As Ethan followed CJ into the demon room, he felt a cool chill fall over his skin and he adopted a militant need to scan the room and look over his shoulder. Nothing followed him down the aisles of dark, dusty bookshelves, nor did he see anything flying above near the two-story-high ceiling. But he was not mistaken that pairs of red eyes seemed to flicker here and there from within the books and haphazardly stacked artifacts.

"Tamatha has been rearranging," CJ said. "It's a bit of a clutter right now. The inner chamber is neater."

CJ pushed open a heavy steel door. It looked like something that should front a bank vault. The dark witch's casual manner relaxed Ethan's tensions. He followed him inside the massive annex room, taking in the musty odor and the many aisles that boasted boxes or small cages with creatures inside. Books papered an entire wall that stretched the length of the chamber.

"Ignore the blaggert," CJ offered as they filed past a small glass-barred cage, secured with electronic locks. Inside, a diminutive red creature with tufted ears bent and waggled his bare ass at them as they passed.

"The *Bibliodaemon* is up on that dais," CJ said. "As with most species, there is a book, or bible, that describes them all, and is constantly updated."

"Like the *Book of All Spells*."

Ethan knew that book was like a living archive of any and all spells created by witches. If a witch was speaking a new spell right now, it was magically being written into that book. There was another for vampires, *The Vampire Codex*, though he'd never been curious about it. Weird, to think that now. Of course, he lived the vampire's life; no need to have it explained to him in text.

"Yes, like that book." CJ skipped up two steps to a steel dais, where a table displayed a huge book that was about three feet high and two feet wide. It sat open to some pages that looked like time-stained parchment. With a sweep of his hand and a mutter of Latin, followed by the demon Gazariel's name, CJ sent the pages fluttering. "It'll take a few minutes to bring up the records. Kind of like the internet but slower and more interesting, eh?"

"Your job must never see a dull day," Ethan commented as he pulled up a stool to sit and watch the book pages move rapidly in search.

"It's a kick, that's for sure. But we could use more help. I've only got Tamatha as my assistant. She's off in the harpie room today. Maybe? I don't know. It's quite the labyrinth down here. A couple more hands would be helpful. We've such a backload of stuff from your retrievers."

"You mean it hasn't all been catalogued?"

"Who has the time? I have a holding room that's warded to the nines. Tamatha and I are working as fast as we can to keep up with the acquisitions."

"You should put in a requisition to the Council. I'm sure they'd approve you hiring more help."

CJ nodded. "Thing is, I'm very particular about who I work with. And I don't have time to vet someone new. So I guess I either lighten up or shut up, eh?"

"Seems to be the case."

The pages stopped moving and CJ leaned over the book and read. "'Gazariel, master angel of the First Void, Creator of Vanity, fallen to Beneath where he became known as The Beautiful One, and was cast out by the Devil Himself.'"

"That demon was once an angel?"

"Many demons were originally angels," CJ said. "When they Fell, those who landed in Beneath assumed demonic form. Others became the Sinistari, who now hunt the Fallen."

"I thought the majority of demons were from Dae-monia?"

"They are. Yet you'll not find a former Fallen One who is now demon who would ever set foot in Daemonia. While Daemonia has its own version of royalty, the Fallen Ones deem themselves highest of all demons since they originated in Above. Daemonia is, literally, beneath them. Looks like your guy has a reason for being called The Beautiful One. Creator of Vanity, eh?"

The demon had been primping when he'd stood before them in the apartment complex. It was as if he couldn't *not* flaunt his beauty.

"Does it say why Himself cast him out of Beneath?" Ethan asked. "Isn't that odd? I thought The Old Lad was always looking for more minions."

CJ leaned over the book and read silently for a while. "Himself was jealous."

"Why, because Gazariel is pretty?"

"Exactly. So he cursed Gazariel with an evil that would not allow him to own love and cast him out to the mortal realm."

"To own it," Ethan repeated, thinking, trying to work this out. "But not necessarily to never know it?"

CJ shrugged. "I suppose. But I assume if a person would have fallen in love with the demon, while he still wore the curse, something terrible would have happened to that person to make them stop loving him."

"Yet Gazariel himself could actually love still." Which would mean that Tuesday could still love. Maybe.

"So the curse came from the devil…" Ethan did not repeat Himself's name. Say the name three times in a row? You've invited the devil for a visit. Not something he ever intended to do. "And obviously Gazariel didn't want that hanging on him, so he pawned it off on a witch."

"Interesting that he was able to so easily give it away."

"Tuesday said she asked for it."

CJ lifted an eyebrow.

"She had been beaten and tortured by a witch hunter, whom she loved, and was very near death."

"Then some demon offers to take love, which hurt her, from her life?"

"Exactly."

"Poor thing." CJ propped his arms akimbo. "Tuesday is dark but she doesn't strike me as evil incarnate."

"If the curse is designed to keep away love, maybe that's all it can get out of her? If she is innately good?"

"Possible. But how is learning this going to help you get a hand on the demon? If he's slipped through your hands once already?"

"I'm trying to gather as much information as I can. And whatever happens I don't want Tuesday getting hurt. She and Gazariel are tied together. He told us if we hurt him she will feel it."

"That makes things difficult. But if she's left the city? She could be at a safe distance."

"But how to know what that safe distance is?"

"Why is Gazariel in Paris?" CJ asked. "If he's got the Final Days code, why not use it? Or is he holding it for someone? Waiting to hand it off? Or has he already done so? There's a reason he's not running far."

"Right. And now that he knows I want what he has…"

"Then he'll make himself scarce."

"Or will he? I'm not sure." Ethan crossed his arms, considering what he'd learned. "There is the connection between him and Tuesday. She is key to calling the demon forth. And there was a moment when I'm sure I saw the desire for the curse in the demon's eyes. When he touched Tuesday, he could feel that darkness calling to him. He said something about love not being what it was cracked up to be. I think he would take the curse back if given the right conditions."

"Which are?"

"I don't know. A bad love affair? Can you perform a tracking spell like Tuesday did? I need to know where Gazariel is right now."

"I'm sure she was using the sigil as a direct conduit. Do you have something from Tuesday that I might use to call up the demon?"

"I…no. Maybe? She was at my place for a bit. I'll have to go see if she left anything behind."

"If you could find some hair strands that would be optimal. That still won't guarantee I can get a fix on the demon. I'll give it a shot, though."

Ethan slapped a hand into CJ's. "Thanks, man."

"Have you considered calling in a reckoner for when you do find Gazariel? Perhaps as a threat?"

A reckoner consigned demons to Daemonia. To threaten Gazariel with going to that place, which he must fear as most mortals feared Hell, could provide some leverage, perhaps even get him to confess about where the book was.

"Good call. I'll have to look up Savin Thorne."

"He's living in the fourteenth. Bit of a hermit. But yes, I'd recommend the man."

"Thanks. I'm heading home to see if I can find traces of the witch. Can I get a copy of that page?" He pointed to the oversized book.

"Why do you people think I'm some kind of a copy machine?"

Ethan shrugged. "You're not?" Then he chuckled. "Have your assistant send me a digital file of it, yes?"

"I can have it to you in a few hours."

"Thanks." Ethan patted his jacket pocket. No phone. Had he lost it in the scuffle at the Bois de Boulogne? Damn. "Send it to my office email," he said. "I seem to have misplaced my phone. Er, will you show me the way out of here? We took so many turns I don't want to end up in the werewolf room."

"Why? Not keen on the dogs?"

"Not so much that as not in the mood to relive some rather sketchy history."

"Blood Wars?" CJ asked.

Ethan nodded.

"I completely understand. Just being in this room creeps me out. Too many memories of an experimental magic excursion to Daemonia gone awry. Let's go."

Tuesday stood in line behind a family of six, who waited with shoes in hand to pass through security at Charles de Gaulle airport. The flight took off in an hour, and she was ready for the eight-hour sleep she would sink into as soon as her butt landed on the narrow seat.

But for perhaps the fifth time, she glanced over her shoulder and gazed out the windows at the stream of cabs letting off travelers or picking them up. Was she really ready to write off this adventure and mark it as defeat? That wasn't like her. She reveled in a good challenge. And if it involved getting down and dirty with some bastard demon? Bring it on. She could stand up to the most powerful of them and win. Every time.

Yes, even the one demon who wanted to rip out her heart.

And there was a certain sexy vampire who had sparked her interest. Was she simply going to walk away from the man without having gotten more than a few kisses? Didn't feel right. Even if she returned, fucked him and left, at least she'd have had that pleasure.

To leave or not?

She knew Gazariel would rely on her fear, on not wanting to lose her heart. And the idea of shivering before the demon did not sit well with her. She was stronger than this. And the demon was messing with her. He wanted to end the world because of...unrequited love? Sounded like a bad romance to her.

It was time to seriously consider transferring this curse back to Gazariel. If he wore the curse, he'd fall out of love and lose the desire to hand off a dangerous gift to goddess knew what kind of malicious entity.

Love? Tuesday clutched her shoes tightly against her chest. Yes, she was ready to welcome it into her life. She wanted it. And if that wasn't reason enough to turn and aim for the exit door, she wasn't about to let that ridiculous fop of a demon tell her what to do. It was time to stand up and show it her teeth.

"Mademoiselle?"

She turned to find the security guard waiting for her to remove her coat then step forward through the X-ray machine. She'd never liked those machines. Something wrong with peering inside a person and seeing their very bones.

"Right." She took one step forward, and then...one step back.

Chapter 10

Ethan opened his apartment door to discover a yawning witch waiting outside in the hallway.

She snapped her mouth shut and put up one finger. "I've got one more idea for a tracking spell on that bastard demon."

"Okay."

"But first, I need a shower." Tuesday strode inside, passing him by, and rummaged through her bag. She tugged out his phone and dropped it on the couch. "Yeah?"

He gestured toward the bedroom, which led to the bathroom. "You know where it is."

She didn't say another word. Didn't explain why she'd returned, or for how long. And he felt it best to let things play out and see what she'd offer him. Because he hadn't found anything of hers to give to CJ for a summoning spell, not even a single strand of hair.

He needed her. In more ways than he was willing to admit to himself.

But this time around, he'd play things closer to the vest. Not go all director-in-charge on her by forcing her to comply. This time, he'd follow the witch's lead. It felt right. It felt as though his heart demanded it.

After a shower, Tuesday pulled on a T-shirt that hung to her thighs, then looked in the mirror. Emblazoned across the shirt were the words, Surely Not Everybody Was Kung Fu Fighting. She'd found it in a vintage store while shopping with Ethan. Ha! And yes, there had been occasions in the nightclubs during the 1970s disco frenzy when everyone had been kung fu fighting. In dance mode, of course. Good times.

She was ready to pull out all her moves against Gazariel. She had no clue how to give the curse back to him, but she would not relent until it happened. If he was in love, maybe she could use that against him. She had to find out who his lover was. And how much she meant to him. Apparently enough to give her a trinket that could end the world.

Tuesday did a few kung fu moves in front of the mirror, then gave it her best fighter's face. That demon wanted to threaten her?

"Let's see what he does when love is taken away from him." And she delivered a knockout kick to her absent opponent.

Grabbing her bag, which she'd filled with a few more magical accoutrements thanks to her rushing around on a hot-chocolate high earlier, she wandered out through the bedroom and set down the bag in the corner between the bed and the living area. An old wood vanity held a record player and a neat stack of albums sat beside it. And on the other half of the vanity a crystal decanter with dark alcohol in it sat surrounded by three wide-bowled glasses.

Ethan sat on the sofa, legs up on the coffee table, bare feet tilted outward. He gazed idly at her.

"Let's do this spell before I fall asleep from utter exhaustion," she said, taking a few items out of her bag. "Get me something to write with. Like a felt-tip marker. Take off your shirt. And lie down in this big ol' salt circle I'm about to make."

She began to pour the bag of ordinary table salt she'd bought at a local market onto the wide plank flooring before the vanity.

Ethan, meanwhile, got a pen from the kitchen and tugged off his shirt. She did notice those washboard abs, and at that moment her circle took a distinct swerve inward.

Shaking off the alluring sight, Tuesday redirected the salt and closed up the circle. It was big enough to contain a very sizable vampire and his nekkid abs that screamed for some hella licking. She gestured toward it. "Lie down."

Ethan scratched his head, then pressed his thumb and forefinger close together. "Just a teeny bit of info first?"

She propped her hands on her hips. Fine. The man was cute enough that he could command that of her. "We want to catch The Beautiful One, yeah?"

"Agreed."

"I am the one who alerts the demon we're near. Not cool. So you need to become the bait or lure or even the GPS. With this spell, I'm going to make you into a tracker. You should be able to turn it on or off when needed. It'll be like you borrowing some of my magic but without having to perform bloodsexmagic."

He shrugged, then stepped inside the circle. "This doesn't require blood?"

"It does, but yours this time."

He put up a hand. "I'm a vampire."

Tuesday gave him a droll look. "I got that. First try, even."

"I don't give blood," he said. "I only take it."

"Get over your bad self."

He crossed his arms. "I refuse to give blood."

Tuesday inhaled through her nose and met the vampire eye-to-eye. All seriousness in those pretty gray irises. For all that she had given thus far, a few drops of blood shouldn't be a hardship for him. And yet, she looked down his face, to his neck, which was tight with tension, and along his arms, that ended in fists. Something was bothering him. And it had to do with the blood.

"It's not going to hurt. Promise," she lied. "And besides, you did give blood for the binding between the two of us."

"That was different. You were a mere…witch. And I was desperate."

"And you're not now?" Though she had caught the vitriol in the way he'd said *witch*. He had not liked her very much when she'd first arrived. A mutual feeling. But her feelings had changed. And she'd thought he was starting to come around as well.

"Why can't we use your blood?" he asked.

"Because you'd get turned on and toss me on the end of the bed before I could finish the spell."

He smirked and shook his head. Not the reaction

she'd been hoping for with the gibe, either. "We've been through this, witch. I don't go from calm to horny with the sniff of a few drops of blood."

"You were aroused by my blood in the car."

He closed his eyes. And Tuesday had to keep herself from leaning forward, moving in to smell his fresh outdoors scent. She wanted to kiss him. Damn her, the stupidest witch of all time. He had a certain allure, not unlike Gazariel's strange pull. But with Ethan it felt honest and even promising.

"The last time I gave blood I killed a woman," he stated plainly.

Tuesday leaned back and met the man's gaze. Stoic and calm, as he had been that first time she'd woken up in the cage to look upon her captor.

"You...killed. You're a vampire—"

"We don't all kill to survive," he interrupted. "I've never killed merely for blood. It is beneath me. It is unnecessary."

"But you have killed before. Many," she said, knowing it to be the truth. For she had walked through the same centuries as he had. No one lived that long and got out of it untouched by foulness or evil.

"I fought in the Blood Wars," he said. "Of course I've killed. It was kill or be killed then. But what I'm talking about is the voluntary giving of blood that results in loss of life. I can't do it. I won't."

"Ethan." She grabbed his hand and held it with both of hers. "Help me to understand. You killed someone by giving them blood? Were you...trying to transform them?"

He made to tug out of her grasp, so she pulled his hand closer and held it firmly. "Talk to me. I shared my ugly stuff with you. I've done desperate things at desperate times. Tell me why donating a few drops of blood is such a big no-no for you."

"A few drops? That's all you need?"

She shrugged. "Yeah?"

He lifted an eyebrow.

"It's not going to be a lot. I need it to trace the spell on you. I'm not going to take it into my veins, if that's got you worried. I don't intend to die today. Swear it by the seven sacred witches."

He studied her, and as he did she suspected he wasn't going to explain to her the whole deal behind his killing someone with a blood transfusion. She wanted to know about that wackiness. But really, this spell did not require a surgical operation or large amounts of the red stuff.

"There's no such thing as the seven sacred witches," he finally said.

Tuesday shrugged. "You got me. Now can we do this? Just a tiny donation is all I ask of you." She pinched her fingers together before him. "I won't even need an athame. Just…" She spun and leaned over to shuffle around in her bag, pulling out the alicorn. "This will be perfect. Yeah?"

"Just a small amount?" Ethan asked. And when she nodded, he sighed and sat down.

"All the way down," she directed, and the vampire lay on his back. "This won't hurt a bit. Maybe a little. You're a big boy. You got this."

But what she wouldn't give to have heard about the person he'd killed. It bothered him enough to freak him out over a little blood ritual. She would learn about it. Soon enough.

With Ethan prone in the circle, Tuesday remained outside the line of salt, and took a moment to admire his physique. What was it about vampires and how they didn't need to work out, yet they all seemed to have the abs and pecs of a bodybuilder? Wasn't easy to disregard. But she would.

For now.

Kneeling, she leaned in and placed a palm to his chest. "Just go with it, okay?"

"I do owe you this much. Thanks, by the way."

"For what?"

"For coming back. You had every right to leave."

"Yeah, well I'm not going to let that asshole demon shove me around and make me feel like the weak one. If he's have relationship issues, ending the world is not the way to resolve them."

"Relationship issues?"

"Yeah. I think the demon wants to give the book to some chick to win her love. Or maybe he already has. He wasn't clear. I just knew with certainty that whoever the woman was, she wasn't in love with him."

"I thought everyone adored him?"

"Do you?"

"He was kind of handsome."

Tuesday couldn't stop some head-shaking laughter. "Right? I mean, it's crazy, but I thought the same."

"That's what makes him so dangerous," Ethan said.

"And why we need to be vigilant. We're strong. We can do this. Together…" She uncapped the red marker he'd found and checked the writing on the plastic tube. Water soluble. Good for him. He'd be able to wash this off later. "We make a pretty decent team. Now I'm going to draw a tracking grid on you."

Ethan put his hands behind his head and closed his eyes as she drew a circle on his chest, and within it, a pentagram. She marked the four compass directions. A copy of the sigil she wore was placed at the spirit peak of the pentagram. Gliding the marker under his pec, she couldn't help but slow down and study the rigid nipple and the sudden goose-bumping of his skin. He was aware she was studying him.

The man would jump if she dashed out her tongue and licked his skin. He wasn't overly hot. Vampires never were too hot, but weren't cold, either, as one might expect. The flesh and muscles beneath her hands were solid and hard. And oh, so delectable. And as the red line journeyed over one abdominal ridge and then the next, she pressed her lips together.

Didn't want to start drooling on the guy. That would be so not cool.

"Are you thinking what I'm thinking?" Ethan asked softly.

She finished her line work with three short dashes above his navel and set aside the marker, but remained leaning over the salt circle and close to his body. "What's that?"

He nudged up a shoulder. "That I like you touching me."

Tuesday lifted an eyebrow. He still had his eyes closed. And from her vantage point, so close to his ribs and looking up over that hard pectoral landscape, she thought she saw his smile grow.

"I am thinking the same thing," she answered truthfully. "You make for a nice drawing board."

"Your breath on my skin is making me uncomfortable."

She glanced down toward his jeans and…oh, yes, he

was growing hard. Well, she didn't need him aroused for this spell—nor did she want to spend too much time considering his arousal because that would only do the same to her—so she gave his stomach a quick smack with her fingers and sat back.

"What the hell?" He lifted his head to seek her.

"Had to be done. We've got to focus. No silly stuff."

"If that's the way you want to play it." He put his head down and closed his eyes again. "But I wouldn't call what I was thinking of doing to you silly."

Mercy. Had he really needed to say that? Because now Tuesday wanted to know what had been running through his thoughts. And how not-silly it might have been. Surely it had involved lots of skin-on-skin contact. And more of his devastating kisses. And if they were forced to do it inside the salt circle without upsetting the perimeter, they might have to get into all sorts of weird yet tight positions.

Hell, she must be overtired if she was slipping into random moments of sex fantasy. What the hex? She shook her head and grabbed the alicorn. The quicker she finished the spell, the sooner she could find out the answer regarding the silly stuff.

Waving the alicorn above the man's chest, she told him to be quiet.

"When will you need my blood?" he asked.

"Oh, uh, soon." She didn't want to freak him out and have him running away before she even got this going. "I'll use this." She waggled the alicorn. "Now. Silence. Just focus on the tone of my voice and drawing in the vibrations that I send to you, yeah?"

He nodded and closed his eyes again. Moonlight gleamed through the big windows to their sides, and fell across his face as if lighting a Hollywood vampire in the big redemption scene. Oh, what a pretty man.

She'd returned from the airport for more than one reason, and she would not forget that.

Soon enough.

Standing, Tuesday first walked the circle widdershins, enclosing it in a permeable violet light that would allow her access to the inside, but wouldn't include her as part of the spell. Stepping inside, she straddled Ethan's legs. She wore only the long T-shirt, but his eyes were closed and she—she had to keep it together and rein in her lusty thoughts. Just for a while longer.

Holding the alicorn in one hand, she spread the fingers of her other hand and leaned forward, focusing her energies toward the sigils drawn on his chest. The words to the spell came by rote and she chanted them over and over, changing her tone to a deeper resonance after a few successions.

The red marker began to glow white and appeared as if it opened Ethan's skin, though it did not. It was a deep and luminous glow. It allowed in her magic. Pointing the alicorn in each direction—north, east, south, then west—she then drew a line down to the center of the pentagram.

Then, with a forceful stab of the alicorn's point, she punctured Ethan's chest.

Chapter 11

Something ice-cold pierced his chest. Ethan gasped, winced. Slapped a hand to his chest, but the witch pushed it away immediately. She'd...staked him?

"Just go with it," she said calmly. "It's only in a quarter of an inch. I need blood, remember?"

She...needed blood? Fuck. Just...what the fuck?

As he felt blood drool from the puncture, Tuesday quickly used the tip of the alicorn to draw with his blood, tracing the sigil over his chest. She'd freaking staked him with a unicorn's horn!

Closing his eyes and letting his head fall back to the floor, Ethan then smirked and snorted. What the hell kind of whacked adventure had he tumbled into? He'd let a witch stake him and...he'd survived. He was still here. Not ash. And she was speaking her witchy voodoo words and humming above him.

When she'd asked for him to give blood, memories of the time he'd killed another with a blood transfusion had almost stopped him from doing this. That had been a different time. A completely different century. Medicine had advanced greatly. And…he hadn't wanted to give her details. To expose his broken heart to her. So he'd dropped his nervous worries and succumbed to Tuesday's wishes.

The witch didn't need to see into that soft and weak part of him. Because apparently she was more into stabbing a man than sympathizing with him. Bloody hell.

Opening his left eye, Ethan spied Tuesday as she kissed the blood-tipped alicorn. Then, kneeling and still straddling him, she bowed to blow across the wet blood. Her magic stirred up a violet fog and with her hands she coaxed it into a malleable cloud over his body, stretching it to encompass him from head to toe. And with a single clap of her palms, the fog dropped over his body and permeated his skin with a sizzle that made him hiss.

Tuesday stood, looking over her work. "That was it. You're such a big boy," she cooed as if he was a child. "That wasn't so bad, was it?"

He would not reply to her mocking tone. Even if he sensed she was teasing him. But it was difficult not to admire the view from where he lay. The woman wore but a T-shirt that was long enough to cover everything, but short enough to make him want to lift his head and take a closer look.

She just staked you, idiot. Right. Ethan pushed up to his elbows and looked over his bloody chest.

Fool that he was, he'd had the thought while in the Archives earlier that he'd like to see what she was capable of when wielding the alicorn. And now he knew.

Twirling the bloodied alicorn, the witch waggled an eyebrow. "Remember when you shoved me against the wall in the alleyway before the dark witch bonded us? You said that was the only blood I'd ever get from you." She shrugged. "Guess you were wrong, eh?"

"I'm doing this to help the mission. Unlike you, who seem to merely want to gloat about taking advantage of a man's kindness. You fucking staked me, witch!"

"And now you can tell everyone you've survived being staked. You don't have to mention it was with a unicorn horn and resulted in you looking like a glitter-bombed clubber."

Her giggle was enough to make Ethan mentally snap a rubber band at his wrist. But he wouldn't get angry at her. He was doing this to help the mission. And if he had gained some sort of magic out of the deal? So be it.

"Now you should have a sixth sense about the demon's location," she said. "You just have to learn to tap in to it. Focus inwardly, keeping the demon's name fore and your intent to find him as the guide. Shouldn't be too difficult for a vampire who has used persuasion on humans. Yeah?"

He had mastered enthralling humans centuries ago. He'd been born innately knowing how to control others with but a tweak to their thoughts, a subtle whisper after the bite, or even a gentle caress that would send a shiver of compliance through their system along with memory loss or even altered thoughts.

"Sounds good to me." Ethan touched the blood on his chest. It sparkled with violet. Was that a condition of using the alicorn? Interesting, and yet a bit too night-club-glitter for him.

"You can get up. But it'll take a bit for it all to soak

in, to really get a fix in you. What would be helpful is…" Tapping a finger to her bottom lip, she stepped out of the circle and gripped the obsidian crystal that hung about her neck from the leather cord.

"Is…?" He stood behind her, and brushed some of the violet dust off his jeans.

"Is what?" she asked.

"You were about to say something would be helpful?" He dismissed the query. "Whatever. Can I wash this off?"

"No, leave it on. The marker, anyway. It'll disappear when the spell has set. But you can wash off the blood that dribbled down the side of your ribs. You got a broom?"

"Stuart, vacuum the living area," he said and wandered into the bathroom.

Tuesday stood aside and watched as the Roomba vacuum cleaner appeared from out of a closet and scurried over to sweep up the salt and random drops of Ethan's blood. Skipping to avoid being attacked by the tenacious thing, she sat on the chair to stay out of the way.

A glance to the bathroom door made her smile. She had freaked the fuck out of the vampire by stabbing him with the alicorn. He might have thought she'd been staking him. Ha!

She shouldn't gloat over that sneaky triumph, but— Yes, she would. She'd caught him unawares, and yet, he hadn't overreacted or tried to push her away. He'd complied and had allowed her to finish the spell. He earned points for that. Not many vamps would do the same, she felt sure. Especially the ones with a bossy, controlling complex.

Yet, he had been not so eager to order her around since she'd returned from her near escape from the country. More points to the vampire for that restraint. Was it a new tactic to get her to ultimately work with him? Probably. Yet he'd given her a clue that there was more between them than mere spellcraft and demon chasing.

He wanted her.

And she was the witch to let the vampire have what he wanted.

When he returned to the room with a blood-free chest, but a few sparkles still in his hair and on his back, he wandered over to the vanity by the wall and poured himself a snifter of brandy. The city lights gleamed against a gray sky, highlighting his physique with a golden glow. He wore nothing but jeans, which he must have unbuttoned to clean off the blood—and he'd forgotten to rebutton them—and tufts of dark hair were visible.

Comfortable? Check.

Sexy? Mercy, could a witch get a break?

"You want some?" he asked as the vacuum rolled off to its closet and shut down.

Hell yes, she wanted some. "Uh…" Turning on the leather chair and pulling up her legs, Tuesday asked, "Oh, you mean brandy?"

"Yes."

"Ugh. That stuff makes me gag."

"Then you haven't tried the good stuff." He held up the goblet and strode over to the window, which was parallel to the bed. An outside light flashed crimson in the glass, winking at them. "A man can drink worlds in brandy. I've tasted Greece and Armenia, Turkey and

Chile. Stravecchio is one of my favorites. It's distilled in copper pots."

"I may have once dated a winemaker," Tuesday said.

"A vintner?"

"Yeah, that's what he called himself. Maybe *date* is too technical a term. More like fucked once or twice. Or a dozen times."

It was either that, or she'd dated a dozen different vintners and fucked them once or twice. Details. He didn't need to know everything about her life.

Ethan leaned back against the brick wall, where the window frame began; the massive pane was but inches from his left shoulder. The moonlight mixed with city lights gave his face a stark quality that Tuesday admired. While vampires as old as he could often look as young as teenagers or twentysomethings, Ethan had a certain seasoning to him that appealed to her centuries-gained sensibilities. He was not young and the years had imprinted on his face. In the line that cut down between his eyebrows when he flashed her the serious look, and in the silver hairs that dashed through his brown hair and beard stubble. A wise toughness deepened his gray irises to a cunning yet knowing stare.

He would be called classically handsome by those who cast Hollywood movies, and probably pigeonholed into the widowed or divorced single-father-with-an-edge role. The man was solid. Physically aware. And comfortable in his skin, muscles and bones that wrapped and formed him into a startlingly exquisite physique.

Washboard abs? Check.

"So, you fucked a lot of men over the centuries?" he asked, as he stared off through the window.

Now he was getting to the interesting conversation. Of course, she had mentioned the vintner.

"A dozen or hundreds. I don't record notches. You?"

"Fuck men?" He shrugged. "Not as often as you, I'm sure."

That nugget of info swirled a deep, hot thrill right between her legs. She could entirely see the man swinging for either women or men. That was sexy to her. A man who was not afraid of his sexuality and who lived his life the way he chose.

"I know the world is vast and coincidence rare," she said, "but if I ever learn we've fucked the same man that would so rock my world."

He chuckled and sipped the brandy. "I never kiss and tell."

And now she really wanted to delve into his love life. The fantasy of him bedding another man put a tight pull at the base of her throat and heated her breasts. And… oh, yes. She shifted on the chair, squeezing her thighs together to catch the flutter of want in her pussy.

"Sex becomes different the longer you live, yes?" he asked.

She nodded. Because it had. In ways no mere mortal could ever imagine.

"It's not so much about the romance and roses," he continued. His gaze was fixed on some point out the window. His rugged profile teased Tuesday's sense of control. "Nothing like what you see in the movies or read in those romance novels."

"Have you ever read a romance novel?"

"No."

"Then don't knock them. I even like the ones about the vampires and werewolves, despite the authors getting their paranormal attributes wildly wrong most of the time. But you're right. As the years, decades and centuries glide by, sex becomes less about the physical. And yet, at the same time, the meaning of it becomes more."

"Exactly," he said with a tilt of the brandy snifter toward her. "It's less about an emotional bond and more about…" He gave it some consideration. "It's about finding yourself in someone else, yet not getting lost there. Knowing that you both are a part of something much bigger. And also, surrendering to the moment, and being able to focus completely on that other person and yourself. Love has nothing to do with sex. It's too messy, and too much thinking is involved."

"I agree. Though—" Now that she'd decided she might welcome love into her life, Tuesday wasn't one-hundred-percent certain anymore what, exactly, sex did mean to her. Though she did know one thing. "It's definitely a soul thing."

"Yes. It's…well, it's worlds." He tipped the glass to his lips for a swallow. "So are we going to avoid the obvious?"

"Which is?"

"That we need to discuss what is going on with us moving forward."

"Honestly? I wish we would avoid it. For now. I'm tired." She pushed her hands through her hair and let the heavy tresses drop over her shoulders. She was aware it was a sensual move, and took all the leisure in drawing her hair back over a shoulder for him to watch. "I just want to sit here and watch you drink your brandy."

He shrugged, then took another sip. That the conversation had turned to sex only spurred her on. She had been thinking the man needed to have sex to make the spell sink in, and had almost said as much earlier, but had wisely stopped herself. And she was very willing to volunteer to assist in the said process of spell-sinking-in.

"Worlds, eh?" she asked.

"Yes, indeed."

"Worlds in the brandy and in sex." She leaned forward, a hand to her knee. Lowering her lashes, she looked up through them. "I bet you've seen worlds unending."

"That I have." He turned to face her. The sleek line of his body stretching his long torso, down his hips and the length of his legs to bare feet screamed out "sex" to Tuesday. "Do something for me?"

She shrugged. "Anything. As long as it's interesting."

He crossed the arm he held the drink in over his chest and eyed her for a moment. That gaze could strip a woman bare. And Tuesday felt it move over her skin as a warm breath that tickled and tightened her nipples. It traced along her side and shivered down the length of each of her legs. And there at her core, it teased her to open herself, to want what she'd been cursed to never have.

Finally, Ethan said, "Show me your world."

Chapter 12

Tuesday lifted an eyebrow. Show him her world?

Now that request was interesting enough to make her want to comply. She had been waiting for this moment. It was time the two of them, indeed, peeked into one another's worlds. Or even went for a running dive.

Yeah, she favored a good splash that would land her all in.

She settled back against the cushy leather seat that she imagined Ethan must have lived in, sat in, perhaps even fucked in for decades. It was so comfortable. And she felt at ease sitting before his soft gaze.

Drawing up her knees, she let them drop apart and to the sides, exposing herself to him. The T-shirt inched above her trimmed patch of pubic hairs, teasing him with the view.

His attention was easy and yet focused. As he tilted

a hip forward, she noticed his erection bulged beneath the dark jeans. He'd been hard for much longer than the few seconds she'd taken to get comfy. It was a good thing for him her limp-dick spell had not succeeded that first day when he'd held her captive in the cage. Good for her, too.

Tapping a finger against her lips, she eyed him teasingly, yet the promise was true. She licked a fingertip and kissed it. Gliding her fingers down between her legs, she watched Ethan as she slid that wetted fingertip along her heated folds. Slowly, deeply, she traced up a slick wetness and skated across her clit, which now hummed with a greedy need for attention. A delicious, erotic thrill shivered in her core and loosened her shoulder muscles.

This was her world, as Ethan had put it. A woman who knew how to gratify herself. She knew what made her squirm, what strokes could make her hum with pleasure, what pressure, speed and the length of time to gauge each touch. And knowing that about herself made her strong and wise. It was a knowledge she had tried to teach those women she had healed over the centuries. The body was theirs to understand. Treat it well, and they would be well. And that included self-care. Which meant jilling off.

Because really, what woman could ever teach a man what she did not first know herself from experience and practice?

Ethan watched without a lusty gape or a smirk. It was his calm, gleaming gaze that made the tease more exciting for her. Everything about him called to her on a sensual song. The relaxed curl of his fingers cupping the brandy snifter. The liquid flame scent of the golden brown liquor. And the tilt of his head that caught the moonlight in the silver strands near his temples. Mmm…

Tuesday moaned appreciatively. The man was something to admire. She didn't need to see fangs to get off on his sexy. Her finger stroked faster and firmer, focusing where she was most sensitive. Wet, swollen and tingling, her body stepped forward to sing its alluring wisdom.

She could do this quickly or draw it out, and prolonging it won the vote.

Ethan tilted his head, turning to study her with more intensity. His upper teeth eased over his lower lip in a tense but wanting slip. The man's abs, still marked with the tracking grid, flexed. And a wince signaled her he was feeling the intensity of the moment in the tightening of his erection. It strained against his jeans. And his fingers curled about the brandy glass more possessively.

Her motions quickened. Tuesday closed her eyes briefly, falling into the sensations, the tightening in her core, the promising jitter of release that seemed to reside at every place within her body at once. And yet… she slowed, easing up on the pressure so that the high began to simmer. Too fast. Never too slow.

"Is this a world you want to learn more about?" she said in breathy gasps. "Ethan?"

"Fuck yes."

"I'm so close." She moaned sweetly. But she wouldn't get herself off. Yet. Not until he joined in on the fun. "Take your cock out. Let me see your world, vampire."

He unzipped and his cock, granted release, sprang up against his tight belly. Still holding the glass, the fingers of his other hand curled about his sizeable hard-on and squeezed, then stroked.

"Turn and face the window," Tuesday directed. "I want to see you from that angle."

He did so, setting the glass up on a jut of wood that was part of the design along the brick wall to his side. He placed the heel of his palm up high on the window, and with his other hand he stroked up and down, slowly, measured, and tightened then loosened his grip. He knew exactly what worked for him. He also knew his body, and so she paid attention to his motions, the pace and the intensity.

"I can't watch you when I'm facing this way," he said.

"You've seen me. It's my turn to watch. Your cock has an inward curve. That's sexy."

He glanced aside at her, smiling briefly, but then his jaw tightened and Tuesday knew he had hit a sweet spot with his pumping motions. She sucked in her lower lip, biting it lightly. Her own motions synched with his, moving faster, more firmly.

"Come over here," he said. "I need your wet pussy to slick my strokes."

She obliged with a teasingly slow stroll over to the window. Leaning her shoulders against a thin connecting steel column, she eyed him from his shuttered eyelids, to his pulsing hard abs, down to his cock. The head of it was red and swollen. Angry and virile. The color of his want and of her desire.

"Take off that shirt," he said.

The T-shirt was abandoned as she flung it to the bed. Ethan moved his gaze over her body, and Tuesday leaned her shoulders back against the cool windowpane, the action lifting her breasts. The nipples were so tight and her pussy demanded touch. Yet she could stand there and soak up his adoration for however long he would give it to her.

Ethan gestured his stroking hand toward her mons. "May I?"

Strangely pleased by his polite request to enter her wanting heat, she nodded and tilted her hips forward. Keeping his gaze pinned to hers, Ethan slid his fingers into her folds. He groaned, and slid them within her moistness. The tease of it, of his welcome invasion into her, was enough to make her gasp.

A glint in his gray irises stole something from her. She gave it willingly.

His didn't remain within her long enough to give her more than a heart-pounding tingle and a wish for him to move deeper. The man returned to the task literally at hand; her wetness gleamed on his length as his strokes about his erection increased velocity.

Sex without the commitment or relationship expectations was exactly the way she preferred it. And it seemed Ethan was completely on board with that. This night was going to be a hell of a lot more interesting than an eight-hour flight to the States.

Slipping her fingers between her folds, Tuesday matched Ethan's rhythm. They held eye contact, mouths slightly parted, gasps punctuating the brandy-tinted air. A dare was volleyed between them with the curl of a lip, or the lift of an eyebrow. Then of a sudden his strokes slowed. His grin revealed bright whites. And in his eyes a question alighted.

Tuesday turned toward him and tapped her finger on his lips. He lashed out his tongue to taste her salty sweetness. She glided it in deeper, skating his tongue, then slipping it under each of his pointed fangs. They were not lowered, but that didn't matter. She knew touching a vampire's fangs was an erotic act. Like touching his cock, it produced the same titillating sensations throughout his system.

He grasped her hand and sucked in her finger, slow, hard... He dashed his tongue firmly at the base, where it met her palm. An exhale heated her skin and she felt the prick of his fang—but he didn't break skin.

"Taste me," she dared. "You know you want to."

He shook his head. "That's not how we're doing this."

"Oh? Is there a guidebook I wasn't allowed to read?"

"There might be."

He kissed her finger and placed her hand about his cock. He moved his fingers to squeeze over hers and show her the speed he liked for her strokes. Tuesday was a fast learner and she took over immediately.

The man cupped her jaw and slid his palm over her cheek. His thumb rubbed her lower lip. With a lash of her tongue she tasted his musky flavor twined with hers. She pulled him closer by his hard-on and touched the head of him to her pinnacle, where she was achingly wet and slick. Leaning into him and lifting one leg to hook at his hip, she hinted at allowing him entrance.

Ethan bowed his head to meet foreheads with her. "Tease me, witch. Don't make this easy."

She gripped his rod tightly, pushing him away from her. Then she lifted her mouth toward his but didn't quite connect, save for with a wink. She liked the tease, too. It was filled with heartbeats and breaths, and silent pleadings that were so loud she felt them racing in her blood. Heated sighs mingled. Skin, moist with desire, slid against skin. And their worlds opened wide, coaxing one another to explore. To learn. To know.

"Kneel," she boldly commanded.

The vampire kissed her lips. A smirk formed behind that kiss, curling on her mouth. A secret he wouldn't allow her to do more than taste. Then he began to lower. His lips brushed her chin, his tongue dashed the pulse on her neck. He held there, scenting her heat, drawing her in, content to indulge himself in her. She wanted to force him lower, but instead she closed her eyes and took in the frustratingly delicious shiver of Ethan taking his time.

Finally, he kissed lower, slowly, and lingered over her breasts, breathing across them—*hush, hush, hush*—but not touching for more than a second. And on his path he veered toward her heart chakra, the center of her being, and kissed the sigil, which didn't glow or pain her in any way. His tongue traced the *S* shape of it, then followed the straight line that dashed from curl to curl. The tickle of his beard on her breasts tightened her nipples. Another *hush*.

The man's journey took him down her stomach. Hot breaths circled her navel. He kneeled and looked up to her, his mouth but inches from her pussy.

Tuesday ran her fingers through his short, spiky hair, reveling in the luxurious softness of it. Yet it looked rough, stalwart. Manly. He begged her permission with his gray eyes. And with a tilt of her hips, she invited him closer.

The first stroke of his tongue to her clit roused a chuckle of affirmation from her. Oh, yeah, the man was on a mission. And his focus did not veer. It required but a few more careful and firm strokes to lift her from the denial she'd been forcing herself to maintain and set her free.

Tuesday came with a throaty growl and a slap of her palms against the window glass behind her. "Yes!" She clasped her fingers tightly against Ethan's scalp. "Oh, you perfect, nasty vampire."

The moon highlighted their naked antics, and she realized that the neighbors were probably getting a good show.

Let them watch.

She bowed forward over her lover as the shivering effects of the orgasm tickled through her system and made everything so much brighter, crisper and fan-freakin'-tastic.

"You taste like many worlds," Ethan whispered against her wetness. "And you come like no world will ever contain you. Powerful witch."

He kissed her there, and there, and then he slid his fingers inside her and groaned with pleasure. "Fuck." He tilted his head against her belly, lashing out his tongue across her skin, then looked up to her. Another request for permission gleamed in his eyes.

"I want this—" she toed his cock "—inside me." She lifted his chin with her fingers. "Now."

He moved backward toward the bed. Tuesday followed, her fingers still under his chin. With a lift, she directed him up and onto the inviting soft bedding. She then straddled him and crawled forward to position herself as if upon the siege perilous. She may not find the Holy Grail, but she would invade Ethan's world tonight.

The man spread his arms across the bed and closed his eyes, giving her the control, the freedom to explore his world. He would take what she would give him.

Ethan slid his palms up her arms and then around to cup her breasts. He thumbed her nipples and pinched them gently, then not so gently. That erotic twinge pulled her forward and hastened her need to feel him within her. Gripping the control stick, Tuesday mounted his thick cock and slid onto him slowly, inch by hot inch, taking him into her feminine power and granting him that secret.

The vampire groaned and squeezed her breasts, but without any purpose, for he was falling into her. Filling her. Being owned by her as she squeezed her inner muscles to hug him tightly. His hips rocked. He swore and insisted she go faster, but she kept her pace slow, lingering, enjoying every hot, thick measure of him.

Bending her knees she settled completely onto him and leaned back, catching her palms beside his thighs. He tilted his hips forward, deepening their connection. She may have opened her world to him, but right now the world slipped away. Only they two existed. Rocking, engaged and finding a harmonious rhythm. Such luxury to feel so full and powerful.

Yet the power was shared. And Tuesday didn't mind that at all.

As the moon slowly glided across the inky night sky, together they rose to a climax that made their bodies shudder. Ethan's chest muscles and biceps flexed into steely ropes. His abdomen clenched. His hips tremored as he spilled inside her.

Shivering with exquisite orgasm, Tuesday flung forward to hug her lover. Nestled in his panting embrace, she smiled with satisfaction.

Tonight she had entered the vampire's world.

Chapter 13

Tuesday rose with the sun, or rather what she expected was early morning. The window shades had drawn down while she had been slumbering. Good ol' Stuart. She could get used to a home butler like that.

"No, never," she muttered. There was something creepy about a robot tending the household duties. She'd seen the movies. It never ended well.

Shaking her head, she wandered into Ethan's kitchen to pour some orange juice. On the kitchen counter, she found one stale croissant in a brown patisserie box so she gnawed on that, thinking to leave the vampire to sleep.

Settling onto the sofa and pulling the bag of supplies she'd purchased onto her lap, she again eyed the bed for movement. That had been some good sex last night. But she didn't intend to sew any strings of attachment between the two of them. It had just been sex. Leave it at that.

Because she didn't belong in Paris, and she most certainly was not in the frame of mind to begin an affair with a sexy vampire who knew how to touch her in all the right places in all the right ways.

Even if she had decided getting rid of the love curse was most important.

She blew out a breath and shook her head.

She wasn't a romantic. Romance had gotten stale for her somewhere around the mid-eighteenth century. Hell, it had been earlier than that. The four days and nights Finnister had tortured her relentlessly had pretty much banished all her idiotic desires for love and romance.

Sex was as she and Ethan had discussed. More than romance, it was a world. And if a person went into a relationship expecting it to fulfill and complete them and make them happy, then they were doing it wrong. Happiness could only come from within. And recognizing that Ethan made her happy—but wasn't the source of that feeling—was key.

However, there was nothing wrong in reveling in the afterglow of a night having been well-fucked.

Pulling out items from the bag, she decided the Tibetan quartz points might come in handy for a summoning spell. She really needed some shungite, something powerful to shield her from the demon's awareness, but the shop had been out. The obsidian she wore was strong and attuned to her body, but it tended to shiver when attacked.

The tracking magic she'd given to Ethan with last night's spell might work. And it might not. Surely, the sex had settled that magic into his very bones. Now, it was all in how he worked with such power. And much as she felt he was a smart guy who could handle this mission on his own, she didn't want to be left standing on the side. Seriously. She liked to participate. And she owed the demon a smackdown that would make his heart crumble and fall from his chest. He'd gotten all the love over these centuries. It was time to tilt the scales in her favor.

"Time to let the witch reign," she murmured, and sipped the orange juice.

Another glance to the bed found the sheets pushed away and the mattress absent of a slumbering vampire. He must have slipped into the bathroom. And she hadn't even noticed. Vampires were shifty like that.

She could only smile at the thought.

Ten minutes later the shower stopped and Ethan wandered through the bedroom with a towel wrapped about his hips. Water droplets glinted on his chest and shoulders, and he scrubbed his hair with a smaller towel until it stood up all over. A slick of his fingers over each side of his head left it styled perfectly. He noticed her watching him and winked at her.

Tuesday experienced a sudden desire to kneel before him and give him whatever he may ask of her.

But she didn't. That would be pushing it. Was she all of a sudden so wishy-washy simply because she'd been considering romance? Silly witch.

"You're an early riser. For a vampire," she commented as he padded into the living area and stood before her.

Tossing the towel he'd used on his hair back to land on the end of the bed, he shrugged. "Never need much sleep. And it's supposed to rain today around noon. I'm getting ready to go out."

"Yeah? You got a date?"

His smile was quick and easy. And it held all the answers to the secrets she'd given him last night. "I'm going to test out this tracking magic you gave me." He splayed a palm down his chest and abs. The red marker was gone, washed away in the shower. The sex had quickened the spell sinking in. The man was now a walking demon compass. "Can't sit around hoping the demon will come knocking on my door, can I?"

"Does that mean I have to stay here?"

"You do know the danger of coming along."

"It's not so much a danger as me being the plague the demon wants to avoid. Do you have your crew ready to go this time?"

"I will." He sat on the sofa next to her, and the towel parted to reveal his muscular, dark-haired thighs and a tease of penis. "Can I kiss you this morning and tell you how beautiful you are? Or are we not doing that lovey-dovey kind of stuff?"

"I'll take a kiss and a compliment any day."

"Good." He leaned in and kissed her, taking his time as he opened her mouth with his and slipped his tongue against hers. Instant recall of his tongue tasting her pussy filled Tuesday's chest with a deep and wanting moan. The vampire ended the kiss with a slip of his thumb over her bottom lip. "You're beautiful, witch."

"You're pretty sexy yourself. Want to have hex?"

"I hope that means what I want it to mean."

"Oh, it does." Tuesday plunged her hand under the towel and claimed his semi-erect cock with a firm grip. "I get a head start."

As she bowed to tug away his towel and lick up his quickly hardening length, Ethan commented, "I think

I'm the one with the head start, if you know what I mean. Oh, yes, this is a good way to begin the day."

Ethan slipped on his Ray-Bans and exited the building. He vacillated on whether or not to drive on his quest to find the demon, then decided against it. On foot he could maneuver quicker and into tighter situations. As vampire he had the ability to traverse the entire city in a swift dash, leaving those he passed only wondering if it was a sudden wind that had brushed their hair across their skin. But he'd start slow as he learned to work with this magic Tuesday had given him.

The training session had been all of a few minutes as she'd explained he had to focus inwardly on his sense of direction and need to stand before the demon Gazariel, while also dividing that focus outward to pick up on signals that indicated he was moving toward that goal. Elementals would work with him, she had explained. He knew elementals were tiny creatures, like sprites, but also not. They were of the elements—earth, air, water and fire—and could resemble their namesakes or not. And they could either choose to be seen or not. A mysterious species that Tuesday had said he should trust would guide him.

So he did.

The forecasted rain was more like a mist, but the sky was clouded and that was all that mattered to a vampire. Still, he kept on the sunglasses so as to notice any wards he should avoid.

Leaving his coat open, and his shirt unbuttoned, he needed to access the invisible sigil on his chest that Tuesday had drawn. Before he'd left, she had taken his hand and placed his forefingers to each of the compass points, between his nipples, above his navel and under his ribs on each side. He had to focus on the demon's name and his intent, so he murmured, "Take me to Gazariel, The Beautiful One."

With a touch to the north direction on his chest, he felt nothing. He slid his fingers down to the south and an inexplicable tug turned him toward the Seine. Had that been the elementals?

"Trust them," Ethan muttered, and he began to walk, following the minute but definite sensation that seemed to keep his feet on track and his eyes on the prize.

If tracking a demon was this easy, he should consider staffing a dark witch to train his retrievers. On the other hand, none in his employ seemed to have too much trouble locating a mission target. It was the adventure and the hunt that fueled a retriever, and he was feeling that old yet invigorating thrill again. He wondered why he'd ever thought settling behind a desk was for him, and now challenged his idea of where, exactly, he wanted his future to go. Perhaps he should participate in fieldwork more often?

When he reached the river and crossed the busy street to lean over the stone balustrade and peer into the inky waters, he touched his chest again and turned his attention inward to divine his next move. This time he was drawn across the Pont de Sully and into the fifth arrondissement to pass before the Arab World Institute. It was a favorite building of his. The facade was paneled with metal squares that were light-sensitive and could regulate the amount of light that entered the building. They mimicked an element of Arabic architecture, the *mashrabiya*. It was gorgeous, plain and simple.

Pulled now with more urgency, he walked swiftly

down a curving street, and turned this way and that until he'd broached the depths of the fifth and the traffic slowed and the number of pedestrians decreased. He dodged to avoid a cyclist on the sidewalk, then abruptly turned to the right.

He stood before a three-story white stucco building hugged by a small patio area with outdoor dining tables capped by red-and white-striped umbrellas. The aroma of roasting meat appealed to him, and he also picked up the delicious caraway scent of baked rye bread. A four-star restaurant?

He supposed demons did have to eat. And the place was large and spacious, so Ethan could enter without being noticed. But also, it was filled with humans. He couldn't risk taking the demon into captivity here. He'd have to get him outside.

He buttoned up his shirt so he wouldn't stand out in such a tony place. At the hostess station, Ethan explained he was looking for a friend and wanted to take a look around. The receptionist with emerald eyes and too much red lipstick started to explain that wasn't the policy and that the place was reservations-only. So Ethan touched her hand and traced his finger along her wrist right above the vein, making sure she felt his persuasion.

She suddenly nodded and gestured him to walk inside. With a sigh, she then turned back to her black leather book of names and tables, instantly forgetting Ethan had been there.

The main room, which hummed with low conversation, was vast and spacious and walled completely in windows, such as in a Victorian conservatory. Massive plants grew up along the walls and hung from the ceiling, and were positioned to give privacy to most tables. It smelled like summer, too. Ethan wouldn't be surprised to see a parrot or even a snake gliding amongst the greenery, but he quickly reined in his wonder and scanned the room from his discreet position beside a tall, bushy ficus.

The pull he felt in his chest was unmistakable. Tuesday's magic had worked. The demon had to be in here.

Methodically, he scanned over every table until he spied a head of dark hair sitting before the far window. A man was talking animatedly to a woman whom Ethan couldn't quite see, for a frond of greenery obscured the view. Didn't matter. He'd found Gazariel. Dressed in an elegant business suit that gleamed when he moved. Like hematite catching the sun, his wavy dark hair looked styled and ready for a magazine photo shoot. Indeed, he was beautiful, and Ethan could admit that.

Now, how to get him out of the restaurant and in position for capture?

He tugged out his phone and texted the containment team leader his location. Five minutes and they'd be outside near the hornbeam shrubbery that demarcated the edge of the property.

Whoever the woman was that the demon spoke to could be a girlfriend or lover. The one he had given the book to? Or had he yet to give her the gift? What sort of gift was a book of angel names and sigils? The woman had to be paranormal. Ethan didn't see the point in a human wanting something like that. Or knowing the value of such a gift.

On the other hand, there were many humans who genuinely Believed, and those sorts could be the most dangerous to his species, to all species.

A waiter neared Ethan and cast him a curious look so Ethan sent out some more persuasive vibes. He needed to remain unremarkable to those around him.

On the other side of the room, the demon clasped the woman's hand from across the table and she leaned forward, a spill of coal-black hair falling over her cheek and veiling her face. Dark lipstick emphasized her narrow mouth as she spoke. Yet when she stroked her hair back with a hand, curling it over an ear, Ethan saw clearly what she looked like.

And he recognized her.

"Holy—what the hell?"

He knew the woman's name. Anyx. She was not human, but rather vampire.

And she was his ex-wife.

Chapter 14

Outside the restaurant, Ethan stalked over to the containment crew waiting for action and told the leader the grab had been called off.

"Not today," he said at the crew leader's inquiry. "There's been…a glitch. Sorry. Thanks for being prompt. But we can't take the demon in hand just yet."

The crew left, and Ethan ran his fingers back through his hair, hoping he'd made the right call. Gripping and ungripping his fingers into fists, he paced before the shrubbery.

Why was Anyx with Gazariel? And how did that change things? He could have taken Gazariel. But without knowing whether or not the demon had given her the book—or Gazariel may have given the book to someone entirely different—Ethan had decided not to move in. Because what if they grabbed the demon and the vampiress got away?

He could take them both into custody. The vicious yet vain demon with a flair for taking down buildings by stealing a witch's magic, and a vampiress whom Ethan had once shared his bed with for decades. Their marriage had lasted sixty years.

Punching the air in frustration, Ethan strode off toward the street, then paused and turned back to the restaurant. This was not how the director of a black ops team that collected dangerous objects from across the world must react in the face of adversity. If he intended to continue with fieldwork he must get this right. Stand up to the challenge. As strange and perplexing as that new challenge had become.

He would wait and track them both. He had to know what connection Gazariel and Anyx had and then he would decide how to deal with this.

Of all the women in the world the demon could be having a relationship with, why did it have to be that particular vampiress?

Tuesday was listening to one of the jazz albums Ethan owned. Having never been interested in the musical style before, she warmed to it now. Swaying to the saxophone's mournful cry, she wrapped her arms across her chest and closed her eyes. She'd dated a musician once. More than once. A handful of musicians over the centuries. But the one she remembered with a self-indulgent smile had been an '80s hair-band drummer. Those guys could keep a steady rhythm going. For a long time.

Smirking, she turned to find Ethan standing before her, smiling widely to have caught her in a personal moment.

She stopped swaying. "I didn't hear you come in."

"The music is on."

"You don't mind? I'm starting to like this stuff."

He tossed his coat aside to the couch and approached, taking her hands in his as if to dance. And then he did start to dance with her, slowly, turning her and finding the beat.

"Billie Holiday is one of my favorites," he said. "I never missed a concert when she performed in Europe."

"Really? You were a fanboy?"

"I suppose. I dated a musician or two."

She chuckled. "I was thinking the same. Two or three, or maybe a dozen. It was all good."

"That it was. We who have lived so long have time on our hands. Time that needs to be filled. So I adventure. Try new things. Keep an open mind about what I encounter. And fuck a musician every once in a while."

"Good life goals, if you ask me. Yeah, settling down in one place, or with one person, only stays interesting for so long. I move around a lot." She tilted her head onto his shoulder because it felt a natural thing to do. He smelled like the cool outdoors. "Just returned to Boston a few months ago after some world traveling."

"You have a permanent residence there?"

"I've owned the place for about forty years. I was thinking I'd open up a New Age shop and sell candles and crystals. Maybe. It sounds…kitchen witch. Yet it gives me something to do, you know? I've lived in the city off and on over the centuries. I always gravitate back to home."

"Never had a hankering to settle in Paris?"

She shrugged and hugged up against him and their footsteps slowed as they swayed. "Too cosmopolitan for me. I like slow-paced and homey. I live in a little suburb at the edge of the city that hugs a forest. We witches do need nature to survive."

He bowed his head and nuzzled his nose beside her ear. The tickle and his warm breath sent a shiver across her skin. A good shiver. But as she looked up at him, she remembered where he'd been and what for.

"How did it go? You're in a good mood, so…?"

"I, uh…" Ethan broke their clutch and walked to the window, his back to her. The shades had risen completely to let in the clouded light. He raked his fingers through his hair. "I didn't apprehend The Beautiful One today. There was an issue."

"But you found him?" Tuesday plucked the needle off the vinyl and set the arm aside, then turned off the record player. "Where did you find him?"

"I tracked him to a four-star restaurant in the fifth. He was lunching with…a woman."

"A lover? I wonder if that's the one he told me he was going to give the book to."

"Do you think he's already given it to her?"

"I don't know. I got the impression he had or would soon. And if he knows we're after it, then he probably wants it out of his hands. What happened? Why didn't you capture him? Did they see you? Was your containment crew late again? Ethan?"

"Tuesday, just—" He turned and took her hands.

And suddenly, heart dropping to her gut, Tuesday felt as if he was going to lay some great confession on her and, whatever it was, she wouldn't like it. "What's going on? You could have had him."

"I made a judgment call. Didn't think the time was right. I want to learn more about the demon's connection to the woman. She's, uh… Tuesday, I recognized the woman Gazariel was with. Her name is Anyx. She's vampire. An old and powerful vampire."

"Yeah? What kept you from taking the demon in hand? You afraid of a vampiress? Didn't want to hurt her feelings by capturing her lover?"

He bracketed her face with his hands and said, "Anyx is my ex-wife."

Tuesday shoved out of his reach. His ex-wife? But that meant he'd once been married. Which—okay, after five hundred years the guy could have been married a time or two. Or even four or a dozen. Shouldn't bother her. Some paranormals who lived a long time had a tendency to collect spouses. And yet…

"Tuesday? I know that's some freaky information to out with, but what's this about?" He gestured toward her stiff posture and open jaw. "Are you…angry? I've lived a long life. There's a lot you don't know about me."

"I know that." She put up a palm as if that could block all the feelings from streaming into her soul. Feelings of betrayal, rejection and downright jealousy. What was up with that? She had no right. And really, she'd decided this was just a fling with the guy. She didn't care what he did, or *who* he did, or when he had done it. Maybe? "You took me by surprise."

"You're upset."

"No, I'm not."

"You—"

He grabbed her by the shoulders and shoved her against the wall. Pinning her with his hips and hands, he kissed her soundly. It wasn't sweet or tender, nor lingering or heady. The man was kissing her in punishment. And as quickly as it started he ended it.

"You don't get to do this," he said. "You have a past, too, witch. Don't go all raging, jealous lover on me. It's beneath you."

He shoved away from her and walked in a half circle, shoving his fingers through his hair. A side glance delivered her a stern reprimand.

Tuesday exhaled. His words were not wrong. But. Just…but.

"Will you let me explain?" he asked. "Or are you going to start calling me Richard again?"

Well, it had been a dick move to slam that one on her.

And yet. Fuck. What *was* up with her? The man had done nothing wrong. Except let the demon get away. Because of his ex-wife.

"Yeah, you'd better explain things to me," she finally said. "I'm having a hard time figuring why some chick could keep you from capturing the one demon you've been jonesing for these past few days. End of the world, remember? That's kind of important."

"I know!" he shouted.

Tuesday toned down her accusatory voice. "Did she see you? Recognize you? Why did you two break up? Ah, shit. I'm sorry, I don't have a right to those answers."

"Yes, you do. And I'll give you those answers. Sit down. I'll get you something to drink."

She could use the whole bottle of brandy right now. Even if it did taste nasty to her. Instead, Ethan returned with a glass of orange juice. She pressed the cool glass against her cheek. When Ethan sat next to her on the sofa, she shifted and pulled up her legs to face him. And also to put some distance between them.

With a nod, he accepted the defensive move. "Fine.

The witch is mad at me. But you haven't managed to bespell my dick limp yet, so... I can deal."

"I would never. I mean, I *can*, but I won't. Promise?"

"You're not so sure about that one. But I'll deal with that challenge if and when it comes my way. And no, Anyx didn't see me, nor did Gazariel."

"Quit saying his name. And hers, for that matter."

Ethan sighed. "Are you really going to do this?"

Ready to swing up and punch him, Tuesday stopped her fingers from curling into a fist by wrapping them around the glass of juice. She reasoned with her shivering inner self that had wanted to believe in the man. To believe that they had started something. She'd wanted love, but maybe this was the universe telling her to back off. Keep the curse. Her heart was safer that way.

When had she begun to think in such a way? Really? She was asking to be let down.

"I was married to Anyx in the sixteenth century," Ethan said. "Right out of my parents' home. The marriage was arranged. We were both vampire. My tribe wanted to form an alliance with another tribe. It was a mutual decision, though. I knew her and had my eye on her before the proposal was even suggested."

Tuesday sighed heavily. She didn't want to hear all this romantic bullshit. Or did she? By the seven sacred witches, she'd listen. He did deserve that much from her.

"We were married for sixty years before we decided to part ways. A couple can only remain together so long before they grow apart and develop different interests. Interests that may oppose one another. And the indifference that grows slowly yet deeply—it's a strong divide. The institution of marriage is not something that lends well to monogamy. We'd both discovered that. We parted amicably."

"Then why the sudden horror at seeing her today? It's been four hundred years. You seem to be over her. Why didn't you march up and take Gazariel out of there?"

"First, because it was in a public place. I required a means to lure him out, and with Anyx there...well. And also, I'm not sure what's going on between Anyx and the demon. And I think learning about that connection may be important. One of the main reasons we parted ways was because she developed a dark obsession with death."

"Coming from a vampire? That doesn't surprise me."

He flicked her a stabbing look. "Really? Is that what you think of me?"

She shrugged. "You're not like that."

"But all the rest of the vampires are walking purveyors of death? You sound worse than I do when I was initially cursing you a witch."

He was right. And she was giving this vampire bitch too much power by hating her for merely having been in Ethan's life. As his wife. For sixty freakin' years. But they'd been apart four and a half centuries. And that did mean something.

"Sorry." Tuesday clasped one of Ethan's hands. "All vamps are not like that. I know you don't kill to survive. It's a stupid myth only made stronger by movies and fiction. I shouldn't buy in to the hive mind's vampiric beliefs. And I don't. It's just a shocker to hear all this. You know?" Bowing her head, she winced and looked up through her lashes. "I gotta know, though... Was she your only wife?"

"Yes." He kissed her forehead, and she lifted her

face up to meet his small smile with one of her own. "I soured on the whole institution of marriage after we parted ways. It falls in the same category as sex with regard to what it should mean and what it really means. A piece of paper uniting two people until death parts them is nothing but trouble waiting to happen."

"So I've heard." She set the empty glass on the floor beside the couch.

"What about you? Any exes I should know about?"

"I've never put on a ring." She waggled her bare fingers. "Never will."

"A ring means so little. A man or woman can have a lover, for years, decades, and it can be a stronger relationship than some marriage certificate could ever forge."

"We are in agreement on that. But love, well…"

"I'm sorry. It must be hard for you if you've never known love."

"Maybe. I don't know. How can one know to miss something they've never had?" She swallowed. That was a lie. "Well, I did have it once. At least, I thought I did. Asshole witch hunter."

And yet, her soul sighed and uttered a longing cry for such an experience. Love?

Best not to think about it right now.

"Okay, I learned something new about you today and I didn't fall apart because of it," she said. "Not yet, at least. I guess I would be stunned if you'd *not* been married. You're quite the catch."

"Why, thank you. But it was a political thing, as I've said. The tribes eventually went back to warring against one another, even though Anyx and I remained man and wife. We did love each other, though. In our own ways."

"What tribe are you in?"

"Right now? I am unaligned. Then? I was in tribe Nava. They are still together to this day, but they've spread across Europe from our humble Parisian beginnings."

"What tribe was your ex-wife with?"

"Sarax," he said. "They disbanded last century. They'd gotten into some really dark shit. I'm pretty sure she was still with them then."

"What did you mean about her having an obsession with death?"

Ethan stood and paced toward the window, arms akimbo. He looked over his shoulder at her. "Anyx began collecting ephemera related to death spells and memento mori. She never used any of the spells—at least, not to my knowledge—but she liked to know what the spell or object could do. After she acquired a plague curse I called it quits. Yet her interest in such dangerous objects may have been what led me to the work I do today. In fact, I know it is."

"A plague curse? Sounds like the kind of chick who would be interested in a book that, when the code is deciphered, could end the world."

"Yes. No. I don't know. I mean, Anyx loved life when I knew her. She was not a vampire who would ever kill indiscriminately. I can't imagine her wanting to destroy the world."

"People change."

"Yes, and she probably has."

"Tell me this. Do you still love her?"

"I did. As I said, in my own way. It was appreciation and admiration. And we were physically attracted to one another. And then the love faded. I don't hate her, but I'm indifferent to her. She would be like a stranger to me now." He placed a hand over his heart. "She's just another vampiress to me."

Tuesday nodded. The hand over his heart had been an unconscious move. He might think that was what he believed, but if she meant nothing to him then why hadn't he walked up to Gazariel and grabbed him? It shouldn't have mattered what the woman meant to him.

"So what's the plan now?" she asked.

"I followed them out of the restaurant. The demon dropped Anyx off on the rue de Rivoli. I then followed him to a parking garage and he joined her in shopping. It looked to be a long day of retail adventure that I wasn't up for. I'll go out again. And next time, I'll take the demon in hand, no matter what. But I'll have to take measures to contain Anyx as well."

"You need me."

"I don't see how that will work if your sigil tips off the demon we're after him."

"I'll figure this one out." She pressed a hand between her breasts. "But admit you might need an uninvolved party to keep you on point."

"Uninvolved?" He leaned forward, close enough to kiss her. "I thought we were involved?"

"You know what I mean." She tapped his mouth. "I have no ties to the vampiress. You need me to keep you steady."

"You do have a manner about you that challenges me, yet also, stills me. Not sure what that is, but I don't mind it. In fact, I might even say you make me better."

"I'll take that. And I'll raise you with this."

She kissed his chin, nipping the stubble and then rubbing her lips over the rough hair. The brush of it tickled across her skin delightfully. So she played at a few more nips to his chin, along his jaw, and then landed on his lower lip and tugged it with a gentle, biting hold.

"You're feisty this afternoon," he said, and pulled her tight against his body. He still wore the coolness from outside on him, and it shivered into her being and ruched her nipples. "Mmm, I like that." He thumbed one of her nipples through the T-shirt, then pinched it, but not as softly as she had been with the nips.

Tuesday squirmed, yet arched her back to lift her breasts, and he took the hint. Bowing to her, he pushed up her blousy shirt and sucked in a nipple. His mouth was hot and his tongue firmly traced and lashed and teased her to a whimpering, clutching, wanting witch.

She shoved at his shirt, but realized it was a button-up. Wasn't going to come off without some pause to make it happen. And she needed to press her bare breasts against his hard pecs.

"Take this off," she pouted, and tugged at the shirt.

"We're going to do this right now?" he asked, plucking slowly at each button down the front of the shirt. He stepped back and pulled it off, exposing a feast to her eyes.

"Oh, yeah." Tuesday veered toward the bed, but Ethan grabbed her wrist and spun her around. She almost walked into the leather chair in the process, and suddenly, he spun her to face away from him, and pushed her forward.

She caught her hands on the back of the chair, and with a grin, leaned forward onto her elbows. A wiggle of her ass received a hard smack from his palm. He pulled down her leggings and gave her another smack that stung yet made her instantly wet.

Behind her she heard him unzip, and seconds later his heavy cock fell against her buttocks. Ethan grinded against her, fitting himself between her legs. She reached down and gripped the head of him, squeezing the length between her thighs.

"Fuck yes," he said tightly, as he cupped a hand over her breast and leaned down to kiss her nape. His hot breath caused erotic sensations that traveled her skin from neck to toe, and danced everywhere in between with the giddy madness of frenzied desire. Turning his head, his cheek hugged her spine. He clutched her breast as an inhale drew in her scent. "Put me inside you." He rocked his hips, pleading for entrance.

Tuesday guided him inside, and he slid in forcefully, pushing her stomach against the back of the chair and pulling her shoulders against him with a hand across her breasts. He kissed her hard again on her nape and bit, but not with his fangs. Just a soft, clinging, feral bite.

He rapidly thrust in and out of her, seeking his pleasure. Yet when his hand slid around to finger her clit, she cried out at the surprising attention. He pushed into her hard while she rocked forward, meeting his finger to adjust the pressure there. Inside her and outside, the man fit her perfectly and knew how to play her to the edge.

"Now," she gasped, hoping he was close to climax. Because she was. And then she decided she didn't need to wait. So she slapped a hand over his finger, moving it a bit to the left, and that was what released her to orgasm. She shouted and gripped the leather.

And behind her Ethan swore again and hilted himself as her orgasm tightened her about him, and with a few more thrusts, he came, too.

Chapter 15

"That was good." Tuesday sat up on the bed and looked over Ethan's bare chest. The soft beige sheet barely covered his cock, yet exposed those gorgeous muscles that pointed to all the action. The window shades had darkened by half to subdue the setting sunlight, and a hazy pale light softened the air.

"Good?" Ethan whistled lowly. "What does it take to rate a great?"

"Are you competing for a better grade?"

"No. Just not sure I can live with a mere good."

"Well…" She trailed a finger along the muscle that led to his crotch.

The sex had been amazing, and it had given her an idea. Together, they could do wondrous things. And if he thought she made him better now, he might be blown away at what a little bloodsexmagic could do for them. She'd already given him some of her magic. With the bite, he could become that much more capable of utilizing that magic. But…

"What would take this to *great* might offend you."

"There's nothing you can do that would offend me. Of course, I wouldn't mind you trying. Over and over." He winked at her.

"Very well. I'm going to ask for something. Something I've never done before but have been curious about."

"Ask away. If it leads to *great* I don't know how I can say no."

She crawled on top of him and stroked the dark hairs that trailed up from his cock to his belly button. Leaning down to kiss his chest, Tuesday lingered there and licked his skin, which had cooled considerably. Sculpted from steel, he was a new plaything that she wanted to learn more about. And she would. In every way possible.

She pushed her hair over one shoulder. "Bite me," she said. "Drink my soul, vampire. And in turn, let me feel yours in the thunder of your heartbeats as we climax together."

Ethan pushed up onto his elbows. His eyes, colored like a rainy sky, held her gaze, searing into her irises so she could feel his thoughts. No fear, yet something made him pause.

"I thought we'd already discussed my nixing the blood-giving stuff."

"I don't need your blood. Heck, I don't want it. Unless it's for a spell. But now that you bring it up, you never did tell me what was up with that. You stopped talking after saying you killed someone. What happened that you're such a freak about giving blood?"

"I'm not a freak." He laid his head back on the pillow and closed his eyes. Still, he winced. "I killed someone I loved, Tuesday, by giving her a blood transfusion. And I won't ever be responsible for another innocent's death by doing the same. No blood from these veins for any reason. Ever."

It was a heavy confession, and she wanted to honor it. Even if a few drops would never harm anyone. But who was she to judge him for something that obviously had hurt him deeply?

She stroked a fingertip over the faint spot below his left pec where she'd stabbed him with the alicorn. No scar, only a slight discoloration in the skin remained.

"This blood transfusion," she said quietly. "I thought you said you weren't trying to transform her?"

"I wasn't. I will never make another vampire. Not unless it is my own child. The woman—she was human. I loved her, but…" He sighed and stroked a hand down her hair. Still, he kept his eyes closed. "It was in the nineteenth century in a little seaside village in Scotland. We were on holiday there, and she'd gone out for a walk in the sunlight, knowing that I was back at the inn buried under the covers, still sleeping. It had rained through the night and the grass was wet and slippery. She fell down a cliff and landed on the boulders fronting the sea. It was hours before I found her and was able to get her to the hospital. So many broken bones. And she'd lost so much blood. And yet, I'd read about blood transfusions, and the medical science behind the operation. I knew there was a possibility of saving her, so I offered my blood."

"Was she your blood type?" Tuesday asked with surprise.

Ethan shook his head. "At that time, the doctors and surgeons weren't aware of blood types. They performed the operation unknowing that the type of blood was important. Unfortunately, we were not a match, and after pumping four pints of my blood into her, she seized and went into a coma. She died an hour later."

Oh, the poor man. "I'm sorry, Ethan."

"I'd been with her for a year. We never fooled ourselves that we'd marry and have children. She knew I was vampire. Had no desire for the lifestyle, either. I did have a moment of thinking I could save her if only I transformed her. But I did not. I respected her choice not to become vampire. And yet, I killed her by giving her my blood."

"That wasn't your fault. Medical science wasn't advanced enough at the time. You could never have known."

"I never should have offered in the first place. I should have let her be. She may have recovered."

"You don't know that. She'd fallen off a cliff? And you said she'd broken bones. It sounds like she would have died no matter what."

"Do we have to talk about this?"

"Of course not. But I have one more question."

"Shoot."

"Did you love her like you loved your wife?"

He wobbled his head. "Love comes in many different forms. You know?"

"Not really."

"Right. Sorry. There are many kinds of love. At least, from my perspective. I loved Anyx because it was something we learned and it grew between us over the years. A certain respect, and yes, sexual desire developed the love between us. But I would never call what we experienced a soul love."

"Even after sixty years?"

"Even after. As for the woman who died, I did love her passionately, but again, it wasn't soul-deep. And I'm okay with that. Whether we are human or creature or other, we love. It's what we do. And I wish you could know love."

"Well, I can love. I just can't receive love. Not for long, anyway. And always to the detriment of the guy who might think he loves me." She shrugged. "I'm fine."

"I don't think you are."

"Do we have to talk about this?" she said, repeating his question.

"Not right now, no."

"Good. And I'm glad you trust me to tell me about the blood thing." She kissed his collarbone and laid her head on his shoulder. "I won't ever ask you for blood. Promise. But…"

"You know when a person tosses in a *but* that means disregard everything I said before that word and only pay attention to what follows?"

Tuesday propped herself up over him. "There's nothing stopping you from biting me. And it could enhance the magic I've already given you. Bloodsexmagic, you know."

"I thought that was what vampires used to steal a witch's magic?"

"It is, but if given freely, and if I control the hex…"

"I don't want to get hexed."

"You've already been thoroughly hexed by me, lover."

He snickered. "Your use of the word has too many meanings to keep straight. I do like hexing you. But I'm not keen on bloodsexmagic."

"Fine. I can deal. But that doesn't mean you still can't

bite me. You know you want a taste. You've thought about it. Don't deny it."

"I have." He stroked the hair along her cheek, and traced her neck where her carotid pumped in anticipation, but then dashed downward to tickle the ends of her hair across her breast.

"I dare you," she whispered, unwilling to back down from the challenge.

Because it was a challenge between the two of them. She'd mentioned to him that fangs got her off, but he had initially been offended by her being a witch. It was an old and innate vampire hang-up. He'd lived through the Great Protection Spell when one drop of witch's blood could destroy a vampire.

"I'm not poisonous," she whispered. "Promise."

"I know that. But you have to know I've never bitten a witch."

"Understandable. But you don't strike me as the type who would carry a centuries-old fear within you."

"I don't fear your blood. But I do think you're a fang junkie."

That was a term vamps reserved for humans desperate for more of the fang. But Tuesday didn't take it as an offense. She shrugged. "Not quite a junkie, but I do love the bite. The orgasm is incredible. Much better than good."

He smirked and humor danced in his eyes. He might buckle...

"You are cute," he said.

She nodded, agreeing.

"And your blood smells different than most."

"How so?"

"Old. Luxurious. Aged, like a fine wine."

"You are not winning points by calling me old, buddy."

"It's the aged vintages that are always best."

Ethan parted his lips and she watched as his fangs lowered. Beautiful weapons. Pearly white. Sharper than most animal incisors. Made for piercing. She tapped one, and then stroked it until the man's hips rocked beneath her thighs. It was a unique way to jack him off.

"Taste me, vampire. Dive deeper into my world."

Ethan dashed out his tongue to lick her finger and she leaned forward, putting her breasts level with his mouth. Offering herself, waiting…wishing for the ultimate connection between the two of them. Because, she'd had it all thus far in life. Sex with so many different species. Bites, blood-sharing and even magic-sharing. But never had she had the bite at the same time as sex. It was a sacred act, and could actually enhance her blood bond with another.

He licked her nipple. And even after making love and having him touch and taste her for hours, she felt it as a new and exciting tingle that shivered through her system. She arched her back, then lifted her breast, putting it in his mouth.

And then the painful pierce of his fangs entered her body. Tuesday gasped at the sharp and intense intrusion. But she didn't flinch or pull away as his tongue lashed after the blood that spilled over the curve of her breast and toward her nipple.

Cleaning it off, he then suckled at the twin pierce marks, drawing out her blood. The sensation was sweet, and wicked. Delicious and deadly. And when his fangs grazed her skin they raised shiver bumps in the wake of his formidable weapons.

"The other," he whispered, and she shifted on her hands, tilting her chest so he could get a firm hold on her other breast.

The second piercing felt as painfully exquisite, and she shuddered, and put a hand to the back of his head to hold him there as he fed from her. Sensation soared through her body, coiling at her pussy and making her instantly wet again. He had penetrated her in a different way, but the feeling was beyond that of simple insert-tab-A-into-slot-B intercourse.

All of a sudden he flipped her onto her back. His strong hand clutched behind her head and lifted her neck to his fangs. With an animal fierceness, Ethan growled and sank his fangs into her carotid. One hand clutched at her breast while he fed ravenously from her pumping life. She could bleed out if he let the blood flow too long, and he might tease at that, but the vampire's saliva was healing and wouldn't allow such to happen.

"Oh, Ethan…" She twined a leg around one of his and let her head fall back, unsupported as he followed her down. "Fuck me now. With your teeth and your cock."

As he shoved into her with his hard-on, Tuesday gasped because she felt that sensation as if…she was the one entering him. Ethan's pleasurable groan ceased his sucking at her neck only momentarily as their gazes met. "You feel that?" he asked.

"I feel…what you feel?"

"Yeah, and…damn." He slapped his chest. "That's amazing."

"We're sharing the blood pleasures. Don't stop. More!"

He dropped his mouth to her neck again and the tug at the wound ached as he touched a fang to it and allowed the blood to flow. And as he greedily took from her, he pumped his hips against hers, gliding in and out. One hand thumbed her nipple, pinching, squeezing, demanding.

Everything was different, and the same, and new, and familiar. The intense squeeze of her insides about his cock…she could feel that as if his steely hard rod was her own. The taste of her blood in his mouth—she experienced that sweet delicacy trickle at the back of her throat. And the coil of orgasm that mastered her core seemed to triple in intensity as it enveloped them together.

"I can feel what you feel," he gasped. "Tuesday… This is… I've never known this before." He hilted himself inside her and then reached down to thumb her clit. "Oh, Christ, that's…wow."

"Invoking a Christian deity's name? You're telling me." She held him at her neck, and rocked her hips upward, meeting his thumb strokes with exacting movements to keep him right where she wanted him. "Give it all to me, Ethan. With my blood you've entered me. And I have entered you."

"Is this witchcraft?" he said on a gasp.

"Call it bloodcraft. A kind of bonding that goes beyond the external. Our souls are touching."

"Yes, that's exactly how I feel it. Some kind of soul bond."

And she didn't want it to stop. But it really was too much. Her mind flew. And her body shuddered uncontrollably. Ethan's teeth had left her neck, his tongue losing its pace lapping her blood. Together they had ceased to rock into one another for they'd become bound in an inner embrace that sparkled and held them at the edge of life and death.

Ethan's jaw tensed. He growled, gasping then searching for the release. And with a flick of his finger across her clit, he surrendered and Tuesday fell into the strange but marvelous experience as her body released. Ethan bucked against her. She took it all in as the world moved through her veins and to her every nerve ending.

They froze together in that penultimate moment catching one another's gaze and peering deep into their reflections. And in that moment the twosome had never known another being so intimately.

Tuesday slid out of bed and padded into the kitchen, where she pulled the orange juice from the fridge. She poured a glass then drank it.

"Tuesday…"

She turned toward the bedroom, but shook her head. She hadn't heard Ethan call out to her audibly. Had she…?

"The bed is growing cold on your side. Come back to me."

Touching her ear, she realized she'd heard him say that to her…in her thoughts. Like a dream, but only it was happening now while she was wide awake.

Let me finish my juice, she thought.

And then she heard him chuckle. Again, not audibly. She felt Ethan's mirth warm her chest and it was almost as if she'd laughed herself. What was that about?

She set down the glass and teased the ends of her hair as she stared off toward the bedroom. They'd been so close in those moments when he'd been drinking her blood and fucking her at the same time. Truly, they had delved into some kind of blood bond.

Walking fast, she entered the bedroom and glided

onto the bed beside Ethan. He patted the cooling side of the sheets, indicating where he wanted her.

"Did you just talk to me in my head?" she asked.

"I did."

"Vampire persuasion?"

"No. I mean, I don't think so. It was a thought that I sent to you, hoping you'd hear. I heard you reply when you were drinking juice."

"We can communicate silently now?" She snuggled up next to him, fitting one leg between both of his as she nudged up her breasts to hug his chest.

He pushed the hair from her neck and studied where he'd bitten her. "It must be residual effects from what we just did."

"Yes. I've never tried it before," she said.

"Really, Miss Fang Junkie?"

"It was either the bite or sex. Never at the same time."

"Wow, you do have a discerning bone."

"Richard."

"That was deserved. But you did say this would bond us and make us stronger together."

"I did say that, didn't I? It was a lark. I've heard it could work, but I was thinking more toward making us a powerful duo tracking the demon. I'm not sure how feeling one another's pleasure is going to help that. Did you feel it all? When I did this…" She reached down and fluttered his forefinger over her folds and then pressed at the peak of them, igniting a twinge of pleasure at her clit.

Ethan sucked in a hiss. "Just the right amount of pressure and, ah, witch, you really fly."

"Yeah? Well, I never knew what it could feel like to do this." She gripped his cock and squeezed, and in reaction she felt her stomach tense and her loins sing. "That is so not bad. Do you think we bonded? I mean, I've heard that vamps can bond with others by sharing blood. I didn't take your blood. And I've been with other vampires before. This never happened."

"I don't have an answer for you. It's weird, but cool. Probably it was a soul thing."

"Would that be okay with you? I mean, you said you've never felt soul-deep toward a woman."

"It's all right by me for now." He clasped her hand and leaned in to kiss her neck, which sent a shiver down her spine. He breathed on her skin, which tickled as well. "Who knows how long it'll last. Let's go with it for as long as we have it, yes?"

"No arguments from this witch."

She settled next to him, both of them staring up at the ceiling. Moonlight shone across a nearby rooftop and glinted copper outside the window.

"Tell me why you pulled a three-sixty from flying back to the States?" Ethan asked. "Was it just to fuck me?"

"That was one reason. But another was that this witch never backs down from a challenge."

"Even if that challenge threatened to end you?"

"Oh, yeah. I could feel that bastard hold my heart, Ethan. He promised to rip it out should I go after him again. But bring it on. This witch is not about to run with her tail between her heels because some pretty demon wants to play piñata with my heart."

"It's dangerous for you to go near him. I've learned more about the demon's curse. I stopped into the Archives while you must have been at the airport. CJ and I looked up Gazariel. I had no idea the curse originated with—"

"Himself." Tuesday felt a catch in her throat speaking that name. "It's something I've always known. Felt. But never articulated. Didn't want to put it into words because I didn't want to believe I was in any way connected to that asshole."

"The grand high asshole of all assholes."

"Exactly. A super Richard." She lifted her head to find his gaze. "Just because I'm primed for the challenge doesn't mean I'm not also freaked the hell out. I can't do this alone. And I know you can't do it without me."

"But now you've made me into some kind of magical tracking device. So maybe I can?"

"True." She smoothed her hand over his abs, where she'd drawn the spell and gifted him her magic. "Of course you can, but... Can we do this together?"

"You've no reason to seek the demon, Tuesday. It means nothing to you to get back the Final Days code. You're free to leave Paris. I mean that. I don't want you involved if the expense means your life."

"Seriously? It means everything to me if the result of having the code enacted means I'll be smothered by angels when they fall. I *am* affected by this, Ethan. This is kind of a world-saving venture, and I do live in the world."

"You've got a point."

"I don't understand why Gazariel would give such a devious weapon to the vampiress. He seems to thrive living amongst the mortals. And without them, he would be left with the angels and...Himself. The very last being I imagine he'd want to associate with. There's something we're missing."

Ethan rolled to his side and absently stroked his fingers along her hip and up her stomach. "So you're in?"

"All the way up to my tits."

"They are nice tits." He squeezed one of them then gasped. "Man, that feels ten times better than when you pinch mine. Yours are so sensitive." He leaned forward and sucked one into his mouth, groaning with the shared pleasure.

And Tuesday closed her eyes, wondering when she'd lost her way. This man was only supposed to be a quick fuck and then she had planned to dash back to the States. Yet every part of her wanted to stay near him, to not lose contact with him. It was as if, with the bite and the sex, they had again bound themselves to one another with a stronger bond than even her magic could manage.

And the word *love* kept bouncing against her brain cells. Well, she didn't have to worry about that. The man couldn't love her. He could, but then it would explode and he'd leave or call her a bitch and hate her forever. True love was the key to breaking the curse? Never happen in her lifetime.

"I have a sort of plan," he said, rolling to his back again.

Missing his heat at her nipple, Tuesday laid her palm over the wet peak. "Tell me."

"First we need to capture the demon. Even if Anyx is with him. I have to add measures to contain her as well. If she's been gifted the book she could be attempting to decipher the code right now."

"So we need them both."

"We do."

"And then what?"

"Then we twist the screws to his thumbs."

"Literally? You know, I've seen people tortured with thumbscrews. It is so not pretty."

"I've seen it too. Metaphorically, we'll twist the screws by threatening to send Gazariel to Daemonia."

"Really? He would not like that place very much. They'd chew up a fallen angel and regurgitate him over and over. And over."

"You knew he was a Fallen One?"

"He told me. Creator of Vanity, remember? Just like the curse has always been inside me, and I've sensed it was birthed from the Big Bad Dude, I also felt the demon's ethereal ties before he cursed me. But how would you put him in Daemonia?"

"I know a reckoner."

"Good to have one of those guys on your contacts list."

"Exactly. So our first step is to track the demon again."

"All right, but I'm hungry, and I probably need another shower after all that sex. Want to share the water?"

"Go get it warmed up for me."

"Aha! Yeah, I don't think so, vampire. Why don't you go warm it up for me?"

Ethan sat up and gave her a mock bow. "Your beck is my command."

"Damn right it is. About time I get to tell you what to do."

"Stuart, start the shower."

And as her lover wandered into the bathroom, Tuesday decided that indeed, it was her turn at command. His plan to capture the demon hadn't worked. He was emotionally stalled by the vampiress and he didn't realize that weakness.

Now it was time for the witch to take control.

Chapter 16

Ethan followed Tuesday up the narrow, spiraling staircase to the fifth floor, where Savin Thorne lived in an apartment building in the fourteenth arrondissement. He'd texted Thorne an hour earlier, asking if he could stop by, and had gotten a return text that he was always welcome. It was evening, but not so late that the streets weren't packed with tourists and the locals were finishing an evening meal.

On occasion, Acquisitions employed reckoners in whatever locale they were needed. Sometimes demons who had broken mortal realm laws, or who were volatile and impossible to contain, required deportation back to Daemonia. That was a reckoner's job. And while Acquisitions wasn't in the business of capturing demons, sometimes that was a necessary by-blow of a job. Nasty demon attached to a toxic or volatile artifact? The retriever may be forced to take both. A helpful demon who refused to leave after the job was done? So long, Sunshine. Or a demon who had stolen a book that could end the world? The threat of Daemonia may be the only thing that could get him to cough it up.

Daemonia was The Place of All Demons. Not exactly *all* demons. But it was where the majority lived and existed. It wasn't Beneath or the hell the humans made up to balance out their religious beliefs. It was simply another realm where demons lived. Much like Faery housed faeries. It wasn't a good place. A mortal, or nondemon, would not care to go there, even for a brief visit. The dark witch Certainly Jones had gone there and returned without too much physical harm. It was the mental damage that could never be completely assessed. Or healed.

Ethan had personally called in Savin Thorne to send demons back to Daemonia on two occasions. Reckoners had a particular tie to Daemonia, yet they were not generally demons. Thorne was mortal, to an extent. Ethan wasn't sure what to call him, exactly. And he didn't want to get caught up in labels. He knew the man was trustworthy, smart, a loner, and could drink him under the table any day. And that was saying a lot, considering vampires generally didn't get drunk unless they literally swam in alcohol.

The sway of Tuesday's coat focused his attention on the reveal of her ass beneath the long alpaca fur. So tight and…he could feel it in his hands.

Using the silent mind communication they'd gained from their sexual encounter, Ethan put out a thought. *You distract me, witch.*

Right back atcha, vampire was her silent response.

She arrived at the only door on the fifth floor and turned to eye him, with a wink. Teasing her tongue along her lips, she lowered her gaze to his crotch. Where a healthy hard-on threatened to make walking difficult if he didn't steer his mind away from Tuesday's sexy curves and stunning kisses to focus on the task at hand.

Ethan leaned in to brush her cheek with his kiss. "Save it for later," he muttered, then rapped on the door.

Just now noticing the strains of bluesy guitar music filtering behind the door, Ethan smiled. The man did like to settle in with a whiskey and his guitar. He collected guitars, and even played the diddley bow, which was a one-stringed guitarlike instrument.

The music stopped and the door swung open five seconds later to reveal a big, hulking man with dark hair, an imposing beard and narrowed eyes, yet a smile that was so overwhelmingly honest he could tease even the most wicked demon to step forward and risk their chances with his unique skill.

"Ethan Pierce! Good to see you, man. Come on in. And let the little lady through first."

"Savin Thorne, this is Tuesday Knightsbridge. Tuesday, Savin."

They shook hands, and Savin enclosed Tuesday's hand with both of his and bowed to her. "Namaste, dark witch. Enter my home with no ill intent and I open my wards to you," he offered.

"Agreed," Tuesday said.

And Ethan felt a tug at his skin as, with a sweep of his hand before them, Savin released whatever wards he had up.

"That one pinched," Tuesday offered. "You're fully warded."

"Not wise to live any other way." Savin gestured for them to follow him through an industrial-style kitchen and beyond to the living area. Dark beams supported the ceiling and bare brickwork fashioned the walls. Steel shelves and wood furniture with faded and cracked leather cushions revealed the place to be the ultimate man cave. Add to that the wall of guitars behind the sofa, and the amps spread out along one wall, and Ethan decided the man could probably get lost in his music and not give a care for the world that bustled outside.

"Can I get you something to drink?" Savin asked. "I know it's still early but I've got an awesome whiskey aged to perfection. You want to try it, don't you, Ethan?"

"Hell yes."

"I'll give it a go," Tuesday said as she sat on the sofa, crossed her legs and shrugged off her coat. A battered electric guitar lay on the cushion next to her and she stroked her fingers down the strings and along the wooden body. "I can feel the power in this one. You practice musicomancy."

Savin returned with two glasses, handing one to Ethan, who stood by a thick beam that resembled a railroad tie, and the other to Tuesday. "I do. Or I'm learning it. Still don't have much control over it. You could feel it in the guitar?"

"Of course." She took her fingers away from the instrument. "Keep working on it. The guitar is infused with your efforts."

"Thanks. I will. So." Savin turned to Ethan, shoving his hands in his back pockets. "What's up? Generally if you need a demon reckoned you shoot me a call and tell me where to be."

"I don't have the demon under control yet," Ethan

said. "But I wanted to put you on call, if that's possible." He tilted back a swallow of the whiskey and winced. "Fuck, this is tight."

"Secret recipe." He tapped his temple. "Got it from somewhere I don't even want to question too much. What demon are you dealing with?"

"Gazariel, The Beautiful One."

Savin crimped an eyebrow. "Not sure I've heard of that one."

"He's a Fallen One," Tuesday offered. "Not originally from Daemonia. But you can still send him there?"

"Of course. But those Fallen bastards are a bitch to deal with. How do you plan on containing him long enough for me to get there and send him off?"

"That's still in the planning phase," Ethan said. "I was hoping you might have some suggestions. I need all the help I can get with this one."

"What's the demon done?"

"It's what he's got. And I may not need you to send him to Daemonia, but rather, offer the real threat of such a thing happening."

"A Fallen One would not want to go to Daemonia. I've reckoned one of them and it was a bitch. They put up quite the fight. But The Beautiful One? What are we dealing with here? A preening poseur?"

"Something like that." Ethan took another swig and still couldn't stop a wince at the burn. But it was a good burn. "The demon has the code for the Final Days. We need to get that from him and lock it away nice and safe."

"Yeah, I'd agree with that. Not much for being smothered by gajillions of angels. You want more?" Savin asked Tuesday.

"No, thanks. This is some powerful stuff."

"Brewed by Scottish trolls."

Ethan raised an eyebrow at that one. The man did have a habit of making stuff up. Just for shits and giggles.

"It's true," Savin defended, noticing Ethan's doubt. "Just ask the mermaid who sold it to me." With that, he laughed heartily, and Ethan joined him. "You want me to stand by for the call should you manage to wrangle this demon? I can get anywhere in the city in about twenty minutes, depending on how traffic cooperates. I assume you'll probably hold him at headquarters?"

"Yes, in the eleventh."

"And what's the witch helping you with? If you don't mind my asking? Or...is she your girl? Tagging along for the fun?"

"She's the operator to my compass," Ethan offered. "She wears his sigil from a curse the demon put inside her centuries ago. They are connected. She gave me some magic that will lead us to him. We've twice already encountered the demon, but... I wasn't prepared for the containment."

"No containment crew?"

"Yes, but...eh, it doesn't matter. I'm preparing for the third time. He won't slip away again."

"Most definitely. I always tell hunters demons are wily. They'll take advantage of everything you hadn't thought they could. So you two are connected?" He looked to Tuesday.

She nodded. "In a working relationship. And while I'm not looking forward to seeing Gazariel again anytime soon, I want to help Ethan get this weapon out of his hands."

"Noble, especially for a dark witch."

"We're not all bitches," Tuesday said.

"No, but the majority of you can't be trusted." He spread out a hand in placation. "Just my call. Take all the offense you like."

"I take no offense. I know what I am, and I don't make excuses for it. So you're on our team now. Great. What information do you need from us to get ready for your gig?"

"As much as you can give me. Though knowing he's Fallen is enough. But…you said you and the demon are connected?" Savin approached Tuesday and nodded, indicating she should stand. "Do you wear the demon's sigil?"

"I do."

"Can I take a look at it?"

With a hefty sigh, Tuesday rose and lifted her T-shirt. "Everybody wants to touch the witch. Just make sure your hands aren't cold."

Savin bent to study the dark sigil drawn between Tuesday's breasts. And with a brisk rub of his palms together, and a questioning gesture, he was given permission to touch. He put his finger on the sigil and traced the lines, then suddenly snapped back and stepped away, shaking the hand that had touched her.

"Yep, you two are connected. That's a nasty one. No wonder you're dark. That curse originated from the Big Guy."

"You know that?" Ethan asked.

Savin shrugged. "Some shit I just know. Like it or not. I wouldn't call her master The Beautiful One, but rather the Dark Prince."

"No." Tuesday pulled down her shirt. "I've never

been attached to Himself. Never felt that pull or such control."

"Whatever. It's what I feel. But, uh…" Savin glanced to Ethan. "You do know if I send the demon to Daemonia, she's going with it?"

Ethan caught Tuesday's gaping look and in his mind he heard her say, *What the fuck?*

"I didn't know that," Ethan offered. "We have to disconnect them before the reckoning?"

"Either that, or bye-bye, witch." Savin shrugged. "Unless she can ward herself to the nines. Not sure it's even possible with a sigil connected to the Dark One."

"Great. Ever since Ethan kidnapped me this whole ride has been one big party of suck."

"Kidnapped?"

Ethan shook his head at Savin's inquiring glance. "A retriever brought her in from the States. She's the only one with a connection to the demon."

"Since when does Acquisitions force others to do their dirty work?" Savin asked.

Ethan raised an eyebrow. The man knew the answer to that one, and he wasn't sure why he was being so openly obstinate.

"Yeah, I get it. Right." Savin sighed heavily. "You give me a call when you've got the demon contained. But I won't hold my breath waiting for the call. This will be a tough catch."

"Thanks for that vote of confidence," Ethan said. "Is there nothing you can offer in way of containing a Fallen One?"

Savin rubbed his jaw in thought. "The witch's dark magic should prove effective, and if you add a familiar into the mix that will only increase the power. But if she's bonded with the demon everything could blow up in your face. I'd suggest keeping her as far from the demon as possible. He could use her magic against you."

"As we've already seen," Tuesday said. "I won't give up on trying to help Ethan. The familiar is a good idea, though. Know of any familiars willing to risk their life for a long shot?"

"Actually—" Savin's generous grin poked dimples into his cheeks "—I do."

"How much does your organization pay a guy like Thorne to reckon demons?" Tuesday asked as they strolled down the sidewalk in a direction Ethan had pointed out.

The city rose around them in three- and four-story buildings, random trees sprouting in tiny courtyards here and there, and the constant car horns squawking at one another. Lights everywhere illuminated the dark streets and touristy areas like a carnival.

Ethan scrolled through the contacts on his phone, searching for the familiar's location. "I'm not sure. I requisition invoices to be paid directly to Savin. I'm not the money guy."

"Is that so? Are you telling me your promise to pay me for helping you was a lie?"

"No. You'll get what you deserve. But I won't be on the negotiating part of that. I don't like to be involved in the money."

"Aren't you going to put in a good word for me?" She turned and fluttered her lashes at him.

And Ethan was taken by that flirtatious move, even though he sensed it was more mocking than a flirt. "Are you worried about what Savin said about you going along with the demon to Daemonia?"

"Why should I be? I thought you said the reckoner would merely be used as a threat to get the demon to talk. Wait. Seriously? You're going to deport the demon with me attached to him? You ass!" She turned and marched onward, furred coat flying out in a rage.

Women! They changed moods like they changed their shoes.

Instead of chasing after her, Ethan sent her a mind message. *Tuesday, you're overreacting. I will never allow that to happen to you. I care about you.* He stopped, pausing to consider those thoughts. Did he really care about the witch?

Ahead of him, Tuesday stopped and turned around, arms swinging out at her sides. In his thoughts he heard her wonder, *Really?* Then her shoulders dropped and she shook her head, and spoke out loud. "Bad move, vampire. I'm not the kind of chick a guy should ever have a care for."

And she turned and strode onward, intent on putting distance between them. Was it because of the curse she wore? Did she believe love could never be hers? What if she did believe in it? Might she then have it?

His contacts list brought up Thomas the familiar's address, which was…in the opposite direction they were walking. Ethan tucked away the phone and ran up to catch Tuesday. She turned a corner down a narrow alley formed by the rough limestone bricks of a small church and a black wrought-iron fence that kept back the leaf-less branches from an overgrown shrub.

He grabbed her by the arm and spun her around, but didn't do the inconsiderate thing of pushing her against the wall and admonishing her for her silly emotional reaction.

"You don't get to tell me who I can care about," he said.

"Yeah? I thought you didn't like witches. If having sex a couple times is all it takes to turn your head I'd tell you to beware your female enemies, big-time."

"Tuesday, I know this is a wall you've created over the years—hell, the centuries—to make life easier to walk through."

"It's not a wall, asshole, it's a fucking curse."

"Right. The curse. But there's a wall, too. I know, because I do it, too. I love my walls. Keeps people at a distance, and makes it easy to ignore the fact that I do have feelings. So I've had a change of heart about a witch that I prejudged incorrectly. I like you. Get over it."

He leaned against the wrought-iron fence, crossing his arms over his chest. Yes, putting up that wall, like she had done. It was something he did by rote.

"What do you want from me, Ethan?"

"You know what I want from you."

She sighed and tilted her head against the wall, turning so her cheek faced him. "And I agreed to help you get what you want because I like to do shit that challenges me. Surprises me. Lures me out of the norm. Chasing a demon who could be my death? Sign me up."

"You think that if you find Gazariel you might get him to break the curse?"

She chuffed. "Only one way to make that happen, and I do like my heart exactly where it is." She turned to look at him and he maintained a cool gaze, arms still crossed defiantly. "This thing we accidentally created between us can only harm us both. You know that."

"Only if we have hope. And we've both lived long enough to know that hope is stupid and cheap."

"So you're saying you're just going with the feeling? That when it ends you can walk away? Wham, bam, thank you, witch?"

"Isn't that how you want it to go?"

She nodded. But he noticed the beginning of her wince before she smoothed away that regretful motion. She wanted more, he knew it. And he did, too. How could he get the demon to break that damn curse for her? She deserved love.

"Right." She lifted her chin. "In it for the ride, arms spread and head thrown back as we scream at the top of our lungs. Then let the chips fall where they may. I like you, too, vampire. There. I said it. You're right. I can do this. And when it's done? I can walk away."

She put out her hand to shake, as if they might seal the agreement to let their hearts stumble against one another, to fall into the experience of some kind of relationship, but knowing full well that it was only until they were both done using one another.

Ethan could get behind that. But not completely.

He gripped Tuesday's hand but then lunged forward to kiss her. She hadn't expected that, and she initially struggled. But he dropped her hand and cupped her head, keeping her mouth at his so he could deepen the kiss, dive in to her and taste her fears as they quickly wilted to allow in desire and want and the very same need he felt.

Her heartbeats entered his and at first they danced in a challenging standoff, but then quickly steadied and began to share the rhythm. She hiked up a leg against his thigh, drawing his hips to her body. Instant hard-on.

Which he crushed against her in a moaning plead for what he suddenly needed right now.

"Yeah?" she said as she tilted her head to catch his mouth at a new angle. "We are away from the crowds."

"Can you put up some kind of shield?"

"You mean my invisibility cloak?"

Ethan pulled from the kiss, meeting her eyes with wonder. "You have one?"

She laughed and then crushed a kiss to his mouth. "No, and who wants the confidence of a protection shield when the risk of being seen is much more fun?"

He unzipped and hissed when her cool fingers wrapped about his cock. The heavy fall of her coat shielded them from curious eyes, should anyone pause at the end of the alleyway and peer down at them. But she was right. The idea of being caught out only made his cock harder.

He slid down her leggings and hugged his erection against her mons. Directing him, she tapped the head of him against her clit. He could feel the tingling curls of sensation with each tap, taking everything she felt into his system and doubling it with his own. He would never regret the blood bond between them. Not even if he had to walk away from her when the demon had been captured and the code secured.

Maybe? He'd just been thinking the witch deserved love. What about him?

No time to think about it. Nuzzling his nose along her hair and down to her ear, he licked her lobe as she allowed him entrance into her hot, wet pussy. With a growl, he clapped a hand about her ass and rocked her onto him as he willed down his fangs and bit into her neck.

She swore and her fingernails clawed at his neck.

That exquisite pain heightened the pleasure, and as her blood spilled down his throat, Ethan spilled into her. He'd never tasted finer, nor had he felt uniquely connected to another.

A giggle from down the way clued him they'd found an audience. Ethan growled and retracted his fangs, but pulled Tuesday in closer, wanting to wrap her about his body until he felt nothing more than her heartbeats envelop his soul.

Chapter 17

Swinging out of the alleyway, Tuesday walked alongside Ethan this time. The man had a way of winning her when she most wanted to push him away. And it wasn't even the power of his cock and kiss. It was something innate. She was a part of him, and she had felt his truth and honesty as he'd kissed her roughly. The desperation in that kiss had made her understand her own desperation for acceptance. It was a long time coming.

But she wouldn't go all moon-eyed for the man and pledge her undying love to him. That way lay broken hearts and regret. Her heart broken. Men tended to wander off and never look back. Because love could never really fix in a man's heart for her. She and Ethan had agreed to go with whatever came their way, and she was good with that. Because life was meant to be lived in the moment, and no one reminded her of that more than Ethan Pierce.

"Is the familiar's place that way?" she asked, as he led her down the street. They passed a crepe hawker and she stopped. "I haven't eaten all day. You got some cash?"

With a smirk he tugged out his wallet and handed her a twenty-euro note.

"You want something? A coffee?"

"I just had a drink. And I'm not talking about the whiskey." His eyes glittered. It was a feeling that hit Tuesday in her very bones. And she couldn't prevent a return smile. "I'll wait over there. I want to check out the musician across the street." He thumbed a gesture over his shoulder, where Tuesday saw a guitarist performing, then wandered across the street.

The night was chilly but not too cold with her big coat to shield from the elements. The instant the hot creamy chocolate and bananas hit her belly, Tuesday groaned with pleasure. No one could tell her this much sugar was not good for her. This gastronomic nightmare spoke to her soul the way no kiss or sex could.

Standing at the curb, watching Ethan listen amongst the crowd as the guitarist performed a dazzling flamenco number, punctuated by frequent cries of *"olé!"* from the onlookers, Tuesday couldn't decide when she'd last been on a date with a man that hadn't seemed like a date. Of course, they were not on a date. They were tracking a crazy demon who was dating Ethan's ex-wife. But it felt date-ish. And certainly they had formed *some* kind of a relationship.

And then she realized she was laying claim to the man in a way that disturbed her. It was her reaction to the ex-wife all over again. What had become of the dark witch who preferred to fuck them and leave them? Who rarely trusted a man, and had been fine with her single no-commitments life over the centuries. Why was the idea of actually enjoying time spent with a man suddenly so alluring? Almost as if it was fulfilling a need she'd never thought to have.

A need she'd willingly sacrificed when at her lowest and near death.

It must be the Paris air. It was making her think. Too much. The City of Light was the city for lovers. So, yeah. Leave it at that, Tuesday. Just lovers.

Catching a drip of chocolate that ran down the side of her hand with her tongue, she traced her skin slowly, thinking to send the sensation across the street and to Ethan. She watched as he lifted his hand, shook it, then swung a glance over his shoulder, making direct eye contact with her.

She gave him a thumbs-up and a smiling wink.

He blew her an air kiss, then nodded that she cross over and join him as he wandered down the sidewalk. Hell, something crazy was going on between her and the man, but she didn't want to overanalyze it. She would take each moment for what it was, as he'd suggested.

"You didn't save me a taste?" he asked as she joined his side.

"I still have some on my fingers." She held out her forefinger and he leaned down to lick it, stopping long enough to suck it into his mouth and draw up a sigh from her. "And here I thought the crepe was awesome."

He winked at her and then clasped her other hand and led her onward. "The familiar lives near the Panthéon."

"Is that the big place with all the dead people in it?"

"It is. Alexandre Dumas is even interred there now.

He was moved a decade or so ago from another spot. Much against his wishes to be buried in his hometown."

"You knew the guy?"

"Of course! Though I never could inspire him to try his hand at writing about vampires. Always the musketeers."

"What's wrong with a sexy musketeer? I knew a few in my time."

"But dating a lawman? Wasn't it difficult for you in the earlier centuries? Seems like the witch hunts have always been a constant."

"I got smart after I got the sigil."

"I bet you did." He swung an arm across her shoulders and hugged her close as they strolled down a cobblestoned sidewalk, avoiding a crowd lingering outside the massive domed Panthéon building. "I never had much of a problem with witches until…"

"Until? Until what? Did one of them look at you the wrong way? Give you the evil eye?"

He grimaced, but they maintained their casual pace. "I had a lover in the early twentieth century."

"Oh, yeah? Someone other than your wife? And the nameless woman with the tragic blood transfusion?"

"I've had many lovers. As I know you have. But this woman was different. She swept me off my feet, you could say. But we were only together six months."

"Was she vampire?"

"Yes."

"And?" They walked a few more paces, Tuesday sensing Ethan's tension tightening the muscles in the arm across her shoulders. But he had brought up this thread of conversation. So… "Ethan?"

"She bit a witch when she was starving for blood.

And you know that's when the Great Protection Spell had rendered all witches' blood poisonous to vampires. I watched her die. It took less than five minutes for the blood to eat her up from the inside out."

Yeah, that had been the cool thing about being a witch before the spell had been broken early in the twenty-first century. A witch need not fear a vampire after centuries of persecution. The Great Protection Spell had been conjured to make all the blood in all the witches lethal to vampires. One bite and bye-bye vampire.

Tuesday had experienced a few occasions when a particularly vicious vampire had thought he was going to take what he wanted from her. No regrets whatsoever.

"She didn't know it was a witch she was biting?" she asked.

"No. And neither did I. We were out partying and she rushed ahead to feed. She was an innocent. And rationally, I know the witch was also innocent of the crime of murder. That witch had not asked to be bitten by a blood-hungry vampire. But at the time I didn't see it that way."

"You murdered the witch?"

He nodded. "I was in a rage. My old warring instincts emerged. I didn't kill her. I…couldn't."

"Of course not. If you would have made her bleed on you…"

"I'm not reckless with lives, Tuesday. You have to know that. But I did do some damage. Of which, I regret."

He must have been a force on the battlegrounds. How times had changed. Not always for the best, but the end of the Great Protection Spell had helped to ease tensions between vamps and witches.

"The past haunts us ever and always," she offered.

"That it does. But now you know about my witch thing."

"Yeah, but I'm not that witch, Ethan. And vampires have no reason to fear our species any longer. So for as much as I can sympathize with you losing someone you loved? You gotta get over it, vampire. Live in the moment, remember?"

"Thanks for reminding me." And then he smiled at her. "And I have gotten over it, apparently so much so that I've drunk from a witch twice within the last twenty-four hours."

Tuesday felt as if the something that had started between them had sunk deeply into her marrow. There would be no walking away from this man after they had dealt with the demon. And how to accept that her staying in his life, possibly allowing him to consider falling in love, could only mean their end?

"You can tell me about all your lovers sometime," she said. "If you want to. I'd like to hear about the women who captured your heart. Even if only for a day, week, month or year."

"Really? You didn't want to hear about Anyx."

"That was…" Not all that different. The man had lovers and a wife over the centuries. Wasn't as if she'd been celibate. Time to drop the jealousy. "We can share. But let's take it slow, yeah?"

"Agreed. Past lovers don't need to be doled out all at once. And they are the past."

"I can agree with that. Been there, don't need to look back."

"But you still owe me a couple lover stories. Which I will collect on later. Right now, I believe that is the familiar's building." Ethan stopped across the street from a nondescript four-story building fronted by stone mascarons and weather-stained pink granite. "I'm never sure how to go about approaching a familiar," he said. "Do I call out 'Here, kitty kitty'?"

"That would be obnoxious," a man's voice said from behind Tuesday and Ethan.

They both turned to find a short man with tousled brown-and-gold hair, green eyes and a confident stance lift a questioning eyebrow.

The familiar bowed to Tuesday, then took her hand and kissed the back of it. Tuesday was not impressed. She could recognize a charmer from a mile away.

"Ethan Pierce," the man said as he shook the vampire's hand. "It's been a few years, yes? How's bites?"

"The usual. I need your help, Thomas. Can we go up and talk?" He gestured toward the building.

"No." Thomas assessed Tuesday carefully, his green eyes narrowing, most likely reading her for powers or skills. Familiars had a thing with witches and could read them fairly well. "I'd prefer to stay outside. Was just heading out for a scamper anyway. Whatever you've got to offer me, make it quick."

Ethan said, "I need a familiar to help summon a demon."

"Nope." Thomas shook his head adamantly. "No can do. I don't do that kind of subservient shit. No witch is going to use me to channel a demon to this realm."

"The demon is already here. In Paris," Ethan explained. "We need to summon him into captivity."

Thomas quirked an eyebrow. "Why don't you go after him? Don't you head a troop of wild and crazy demon hunters?"

"We don't hunt demons. Exactly. Besides, we tried that."

"And failed? And why are you, the director of Acquisitions, asking me about this? Are you doing fieldwork now, Pierce?"

"I am. This is an important case. I don't want to cock it up."

Tuesday held back from mentioning that he'd already managed to do just that. She'd give the man a break. He was particularly cute, and she was still riding all the warm feelies after that quickie in the alley.

"You do have a partner that works with you, yes?" Ethan asked.

Thomas lifted his shoulders in affront. "Whether or not I do is none of your business. I won't do it. I do have my dignity. Good day to the two of you."

The familiar turned and strolled away, shoving his hands in the pockets of a summery white linen jacket.

Ethan called after him, "It pays!"

Thomas performed an agile turn—as graceful as a feline—and walked back up to them. "How much?"

Ethan shrugged. "How much do you charge?"

"A hundred thousand," Thomas said without pause.

Curious to see how the man who had explained to her that he didn't have a handle on the money would play this one, Tuesday listened avidly.

"Can't do that," Ethan said.

"Fifty grand."

Ethan winced.

"Oh, come on! What can you give me, man?"

"Ten," Ethan said.

Thomas turned and stalked away from them, but he flung out his arms and called without looking back, "Fine!"

"I'll need you after dark. Tomorrow!" Ethan called after him. "At headquarters. Ready to go."

Thomas delivered a thumbs-up over his shoulder and kept on walking.

"Ten grand?" Tuesday asked.

"His job isn't that complicated. Having sex until he's sated?" Ethan blew out a breath.

"Yeah, but it is dangerous. When the demon comes through, the familiar will shift to cat form and be left vulnerable. Not to mention whomever he works with will be in danger." Meaning, the person he'd be having sex with in order to become sated.

Familiars were conduits for demons to bridge into this realm. A witch could summon a demon via a familiar by invoking a spell at the point in which the familiar was sexually sated and open to receive that demon into this realm. Bridging a demon already in the same realm? Should be a piece of cake.

"You want me to invoke the spell?" Tuesday asked as she joined Ethan's side and they walked again. "I've conjured a demon or two in my day."

"Yes, and I've met one of them," he replied. "He almost brought down a four-story building on our heads. No, I'll have Certainly Jones do it. I don't want you anywhere near when the demon Gazariel is summoned."

"Don't you trust me?"

"Tuesday, I thought you said he'd rip out your heart if he saw you again. I'm trying to keep you safe."

"I appreciate that, but I think you'll need me to be

there. My sigil will focus CJ's and the familiar's magic and abbreviate the process. The familiar might not even have to go through all his…gyrations, to achieve bridging mode."

"You have something against watching a familiar have sex?"

"Do *you* want to watch? Kinky. The things I'm learning about you."

Ethan grabbed her and kissed her. Hard. Claiming. Just long enough to make her glad for his need to silence her in such a manner.

"I'd rather not watch, if truth be told," he offered. "Fine. I'll talk to CJ about the possibility of having you close. But I need you to be protected. If we can't ensure your safety, you're out."

"My, how your attitude toward me has altered in but a few days. Is it my dazzling personality? Or merely that you like fucking me?"

"Both." The wink was the killer move to seal Tuesday's crazy fall into something she wasn't about to name. No, never. "Now come on," he said. "We've a little over twenty-four hours until tomorrow night. I'm going to call CJ and get the ball rolling, then set up things to ensure the reckoner is on-site as well. After that, we'll have a little time to spare."

"I'm hungry."

"Again? You just ate a monstrous crepe stuffed with an entire banana and enough chocolate to feed a classroom."

"Are you judging my eating habits?"

He laughed. "Not at all. Let me make the phone calls, then I'll take you to a place on the island. I've always wanted to taste their food."

Chapter 18

The meal featured tiny jewels of savory-flavored gelatin and a salad that would have starved a baby bunny. Tuesday had been forced to order two desserts. When the waiter delivered the cherry cake laced with rum he winked at Ethan. But Ethan's attention remained on Tuesday as she teased her fork at the decadent, moist cake.

They'd talked about familiars and what a weird life that must be. To be able to shift to such a small animal, such as a cat, bird, insect, or snakes and worms, and then to transform back to a human shape. Had to fuck with the insides and internal organs, yeah? The paranormal realm was truly wondrous.

The first bite of the cake made up for the pitiful meal. Lush, rum-soaked cherries burst on Tuesday's tongue, and she moaned in appreciation, savoring the wicked dark flavor.

Ethan leaned forward, his interest suddenly intent. "That good, eh?"

"You want a taste?"

"I think I'd rather experience it through you."

"I don't think the mutual-sexual-vibes thing works with food. On the other hand…"

She forked in another bite and this time closed her eyes to really enjoy and experience the flavors. Sweet and tart, dense and creamy. Kind of how it felt when Ethan ran his tongue over her swollen, wet pussy. The man was always intent on her pleasure. Just thinking about it, combined with the cherries and cake, made her nipples tighten.

Ethan groaned.

She opened one eye to see the vampire silently pleading with her from across the table. She slid her hand over the table and clasped fingers with him. The touch shivered over her skin.

"I felt that," he said. "The way you felt it. Really? That good?"

"I'm using my imagination, and thinking about you…with your head between my legs." She dipped into the cherry syrup and touched the fork to her lips, licking it off with a slow draw of her tongue.

Ethan sucked in his lower lip and eased his free hand down to his lap. Tuesday felt the rub of his palm across his cock as a visceral hum in her loins. The man's sexual energy was focused and targeted to his core. Acknowledging it started an aching throb at her clitoris. She stabbed another syrupy cherry onto the fork and this time held it between her lips and slowly crushed it. Cherry juice ran down her chin.

"I'd crawl under the table right now if there weren't

people sitting but five feet from us. But can you feel this?" Ethan's hand under the table must have squeezed his erection because Tuesday reacted with a gasp.

"Sweet bloody cherries, yes. You're so hard, vampire."

A sudden throat clearing beside them darted Tuesday's attention to the side. The man sitting at a table by himself, a small cup of espresso steaming before him, gave her a snide look down his nose.

The voyeur did not approve?

Tuesday pulled up Ethan's hand to trace the cherry juice on her chin. He then dipped that finger into her mouth and she sucked it. With a tender bite to the tip of his finger and a lash of her tongue, she was gifted with the exact right pressure to her clit that set her off. A deep and concentrated orgasm clasped her for a few seconds. Enough to lift her gasp to a vocal cry of "Oh!"

For his part, Ethan pulled his hand from her mouth and muffled his groan behind a napkin.

Tuesday leaned forward, panting and squeezing her thighs together to milk one last shock of vibrant sensation from the orgasm. Yes, right there. She bowed her head and said in a tight whisper, "That was so fucking good."

"I am suddenly a fan of rum-soaked cherries." He clasped her hand and they stood to leave. Ethan gave the voyeur a smirk.

And Tuesday said as they passed him, "Let them eat cake."

Hand in hand, they walked to Acquisitions headquarters, and entered through a nondescript door in an alleyway. The same door that Tuesday had walked out of days earlier and then had been bound to Ethan. Now they were bound in a different manner, and because of the choices they'd made to do so.

A dark hallway led to an elevator, which rose four flights. It was near midnight so the building was mostly quiet, though Ethan mentioned that there were always people in some department doing something at all hours of the day.

A small reception area let in moonlight across the single desk and curved walls. Tuesday stepped behind Ethan as he waited before a steel platform and some kind of electronic reading device that resembled the scanner a person walks through at the airport. He waited for green LEDs to blink, then grabbed her and rushed across the platform.

"You don't have access," he said as he punched in a digital code on a massive wood door before them. "But that sneaky move worked better than I expected."

"You've never snuck a girlfriend into your office before?"

"You're the first," he said as he opened the door and she walked through.

Though she had been in here briefly before, she'd not taken the time to look around because she'd been seriously in need of a bathroom break and had also been focusing on the sigil burning through the shackle rope Certainly Jones had placed on her.

Eerily quiet, and barely lit by pale moonlight, the dark room smelled like cedar. Tuesday slipped off her coat and let it drop to the floor as she walked up to the desk. Dim lighting blinked on and highlighted the hexagon structure of the room. An excellent shape for creating magic. The walls were solid, dark-stained wood, and the windows had a view of the city lights, yet she wouldn't be able to pinpoint a monument or tourist attraction for the life of her.

"A vampire's retreat," she decided. "Cool, calm and dark."

"I spend a lot of time behind this desk. Might as well make it comfortable."

"Doesn't look very comfy to me." She swung around the desk and sat on his chair, which— "Oh, mercy, I change that statement. Is this the most comfortable chair on the planet?" She wiggled on what felt like a living material that conformed to her shape and curves and… was that a sudden warmth? "Is it one of those massage chairs? Tell me it is, because I am so in to that."

Ethan reached under the desk and the chair suddenly began to vibrate and undulate.

"Oh, fuck yeah." She closed her eyes and put up her feet on the edge of the desktop. "Don't mind me. I'll fly to seventh heaven while you're doing whatever it is you have to do."

Standing beside the chair, Ethan opened the laptop on the desk and began clacking away on the keys. "Just want to make sure the holding room is cleared for tomorrow night. And that no unnecessary personnel are on sight. I've decided we're going to summon the demon with the familiar directly here to headquarters. It will work if we make the proper preparations. Looks like CJ is the only one scheduled to be in the building, save the tech guys, but they're on the first floor. I'm bringing in Cinder on this one. He's IT. He'll grant us access and make sure all wards are down."

"Mmm…" Tuesday let her head drift off the back of the chair and twisted to sit sideways, catching a particularly deep kneading motion at the base of her spine. "This chair could probably fuck me if I found the right position."

Ethan laughed. "You're a lot easier than I'd initially thought."

"Oh, come on, don't tell me you've never gotten off on the vibrations from this fabulous thing?"

"Can't say that I have. Though, what is it with you women and vibrations?"

"Hit us in the right spot and we will sing, baby, sing. You don't feel it?"

He frowned then. "No, I actually don't." Was that worry in his eyes? "Huh. You think our bond is wearing thin?"

"It's possible. I would guess it will last so long as my blood served you. But we can always refresh it." She slid a hand up Ethan's leg, aiming for the front, where his dark jeans did not conceal the erection. "Maybe I can make you hum a little tune, eh?"

"I won't stop you from trying. I have to verify the security locks are activated in a few sectors for tomorrow night…"

She squeezed his erection through the rough fabric and then unzipped him. The man always went commando and his penis jutted out as the zipper teeth separated. She wrapped a firm hand around the stick shift and began to drive, even while his attention was focused on the laptop screen. But he did move his hips to give her better access, and soon enough he closed the laptop and leaned against the desk.

Sliding forward on the wheeled office chair, Tuesday licked up from the base of his thick rod, slowly, following the pulsing vein to the sensitive foreskin below the crown. She took her time, making sure every bit of him received her tongue. His fingers slipped through her hair, clasping greedily, and he groaned and rocked his hips slowly.

He was right. She didn't feel every slow, lazy lick reciprocating on her pussy as she would expect because of their blood bond. Their connection had depleted. But that didn't make this any less exciting.

"I'm going to make this better than cherry cake," she said.

Ethan bent forward, pressing his hand over her crotch and finding her aching pinnacle with a firm touch. "I'll help."

The pressure of his fingers over her clit prompted her to answer with a careful nibble to the side of his mighty shaft. With a growl that must have birthed in his core, he bent his head over hers and muttered, "Take me in your mouth, Tuesday. Please."

The desperation in his tone would not allow her to tease at him, nor would her own desire to take him past her lips and feel the press of him against the back of her mouth. Cupping his testicles with her other hand, she fed on him greedily, slicking and lashing and sucking.

He slid his hand inside her leggings and slipped a finger between her folds, curling into her and gliding in deeply. She pressed up her hips, hilting him within her pussy and her mouth. Having lost direct contact with the vibrating chair, she could still feel subtle movement from it, and that coaxed her body to the high from which she wished to fall.

Ethan's fingers in her hair gripped and squeezed and his body began to tremor. Control was impossible. Surrender unthinkable. Meeting at a mutual peak and then plunging together was the only option. He swore, and came in her mouth. She, in turn, came in bucking thrusts against his hand.

Dropping to his knees before her, Ethan buried his face in her hair, his fingers caressing over her pussy and maintaining a firmness that extended her orgasm.

"Witch, you own me."

She liked the idea of owning him. Sexually. But no other way. He was a fierce, powerful vampire. The only kneeling she required of him was to satisfy her sexual needs.

"I'll share myself with you, lover. But let's never take ownership. Agreed?"

He nodded, then kissed her hard and deep, showing her an exquisite glimpse of the control he masterfully claimed as his own.

A knock at the door paused them both. Ethan hastily stood and zipped with a wince and a curse. "Sit up," he muttered as he approached the door.

Fluffing her hair and tugging down her shirt, Tuesday sat up on the chair and grabbed a pen, assuming... well, she wasn't sure what she was trying to reflect but the fake-secretary-looking-busy act seemed like a good move.

Ethan opened the door. "Cinder. I didn't think you were coming up. I don't need you until tomorrow night. I thought I made that clear in the text. Is there a problem?"

The tall, dark-haired man entered the room and Tuesday saw his red, ashy aura. But also...hmm—he was something beyond vampire, but she couldn't quite make out what that *else* could be. He eyed her a few seconds, sniffed, then smirked. What was that about?

"No problem," Cinder said. "Just wanted to ask you about the outer wards on the building and your phone was on forward."

"Right." Ethan took out his phone and tapped a few keys.

"If you're trying to pull a demon in," Cinder said, "you need the building to be open. But I'm not cool with letting down all the wards. The Archives could go crazy. All the captive beasts on the premises suddenly set free?"

"It would be for a brief period," Ethan assured him. "Is it possible to let them down only around the holding cell and then be on standby for immediate reinstatement?"

Cinder blew out a breath. He didn't look like any kind of tech guy Tuesday had ever met. Broad-shouldered and built like a bruiser, but oh, so pretty. Her sigil warmed. And that alerted her.

"Angel?" she suddenly said.

Cinder turned to her. "What?"

"I, uh…what are you?"

Cinder chuckled and swung to face her, crossing his arms high on his chest. "What are you?"

"I'm a witch. Your boss had me kidnapped from Boston, and flew me across the ocean while under the influence of a nasty but powerful drug to help him track the demon. Didn't you get the memo?"

The tech guy swung a look to Ethan, who shook his head. Then he offered his hand toward Tuesday, so she got up from the chair to shake it. And then she knew.

"Demon," she said. "But…you've fallen."

"Labatiel, the Flaming One, Angel of Punishment," he explained. A bit of pride in his tone, though. Expected of demons. "Used to be trapped under Paris until a sinkhole released me and I came to ground."

"Cool. Maybe. But…you're also vamp?"

He nodded. "It's a long story."

"I bet it is." Angel of Punishment, eh? That could prove an interesting history. "You got any suggestions for how to handle the demon we're going after tomorrow night? I mean, you two do hail from the same place."

"I don't know who you're after. The boss didn't enlighten me."

"It's need-to-know. Or it was," Ethan said with a glance to Tuesday. Oops. She'd said too much. But Ethan relented. "Demon's name is Gazariel."

Cinder hitched a clicking sound out the side of his mouth. "The Beautiful One. A primping idiot. That's who you're after? Why are you finding this so difficult? Just hold up a mirror and catch him while he's preening."

Tuesday giggled. "Oh, you men. Always thinking there's an easy button for everything."

"He's proving an evasive catch," Ethan said. "And the witch I thought could lure him to us is actually repelling him."

She did not miss Ethan's admonishing glance. She'd take it in retaliation for spilling the intel beans.

Cinder's gaze took her in none too kindly. "Then why is she still around?"

"She's, uh…" Tuesday could sense Ethan's sudden discomfort yet he hid it with an authoritative lift of his jaw. "Can you do it or not, Cinder? You'll have a day to figure this out. I'll need you to be on call to drop the wards only around the holding cell and then set them back up."

"The building wards will need to be briefly shut down as well. It's not as easy as flicking a switch. Dropping them is. But resetting them?" He shook his head. "That'll require a witch."

Tuesday stepped forward. "I, myself, happen to be a witch."

"I will only work with a witch who works for and has been approved by the Council. I can't do it, man," Cinder said to Ethan.

"I'll send CJ to assist you. That will work, yes?"

"The dark witch." Cinder exhaled heavily. "Fine. I've got to get things started. This is going to be a bitch." The vampire strode out, leaving the door open behind him. "You owe me, man!"

Tuesday looked to Ethan and said, "Now *he's* a Richard."

Chapter 19

Back at his place, Ethan wandered into the living room after kissing a sleeping Tuesday on the cheek. She had muttered something about needing to catch a few winks, had hit the bed as soon as they'd gotten back, and two minutes later she was out. The woman had a talent for dropping into a dead sleep.

Tugging off his shirt, he tucked it behind his head and slumped down on the sofa into a comfortable position. Then he took out his phone and checked texts and emails. He'd gotten an email marked urgent from CJ with intel about Anyx. The dark witch had looked her up in the Archives' vampire room. He'd checked *The Vampire Codex, the* book on all vampires—similar to the witches' *Book of All Spells*—and this was what he'd found:

Anyx—no known surname following marriage to Ethan

Pierce in 1540 and subsequent divorce in 1600—has been observed to collect memento mori and death spells. 1720, she was stopped from using a plague hex on a village and was added to the Council's watch list. One incident in 1878 with a volatile organic poison resulted in the Archives seizing her eclectic collection from home in London, but other residences were not checked.

The vampire has remained under the radar but must always be kept on the watch list for occult fascination with bringing pain, suffering and death, or even possible experiments that could lead to mass genocide.

Known residences in Tampa, Florida, and Paris, France. Known former love affairs with Wolfgang Amadeus Mozart, Rasputin and Henri Telluir, a geophysicist of little renown. Current relationships unknown.

Ethan slapped the phone against his chest and muttered, "Anyx, what the hell have you gotten in to over the centuries?"

And had the book on vampires been updated recently? He'd thought it was a living book, always updating and rewriting the vampire history. Yet if Anyx was involved with Gazariel, the book had missed that. Unless Gazariel had lied to them about their relationship?

No, Ethan had seen the two in the restaurant. There was something going on between them.

As he'd told Tuesday, he'd witnessed Anyx's strange fascination for death early on and had extricated himself from a relationship that had no longer felt comfortable or safe for him. He and Anyx had lived as husband and wife for sixty years! And for the most part, they had loved and enjoyed one another's company. But they had spent a lot of time apart as Ethan served his tribe elders and fought in the Blood Wars. And Anyx, well, she'd traveled and tended her collection and kept it away from him until that one night he'd stumbled upon it.

Perhaps Gazariel was doing much the same after learning what a morbid and wicked vampiress he'd gotten involved with. Surely, for a demon who thrived on love and adoration, Anyx would present a challenge to his vanity.

It saddened him now to know that his ex-wife was so…strange. So dark and apparently evil. Was there a way to appeal to her? If she had been gifted the book with the Final Days code by The Beautiful One was there a chance Ethan could talk her into handing it over to him?

Judging from the report he doubted that would happen. She didn't seem mentally stable. So he had to set aside any lingering compassion he may have for the vampiress in order to help the greater good. And he could do that. He just…didn't want to know her reason why she had such a morbid fascination. He really didn't.

He texted CJ back with a request to recheck *The Vampire Codex* for updates, and for Anyx's Paris address. The report did not list it, but it should be entered in to a database somewhere in the Council's vast system. He'd send out a team to bring her in, but he didn't expect to find her. Something in his gut told him she had already received the gift. And that she may very well be trying to crack the code right now.

Heart sinking, Ethan clicked off his phone. He should be out there, looking for Anyx and Gazariel. But he had a solid plan for tomorrow, and it would work. He had to be patient.

There was one thing he could do. He paged through the dossier on the mission file on his phone and landed on the name of the muse who had created the book of names and sigils.

"Cassandra Stephens."

Stephans' location was currently unknown, but she had formerly lived in London and Berlin. Generally, phone numbers remained the same if the move was not a long distance. It was late, but he'd give it a try.

He dialed up the muse and as the phone rang he thought how odd it must be to know, as a muse, you were a human female—not immortal—who had been born to this realm and were connected to a specific fallen angel. And that angel's only goal was to find his muse and impregnate her in hopes of birthing a nephilim. Nephilim were monsters, and one had actually been born years ago. Cassandra Stephens and her Fallen One had helped to destroy the monstrosity. It was a long story, but Ethan could be thankful the woman was obviously kick-ass and determined not to let a label stop her from rising above her terrible fate.

After five rings, a sleepy voice answered. Ethan apologized for the late time. He told her who he was and who he worked for. "I don't know where you are, and I won't ask. But I need some information about the book of angel names and sigils you created."

"I…" A yawn was abruptly cut off. "Sorry about that. Uh, the book. It's been a while since I've had my hands on it. I thought it was with Raphael?"

"It's been stolen."

"Ah, shit. You need my help?"

"No, we've got things under control. But you wrote

the book. Can you tell me how you created the code to enact the Final Days or even give me the code?"

"I'm sorry, Mister Pierce. I didn't think I was creating any such thing while writing the book. The code sort of magically formed and became the awful thing it is now. You know how this weird paranormal stuff works. Add in angelic magic and you've got some mysterious ineffable shit going on."

"So, not a clue what the code is?"

"I'm really sorry."

And if she hadn't created the code she certainly wouldn't have an idea if there was a way to stop it or call the whole thing off.

"I had to check."

"I understand," she said with another yawn. "Are you sure you don't need help? I can hop a flight and be… heh. I don't even know where you are."

"I'm in Paris, and I'm not sure what you could do to help. I've got a crew ready to take down the demon who has the book."

"I wish you much luck. But if the demon is no longer an angel, then you won't be able to attract him with his muse."

"I don't think he ever had a muse. He fell directly to Beneath."

"Then no, he wouldn't have a muse. If you've got a Sinistari blade lying around that could prove useful as a threat against the guy."

"Good to know. We may have one of those. Thanks, Cassandra."

Ethan hung up, and texted CJ to check the demon room for a Sinistari blade. He recalled Bron Everhart, the same retriever who had brought Tuesday to Paris and had taken such a blade in hand a few years ago on a mission to obtain the Purgatory Heart. Such a blade was formed from the halo of the fallen angel. Those specific angels fell beyond earth and to Beneath where they became Sinistari demons, those who hunted the Fallen Ones. An angel blade was supposed to be the only thing that could kill an angel, besides a halo. It might not have the same effect on Gazariel, but it could provide another good threat besides the reckoner. It wouldn't hurt to go in fully armed.

Prepping for tonight's adventure involved warding herself with the obsidian and a smoky quartz, both on leather cords hung around her neck. Tuesday had found a pair of spangled black leggings at the thrift shop the day she and Ethan had gone shopping. Perfect. On top, she wore a plain black T-shirt. Because when combined with her spangled fur coat, she certainly didn't want to overdo the sparkle.

On the other hand, some sparkly black eyeshadow was necessary. And she loved the matte violet lipstick. So did Ethan. It drew his hungry gaze, and that was all good.

She rarely drew wards on her skin, and wasn't going to put any on until she got to the headquarters and talked with Certainly Jones. If they were going to cast a spell together, they'd need to sync wards.

Blowing herself a kiss in the mirror, she checked for the alicorn, which she'd tucked at her right hip in the waistband of her leggings. And the athame she would carry in her coat pocket. Ritual weapons, not things she expected to use in defense. Maybe? She could poke an eye out with the alicorn, if necessary.

She strolled out by the bed and paused. Ethan paced before the window, back and forth from there to the record player. He didn't notice her, and his brow was furrowed. Of course, the man must have a million things going on in his brain right now. But he seemed different than his usual stoic, controlling boss-man self.

Padding over to him and waiting until he noticed her, when he did, she tilted her head. "Tell me why you chose this particular mission to step back into fieldwork," she asked. "Was it because the bait was so sexy and you couldn't resist spending time with her?"

His smirk softened his tension and his shoulders dropped. He reached out a hand and she clasped it, but he didn't tug her into an embrace. Instead, he turned to look out the window. They stood there, side by side, hand in hand, unable to pick out a star in the night sky, as the evening, while dark, was illuminated by millions of neon lights and streetlights.

"I needed to prove to myself that I wasn't washed up," he said quietly.

The confession surprised her. Coming from such a confident and strong man? He had it all together. Except when he was winging it without a plan. Okay, so he might need some practice to get back to where he once was with the fieldwork. But washed up?

"That's crazy. You've impressed me at every turn on this mission," she said.

"I missed capturing the demon. Twice," he said. "And I can't seem to quit fucking the bait. Does that sound like a professional retriever to you?"

She shrugged. "Not sure the qualifications for a retriever. I assume hexing the help isn't one of them, but it doesn't seem to be dragging you down."

He squeezed her hand. "I've become lax in my methods. My targeting and reconnaissance. I don't follow protocol—I make up my own. And—"

"And it's been a while, so give yourself a break, will you?"

"Any breaks I take may result in the world being smothered by myriad angel wings."

He did have a point there.

"You've got me by your side. That's got to count for something."

"It does. It really does."

"Then we're good to go? All confidence levels are high and alpha-charged?"

He turned, and with a sweep, lifted her by the legs and tossed her over his shoulder. Heading toward the doorway, he said, "Alpha-charged and ready to go."

Watching Ethan organize the players in this demon-hunting mission was like watching a commander order his troops. He exuded a control and knowledge that impressed Tuesday. And everyone knew exactly what their roles were.

Far from washed up. But that he'd told her as much meant he trusted her with such knowledge. And that was something she'd treasure. His confidence.

The familiar was already on the other side of the steel door in the clean room, inside the cage with his partner, having sex. Thomas had said he'd need half an hour to accomplish the task of getting sated, then the witch could go in and invoke the spell to capture Gazariel. And Cinder, the tech guy, would then take down the building wards to facilitate it all.

Certainly Jones, the witch who would perform the invoking, paced the hallway outside the main room, head down and arms crossed over his chest. Long dark hair spilled forward and covered half his face. A particularly bold tattoo right over his carotid clued Tuesday it was a ward against vampire bites. Smart witch.

Unless of course, the witch enjoyed a bite now and then.

She should have had Ethan bite her before they'd set out for this adventure. Might have come in handy to reinforce their blood bond. As it was, she decided it was a temporary thing that only lasted about twenty-four hours. It was fun while it had lasted.

The dark witch's pacing moved him past her.

"You don't think you should be in there so you know when the time is right?" Tuesday asked him.

He tapped his ear, and she noticed an earbud. "I've got audio. And trust me, that's as close as I need to be right now. That is one noisy woman the familiar brought along with him."

"Well, if you need any help?"

"You stay back and keep the wards on you. If we need your assistance, we'll ask."

She nodded and strolled back to the steel door to lean against it. Certainly had warded her to the nines against angels, demons, light magic and dark, as well. She felt as if a suit of armor sat on her shoulders. And it was only slim protection against Gazariel's influence should he breech the cage wards.

She'd felt those wards. They were strong. They should subdue the demon. With hope.

Glancing over her shoulder, she eyed Ethan. He was speaking to the reckoner, Savin Thorne, who had just arrived. The big man wore a bowler hat over his messy hair. A loose-fitting coat that looked cobbled from different fabrics, something a gypsy might wear, barely hung to his hips. And as he nodded and gestured with his hands while talking to Ethan, she noted the sigils, or possibly wards, drawn on the back of each of his hands. They hadn't been there when she'd met him yesterday. She hoped he wouldn't have to resort to actually sending the demon to Daemonia. Because without the curse lifted from her, that meant she would have to tag along.

No witch could survive in Daemonia for long. It would be a fate worse than any torture a vindictive witch hunter could mete out. She should have made it clear to Ethan that she was out if it came to that. But not like she could protest now. Such refusal would shut down the whole demon-summoning operation. Her presence was needed and it was not. Be here to sync all the magic and connect with the demon, yet don't get so close that she scared off the demon, or got sucked into his vortex of wicked magic.

This unexpected trip to Paris had become quite the adventure. Kidnapping aside, she was glad to be here. It gave her purpose. And often, when living for so long, there were days she wondered what good she was doing the world. And since her magic was dark, it was rare she felt she *did* serve the world goodness.

Once, she'd been a healer and had educated women. Why had she ever stopped? Oh, right. Lack of love did tend to change a person as the years grew long.

It had never mattered to her before, but lately she wanted to do good. To change. To rise up from the darkness she had caressed and made her own over the centuries and become someone worthy of giving and receiving goodness.

And love.

The thought startled her so much that she didn't hear Ethan call her name. Only when he gripped her wrist and bent to meet her eyes did she slip back into the present moment.

"You okay?" His gray irises were clear and focused. He may have felt washed up, but he was far from that. "I called your name twice and you're standing right here."

"Sorry. My mind was wandering. Yeah, I'm good." Or at least, she was trying to be. "What if the demon won't tell us where he put the book? Do we have a plan for bringing in the vampiress?"

"I have a containment crew on call to bring her in, but we're having a time locating her address in the database. I have hope, though."

"I hope your hope is effective. Because I thought you were using the reckoner as a threat."

"CJ has some magical thumbscrews to twist if Gazariel doesn't want to give us the information. We've done this before."

"The Beautiful One is not going to give up anything without a sacrifice from me."

"You don't know that."

"Yeah, I kind of do. He's an asshole."

"A Richard?"

"The number-one Richard of all Richards. He'll ask for my heart in exchange for the book, I know it."

"But that doesn't make sense. If he takes your heart, it'll return the curse to him."

"Maybe, maybe not. Maybe he can simply tug out my heart and crush it and the curse along with it. But better he suffers and I die, than I live and he suffers."

"Let's not think like that. I'm going to protect you, Tuesday."

"I can take care of myself. I've some powerful magic. Probably more effective against the blood demon than your dark witch pacing over there like he's headed to his own funeral."

"The man has a wife and children. I'm asking a lot from him."

Yes, she recalled the feeling of overwhelming and true love she had gotten from CJ when she'd done a soul gaze on him. She wanted that kind of love. She really did.

"I still can't allow you to work the summons," Ethan said. "Gazariel will use your magic against us all."

"Not if the wards on the cage hold up. Let me go at him first. Break him down."

Ethan shook his head. "We're doing this my way. And besides, what if he's already given the book to Anyx? We're going to need him intact. And no magic you can throw at him will ever convince him to talk. You know that."

Tuesday nodded reluctantly. He was right.

"I expect to have a location on Anyx soon," he said. "I've got everything under control. This is what I do, Tuesday. Trust me."

"I do trust you. Completely."

"Thank you. Now, you stay back and out of the way. You've got all the wards on?"

"I'm loaded with them. You wouldn't be able to bite me if you wanted to."

"I can feel that repulsion. Which is why I haven't kissed you."

"And here I thought you were against PDAs."

"You can actually think that after our tryst in the alleyway? Or almost getting caught by Cinder in my office? What about in the restaurant?"

"I stand corrected. I see you're warded as well. The reckoner do that?" She tapped his throat.

"Yes." He stroked the lines drawn on his throat with a black felt-tip marker. She interpreted them as protective and closing, perhaps to keep him from speaking things the demon might try to trick out of him. "He suggested some additional protections to the ones I already have."

"Tell me one thing about the vampire chick you said you loved? The one who died by biting the witch."

"Huh?" Ethan glanced around to see if the other men were listening. They were not. "I don't understand."

"Did you promise to protect her always?"

"I, uh… Tuesday, you think I'm going to let you down?"

"No. I want to know if you let her down."

"That's cruel."

"It might be but… I need your truth, Ethan."

Ethan glanced to the men lingering in the hallway. None met his gaze. He lowered his voice and spoke near her ear. "I feel as though I let her down. But no, she chose that witch on the fly. I'm not sure I would have known he was a witch before she bit him, either. But I would have given my life to change it. To have been the one who took the bite and not her."

"You loved her that much?" Tuesday slid her hand along Ethan's cheek. Her heartbeats thudded. "More than your wife of sixty years? What about the chick who died from the blood transfusion?"

"Tuesday." He shook his head. "As I've told you, I've loved many."

Yes, and he'd loved a woman so much he would have died for her. And after knowing her but six months. Tuesday imagined such deep and abiding love happened only once in a man's life. Or a woman's. Yet he'd gone on to love others. And to experience heartbreak. And through it all, he survived. Perhaps Ethan's heart was capable of giving love to yet another?

She daren't dream. He would only be hurt if he fell in love with her. And he had been hurt by love more than enough times.

"You're a good man, Ethan." She kissed him quickly, then they turned as CJ spoke.

"The familiar is on target," the dark witch said. "Sated and open to bridge the demon. Ethan, notify Cinder to let down the wards. I'm going in. Everyone else follow, but stay back."

As Ethan called Cinder, they entered the clean room. The cage bars did not glow and the door was wide open. A naked woman gathered her clothing while a very naked Thomas lay sprawled on the center of the cage floor.

CJ approached the cage door. Standing aside to let the woman flee, he then gripped a bar in each hand and began to chant.

Tuesday helped the woman pull on her dress over her head. She nodded a quiet thanks, then looked to Ethan.

"You remember the way out?" he asked.

She shook her head.

"Thomas will be out shortly. Stand outside the door and wait for him. Thank you."

He held the door open and closed it behind her. Stepping up to stand beside the reckoner, Ethan crossed his arms and observed. Tuesday, back to the wall, kept a keen eye on the familiar in the cage, but also listened carefully to the Latin incantation CJ spoke. It was a standard demon-summoning spell with an adjustment to focus the reach within this realm. He battened it with protective sigils he drew in the air using a crystal wand. A white light trail followed in the wake of his movements. He traced a few of the spell tattoos on his left hand and then thrust his palm downward, facing it toward the familiar.

Thomas's body jerked and convulsed. Naked and sweating, he was open to allow a demon entity to inhabit his body only briefly before it apported into corporeal form. A spume of red smoke spiraled up from the familiar's pores, forming a tornado above him. The familiar opened his eyes, saw the red cloud and scrambled toward the cage door. As he fled, his body shifted, contorting and growing fur. A calico cat meowed and slipped out just as the cloud began to take human form.

Ethan rushed over and slammed the cage door shut, slipping a heavy bolt through a lock and activating the electronic security system with a few taps on the digital keyboard. The cage bars briefly glowed green then blinked out.

And within the cage formed the demon Gazariel, The Beautiful One. Long black hair spilled down his shoulders and to his elbows. Bare feet were marked with faint blue sigils. On his open palms glowed more blue markings.

He lifted his head, his red eyes glowing as he took in the cage and those standing around watching. On his cheek, Tuesday saw three long scratch marks. They bled black.

And when Gazariel's gaze met Tuesday's, he said, "You will suffer for this, my witch."

Chapter 20

The demon inside the cage stood tall, fists out at his sides. He wore black leather pants and no shirt. His abdomen was carved as if from stone and his muscles were many, forming him lean and imposing. Long streams of wavy coal hair hung over his broad shoulders and his red eyes glinted like rubies.

Slowly, the scratches on his cheek closed up, leaving but a spill of black blood trickling down his jaw.

With a hiss he released his wings, which spread to the cage bars without touching them. Black feathered wings that flashed like mirrors with each movement and seemed made of silk and sewn with silver threads. They were iridescent with all colors, much as a raven's wings.

Tuesday knew that angels rarely wore feathered wings, but demons often did. Had this angel's wings taken on a different form when he had fallen to Beneath and become demon? No matter. They were beautiful. He was beautiful.

And her sigil burned as if pleading with her to rush forth and touch those wings. To make contact with something that could both harm her and equally embrace her. The invitation felt so real.

She squeezed her hands, fingernails digging in to her palms to stop the urge.

The demon let out a guttural yell, retracting his wings when they touched the electrified bars. He swung about, his wings sending a rush of icy wind across the observers, lifting their hair and stirring up a bone-deep shiver that made Tuesday gasp.

Stomping a foot, Gazariel tested the steel cage floor. Thrusting out his hands, he sent demonic magic hurtling toward them, only to have it deflected by the wards. He took the brunt of that repulsed magic with a stagger backward and a screaming trill of swear words. He ended his tirade with a flip of his middle finger toward Tuesday, and a simple "Bitch."

Tuesday met CJ's eyes. The dark witch who had summoned the demon stepped back to stand beside her. "We'll leave him to the boss," he said quietly. "But stand on guard."

Always. Holding the alicorn in one hand and her athame in the other, she was prepared to fling some wicked magic toward the demon. Tuesday watched as Ethan questioned the captive.

"You'll get nothing from me that you could not get before," Gazariel announced. "How dare you steal me away from my very life?"

Tuesday had felt much the same upon waking inside this cage. But she would not sympathize with the demon. And yet, the compulsion to step forward and embrace him only grew stronger. This time a snap of the rubber band around her wrist was necessary.

The cat meowed and slunk toward the door. Tuesday leaned over to open it and the feline scrambled out.

"If you would have given me what I wanted during our first encounter I wouldn't have had to resort to such tactics." Ethan stood stoic before the cage, shoulders back and head lifted. A commander protecting his troops and interrogating the enemy. He wore wards drawn on the backs of his hands, beneath his chin and down his throat. But his true strength came from within; his courage and integrity. "You need only hand over the book, written by the muse Cassandra Stephens, which contains the code for the Final Days and I will release you. Simple as that."

Gazariel swiped a hand over his cheek, studied the black blood on his fingers, then gestured dismissively. "I don't have it."

"You are lying."

"I had it," the demon said with a sly red glance to Tuesday. "But now I do not."

"Then where is it?"

"In a safe place."

"Tell me where it is, and once I've retrieved it, you are free to go," Ethan stated. "Did you give it to Anyx?"

That caught the demon's attention. He gripped the cage bars, but released them as quickly with a hiss and a string of vile oaths that never would have been allowed Above. "I knew someone was watching us! Did you follow me, vampire? Why didn't you take me in hand that day when we were dining?"

"Did you give it to the vampiress?" Ethan repeated.

"Maybe." The demon rubbed his cheek again.

"You two had a lover's spat," Tuesday said, realizing now where the claw marks had come from. "Did she take the book from you and run?"

Gazariel flipped her off again. "Not worth my breath to converse with you lot of miscreants. I need something in exchange."

"How about your life?" Ethan offered. "You do know that if the Final Days is activated we will all die?"

Gazariel shrugged. "Assuming you remain in this realm. I, on the other hand, have made preparations to be located elsewhere."

"He doesn't have leave of this realm!" Tuesday blurted out. "He's as much a captive of the mortal realm as we all are."

Ethan cast her a castigating glare, which she took with a huff. She did not need a reprimand for providing him the facts.

"You know nothing about me, my witch," Gazariel growled through a tight jaw. He curled his wings forward, tucking them until the points crossed before his feet.

"I know everything about you, as you know everything about me," she said, and once again got *the look* from Ethan. She was supposed to stand back and keep quiet? She could not. Thrusting out an arm, she pointed the alicorn at the demon. "You are a vain and insignificant reject from Above, and then you were also rejected in Beneath and cast out to live in this realm. You, who couldn't bear to carry the curse of a loveless life so you put it on a helpless, dying woman. Some demon you are!"

Gazariel gripped the cage bars, and the action transferred mighty amounts of voltage through his system. He managed to hold on for much longer than Tuesday imagined any normal creature could, and as he did so, his eyes flashed brilliant crimson. Was he feeding off the electricity?

Ethan kicked a control button at the base of the cage, and the demon was propelled backward to collide with the bars at the back of the cage. Those bars hissed with smoke and sent the demon stumbling forward, so he almost landed on his knees, but he caught himself. Bent over, huffing, his wings slowly curled about him, enclosing him in a cocoon.

"Is she right?" Ethan asked. "Are you but a feeble reject from both Above and Beneath? Is it that your lover took off with the book, leaving you a simpering reject in her wake?"

"I don't have it. Not anymore. I was going to give it to her to—"

Tuesday filled in the words he probably couldn't bring himself to say—*to win her love*. Was the vampiress the one creature from whom Gazariel could not be loved?

"No." The demon stomped a foot. "I'm not going to utter a single word about that…bitch of a vampire." Gazariel lifted his head from the glinting cove of wings. His jaw was tight. He'd felt that pain from the cage bars, Tuesday knew. "Serve me your worst, Ethan Pierce."

"Very well." Ethan stepped back and gestured for Savin Thorne to step forward. The man tossed his hat aside, and shrugged up his shoulders, as if preparing to step into a boxing ring.

"Who is this mortal you've put before me?" Gazariel asked. "He may look imposing but I can feel no power within him."

The reckoner chuckled and rubbed his palms together before his face. When he spread his hands to face toward the cage, the wards on his palms took to flame. "I am Savin Thorne," he said to the demon. "I'm here to reckon you to Daemonia."

Ethan stepped aside to give the reckoner room to work. Tuesday stood just behind him. He could sense her in him. Because she was in him. And he didn't feel fear in her, but rather, indifference and a righteous anger. She hated this demon and wanted him gone. But he also knew they could not send him off to Daemonia until they'd gotten the information they needed from him. Nor could they actually send him away without also sending Tuesday along with him.

Thorne knew that as well.

The reckoner clapped his hands together over his head and began to chant something that sounded like a Polynesian tribal rite. It had a beat and a low, bellowing caw that sent chills up Ethan's spine.

Inside the cage the demon narrowed his gaze on the reckoner. With a shrewd sneer, he folded back his wings. He wasn't standing so tall and proud anymore. And it wasn't curiosity that bent him forward to better hear the reckoner's deep and loud voice. It had to be a nervous fear.

To Ethan's right stood CJ. The dark witch had crossed himself and touched some of the tattoos on his hand the moment the reckoner had started to chant. Ethan wasn't aware of any protections he needed against a reckoner. He'd worked with Savin twice before and had witnessed the man send a demon off to Daemonia in a cloud of black smoke. It had taken but ten minutes of chanting.

And they were nearing that mark now.

"All right!" the demon suddenly shouted, yet the reckoner kept up his wicked chant. "Make him cease and I will tell you where it is."

"Savin," Ethan said.

The reckoner silenced, closed his eyes and thrust his hands above his head again, but this time only touching together his forefingers, as if to pause something he could then continue when required. With a nod, he stepped back beside CJ.

Ethan stepped up to the cage. "Tell me."

Gazariel peered past him to Tuesday. "I will only tell my witch."

"That's not going to happen. She's not involved in this interrogation."

"I won't do anything to her. These damn wards have drained me already. And that bloody chanting. Ugh. I could almost see the gates to Daemonia. She knows she'll be safe. Yes?"

Behind him, Ethan felt Tuesday's nod more than saw it. He'd promised to protect her, and he did trust the efficacy of the wards in the room. And she was warded fully as well. He turned to look at her and without so much as a flinch, her confident posture conveyed to him that she was ready.

The woman was brave and strong. Of course she could handle this. Ethan nodded once, and Tuesday stepped forward.

Chapter 21

The leering look of satisfaction on Gazariel's face was slightly challenged by the fact that he was subdued, unable to reach through the bars and grab for Tuesday, as she knew he wished to do. So she walked up and stood but inches from those bars, and he did the same. She could feel him inside her. Feel his haughty vanity and his complex anger at the imprisonment.

And she well understood his pride in knowing that he had control over her, no matter the safeguards and wards. Because she would never have freedom so long as she wore his sigil.

And a larger part of her than she was comfortable with…wanted him. Close to her. Inside her. A part of her, as the sigil's burning caress promised.

"Where is it?" she asked, curling her fingers about

the alicorn and athame. "Come on, it's late and I need to go home and wash my hair."

"Snark does not suit you, witch. I prefer those times when you are raging in your dark beauty, calling down the rains to chase away the dust storms, or sending out an army of gargoyles to defeat a band of marauders. Or what about that time you burned out a lecher's tongue for harming a child? You think I haven't watched you over the centuries?"

Behind her, Ethan cleared his throat. He wanted her to get on with it, but she couldn't force the demon when grandstanding was obviously his thing.

"I've never sensed your presence," she offered honestly. A creepy discomfort kept her from prompting for the details.

"I'm sure the sigil did. But you were focused. Honed to a precise and elegant weapon. And now look at you. Being led on a leash by an insignificant vampire and his band of not-so-merry men."

"The reckoner fucked with your sense of safety," she observed. "If sent to Daemonia you wouldn't last a day. And how long is a day in that place? Decades? Oh, the fun they'd have with such a pretty, spoiled Fallen brat such as you."

The demon reached to grab at her but recoiled when his fingers connected with the electrical field. "Bitch."

"Actually, it's witch. Get it right."

Gazariel chuckled. "I like your moxie, my witch. Despite your reliance on that silly plaything. An alicorn? Really? It's been tainted by vampire blood. It will no longer serve you in any significant manner."

She looked at the pearlescent twist of horn. It did seem a bit duller than when she'd first claimed it. But she wouldn't set it aside. That's what the demon wanted her to do.

Gazariel bowed his head toward her. "We might have made an interesting pair."

"Seriously? Nope. I prefer my men with balls."

The demon gripped his crotch defiantly, gnashing his teeth as he did so. "Words—"

"*Do* seem to bother you. But now let's get this done with, shall we? The sooner you tell me where the book is, the faster me and the band of merry men will let you go."

"You don't actually think they'll release me, do you? The reckoner stands greedily waiting. I can see the lust for revenge in his eyes."

"Revenge? You've done nothing to him."

"It is revenge for all of our kind. A secret he holds so tightly it keeps him from his true powers." The demon's eyes glinted as he met gazes with the reckoner.

"I was promised you would be released as soon as the book with the code is handed over," Tuesday said, not wanting to get into whatever issues the reckoner had with demons right now. "I won't allow them to go back on their word to me. I do have your word, yes, Ethan Pierce?" she said loudly.

"You do," Ethan said. "He gives us the location of the book. We retrieve it, verify it's intact. We let him go. Simple as that."

Gazariel considered it for a moment, his eyes flicking from red to the brilliant azure that must have lured thousands of women to their knees before him. So damn pretty.

But also a Richard.

And it was only with that thought Tuesday was able

to keep it together and not attempt to reach for his chiseled abs.

"As the mean vampire guessed, I gave it to my girlfriend," he said quietly. Tuesday suspected none could hear but her, though the vampire should be able to with his heightened senses.

"She didn't love you," Tuesday said, trying out her earlier suspicion. "You thought by giving her the book you could win her love."

Gazariel lifted his chin imperiously.

"There was actually one creature in this realm who did not fall on her knees in adoration before you," she declared. "Must have been tough for a poseur like you."

"Enough!"

"Apparently, you were not enough for Anyx."

"I care little about that somber, death-obsessed vampiress. Besides, we broke up recently."

"Let me guess. Just before you were whisked away to this cage? I saw the claw marks," Tuesday said. "And you bleed black blood. No angel left in you, Beautiful One."

Gazariel's upper lip flinched.

"Why that book and that particular vampiress?"

"I had no idea, when first we met, that she had a disturbingly dark obsession."

"So I've been told." Tuesday kept herself from glancing Ethan's way. The vampiress did not sound like the sort any man could love. She must have some serious skills when it came to pleasuring them. "So you gave her a book with a code that could end the world as a sort of…love token?"

"I gave it to her days ago. She thanked me, but…she didn't say she loved me. Can you believe that?"

"Shocking," Tuesday said with all the snark exploding in that one utterance.

"I thought she would merely add it to her collection," Gazariel explained. "She collects death. Remnants from the *Titanic*. The leather straps from an electric chair that ended the lives of so many. A charm to give the bearer instant necrosis. Et cetera. So a code that could enact the end of the world? She was excited. It was the most powerful item she'd ever heard of. She was thrilled to have it. Little did I know she was using me to get what she wanted." He looked aside, and for a moment Tuesday almost saw regret cross his perfectly symmetrical face. "She's a bigger bitch than you are. Good riddance, I say."

"Along with the means to end the world? Gazariel, please."

He closed his eyes and sucked in a breath through his nose. "I do love it when you speak my name. It shivers through me like a teasing yet unrequited orgasm. Always promising yet never fulfilling."

Now she was ready to poke him in the eye with the alicorn, but Tuesday knew the wards worked on both sides of the cage bars.

"If you two are on the outs, then why the hell won't you give her up to us?" she asked. "Why not get the ultimate revenge against the one person who doesn't love you by sending us after her to claim the book?"

"Do *you* love me, Tuesday Knightsbridge?"

Pressing her lips together, Tuesday prevented an oath, but oh, did it tangle with her tongue for release. She needed to play nice with the demon, or they would never get anywhere with him. She pressed a palm over the sigil and said what she knew to be partially true, and what she hoped wasn't deeply true. "I do love you, Gazariel. You are beautiful. I adore you."

"Of course you do." Another deep inhale of satisfaction and he opened his eyes to beam a soft blue gaze upon her. She almost thought to see compassion in his irises. "I gave you freedom from death. And from love."

"Yeah, well… I would like to know love," she admitted.

"It is exquisite. I have it all the time. You are missing so much."

She tilted her head and couldn't stop the truth from spilling out. "I don't think what you believe to be love is really quite the thing. You are adored and worshipped. But that's not love. Love is…something different. It comes from the soul. It connects two people not out of desperation, or a worshipful lusting desire, but here." She beat her chest with a fist. "Deeply and to the bone. It is blood, bone and spirit."

The demon sniffed. "You think to know so much?"

"I know a lot, but certainly not everything. What I do know is that the manner in which I love you is not abiding or deep. It is only surface. You will only ever have surface love, Gazariel. And that makes you a sad, pitiful, impotent demon."

This time Gazariel's hand plunged through the cage bars, and even as he screamed at the pain of the wards burning his skin, he managed to grasp her throat.

Tuesday's body was pulled away from the weak attack, and she turned to shove Ethan away. "I'm fine. Just let me do this. I've got him. I do."

Ethan nodded. "You do. But I'm close."

Stepping back up to the bars, Tuesday waited for the demon to stop groaning and look up from his burned hand. The angry red skin smoldered, but they both watched as it healed, forming new, pale flesh and re-shaping his broken fingers into long, elegant append-ages.

"Admit you did a bad thing," she said to him. "Your ex-girlfriend has something that no one should be al-lowed to touch. And really? If she does manage to ac-tivate the code and brings down all the angels from Above, they'll smother you, too."

Shaking out his newly healed hand, Gazariel lifted his chin with a haughty thrust. "Assuming I remain on this mortal realm."

Tuesday crossed her arms, and stated flatly, "You can't go back to Beneath. Or even Above. You're stuck here." It was a guess, but she figured it was a good one.

Yet Gazariel looked down his nose at her. "It is as simple as going belowground. The angels won't fall through the earth. Not too far, anyway. Their wings will burn up the surface and the bodies of all those walking this earth. But Paris is a virtual maze of passages and tunnels beneath the manmade clutter."

Tuesday glanced to Ethan, who was hearing all of this. He didn't make a move or give her a sign that he understood what the demon was talking about.

"You think you'll be safe when your bitch of a girl-friend releases Above's angels as long as you're under-ground?"

"The catacombs are where Anyx said she intended to be when she set off the spell." Gazariel hung his head. "I thought she'd put it on the shelf next to her other collectibles."

"No, you didn't. You're not that much of an idiot."

The man sucked in his lower lip. The move reduced

him to such a human thing. Truly, an impotent loveless creature. She was right; he had not known true, soul-deep love. And she knew that because she was exactly the same as him.

"Maybe you are an idiot," she said quietly. "Love dumb?"

"If you wish me to continue speaking to you so openly you should try a little kindness, my witch. I happen to know you and that vampire are currently engaged in a frenzied affair. Does he know the *other* way to break your curse? The one that doesn't involve my ripping out your heart?"

Tuesday closed her eyes and sensed that Ethan was listening, carefully. He didn't say anything. And she could not allow him to learn the truth.

"It's not something that's ever going to come to fruition," she said quietly. "And if I could rip out my heart and give it to you without dying, believe me, I would."

"I do tire of so much love some days."

"You've never been lovable a day in your pitiful life."

"I am an extremely lovable demon. Adored. Worshipped. Ugh. It can get tiresome, let me tell you."

"I wouldn't know."

"No, you would not." The demon glanced to Ethan. "But…you could."

Enough of the sly entendres about her love life.

"Come on. Where is Anyx and what sort of booby traps do we have to wend through to get to her?"

"She intends to enact the code under the full moon."

"That's tonight."

"I believe so. At the stroke of midnight." Gazariel rubbed his knuckles against his bare chest and blew on them. Casual. Just playing for time, now that he realized he might have the upper hand.

"Thorne," Ethan said from behind them.

The reckoner clapped his hands loudly and again set into his chant.

"Guess your time is up," Tuesday said, as calmly as she could manage. But really? She wasn't in any mood to get transported to Daemonia with this vain angel-turned-demon-turned-love-sick idiot.

"What do you want from me!" Gazariel shouted.

"Where is she?" Ethan demanded.

The reckoner's voice rose. The cage bars began to shudder.

"Fine! She's beneath the Temple of Reason."

Tuesday turned to face the men behind her, and as one they said, "Notre Dame."

Chapter 22

Outside in the hallway the crew gathered to discuss their next move. They needed to find Anyx STAT. Since she'd only had the book a few days, Ethan wondered if the vampiress had figured out the code. Gazariel hadn't known. They convened outside the clean room, leaving Gazariel inside the cage after he'd given them Anyx's address.

"Now what?" Savin asked.

"I'm routing the containment team to the address I just got for Anyx, but I suspect we won't find her there," Ethan said. "The demon is telling the truth. We need to go below Notre Dame."

CJ whistled. "Beneath holy ground?"

"This adventure gets more fun by the minute," Tuesday said with little sincerity.

"Isn't it old Roman remains below the church?" Savin asked.

"That's the public level," CJ explained. "There are tunnels beneath the church that snake down much deeper, perhaps five or six stories. We might have to do some spelunking."

"I know a guy who'll grant us access through the church. Want me to call him?" Savin asked.

"If you can get him here immediately," Ethan said.

Savin tugged out a cell phone. "I'll go along, but only if you need me. Or do you want me to hang around here? Babysit the demon?"

"We need to take Gazariel along," Tuesday said.

"No." Ethan shook his head. "We can't risk it."

"With a little blood magic the demon will lead us straight to her," she said.

"Like drawing a compass on his chest?"

"More complicated than that, but very doable. And CJ and I can shackle him and make him utterly incapable to do anything but walk and breathe."

Ethan looked to CJ. The dark witch nodded. "It's possible. If he's had sex with Anyx recently—and she drew his blood—we could work the spell. Remnants of her DNA would still be on or in him. But we'd have to combine our magics," he said to Tuesday.

"Not a problem. And if we bring along the reckoner he remains a threat to the demon to stay on his best behavior. But you're not going to send him to Daemonia as long as I'm wearing his sigil."

"Of course not," Savin offered.

"Tuesday, can I talk to you over here?" Ethan nodded down the hallway. "CJ, you and Savin prepare for our adventure."

"Will do," CJ said. "But first I've to head up to tech

and make sure Cinder has the building wards back in place. Come on, Savin."

When the two men had left, Ethan took Tuesday by the arms and looked into her eyes for the longest time before he finally asked, "What's the other way to break the curse?"

"What?"

"I heard every word the two of you spoke. The demon said there was a way to break your curse without ripping out your heart."

She looked away from him, but he moved to the side and blocked her in by the wall, tipping up her chin and forcing her to meet the challenge in his eyes. "Tell me. You've known there was another way all along?"

"I've known since the moment the curse settled into me. He told me then. It's not something that will ever happen. And I will not tell you what it is, so to use one of your favorite lines, you don't get to tell me what I can and can't do." She shrugged out of his grasp and walked a few steps away. "You did promise to release Gazariel after we got the code. So the reckoner shouldn't even be an issue. I needn't worry about being tugged off to Daemonia. And I'm resigned to carry the curse within me for the rest of my days."

"Don't you want love, Tuesday? If there's a chance to break the curse in some other manner—"

"I said we will not discuss this anymore. Can you give me that?"

Ethan raked his fingers through his hair and gave her a nodding shrug. "I guess I have to. But will it interfere with the task we have before us?"

"Not at all. I swear it to you."

"Then you and CJ need to bespell the demon in whatever manner will help us, and we'll set him loose to lead us to Anyx. Do you have a means to stop the spell should she have already enacted it? Do you know how the code is activated?"

"I've not seen the book or the code. And I thought you were the man in charge. Don't you have information about how the code is activated?"

"It's a blood spell."

"How do you know?"

"That's what I was told."

"By who?"

"The one who ordered I retrieve the book," he said angrily.

"Who is?" Tuesday insisted.

Ethan looked away from her.

"Ethan? Who sent you on the quest for this book? Was it the Council? Because it doesn't feel right to me. You'd have more information if the Council—"

"It was a direct order from Raphael," he finally said.

"Raph— An actual—" Shivers traced Tuesday's nape. This was getting a bit too deep into angeldom and their mysterious ways for her comfort. "You got an order from an archangel?"

He squeezed the fingers of one hand before him and nodded. "Came to me a few days before you arrived with a demand we locate the thing."

"Why are you acting so weird about it? It's like you're embarrassed or—"

"I am not embarrassed. This is a need-to-know mission. And you don't—"

"Do not give me that excuse. I'm in this. Deep. And you couldn't have gotten this far without me. What's going on, Ethan? Do you often take orders from angels? How is Raphael involved?"

He gripped her by the shoulders as if to steady her, but he was actually finding his ground and forcing up calm when he wanted to walk away from her right now. His confession about not being up to snuff on fieldwork returned to his thoughts. Had he stepped into a mess too deep for even him to struggle out of?

"Raphael was keeping track of the book," Ethan said, "and…he misplaced it. That is confidential information. But you won't say anything, right?"

"Why would I? And to whom? I just think it's kind of weird that an angel allowed a demon to steal something so valuable from him." She tilted her head, and tried to read Ethan's gaze. "In fact, I find it nearly impossible that one so all-powerful could have had something taken from him without noticing. The only other option is that Raphael gave it up freely. And why would he do that?"

"I don't…" Ethan squeezed his eyelids shut. She was pressing him, guessing at scenarios that were turning out to be dreadfully true. And he'd never considered it, but had the archangel *purposefully* allowed Gazariel to steal the book?

"I think it's a test," Ethan finally said. "I don't know much, Tuesday. You have to believe that. I thought it was suspicious, too, after getting the command from Raphael to search for the book."

"But that could mean the angel might actually stand back and allow it all to happen. End-of-world stuff. Yeah?"

"I don't know about allowing things to go to completion," Ethan said. "I should hope not. But I don't know much about angels."

"Except that you take orders from any random angel that happens to request your services."

"He is an arch— Tuesday, we don't have time for this argument. Do you really want to do this now? Because it's not going to get us anywhere, and it will give Anyx more time to crack the code and enact the spell."

Frustration tightening her fists at her sides, Tuesday blew out a breath. Neither of them was helpless. They did have the power to stop this. Whatever *this* was.

"Fine. This whole adventure is fucked. Just like I knew it would be. But I'm with you. I promise. You got my back, I've got yours. Let's get to it. I can do blood magic, which is helpful if the code activation truly requires blood. And Gazariel is a blood demon. But I should go armed with supplies. Can I take a look around in the witch room and see what I can find?"

"I'll show you where it is." He held his hand out for her to take and she looked at it a moment. "I should have told you about Raphael from the start. But it wouldn't have changed things."

"I realize that. Maybe."

"I want things to be good between us, Tuesday. Don't block me out, please. We'll need to be strong and stand as one against whatever we next face. Can we do that?"

She slapped her hand into his firmly. "We can. And when this is over? I want to talk to that Richard of an archangel."

He pulled her to him. "When this is over we're going to talk about breaking your curse. For my sake."

"Why? Oh. Don't fall in love with me, Ethan. It won't end well for you."

And she strode off, but not before Ethan saw the tears forming at the corners of her eyes.

With CJ's permission, Ethan left Tuesday to ransack the Archives' witch room for whatever magical items she may need, then headed back to the clean room, where the demon was still caged.

He could not get the fact that Tuesday wasn't willing to tell him what could break her curse from his mind. Was it so much worse than having her heart ripped out? Nothing was worse than death.

The demon lifted his head as Ethan entered the room. Eying the base of the cage, Ethan verified that all the wards were lighting up the control panel. And he still wore the demonic wards on his hands. The wards on his throat would keep the demon from trying to trick useful information out of him.

The demon hooked his arms akimbo and inhaled deeply, expanding his chest. With a flip of hair over a shoulder, he asked, "You lied to her, didn't you?"

Ethan stepped up to meet the demon's blue gaze between the bars. "What do you think I lied about?"

"About releasing me."

"That wasn't a lie. Should we find the book, you're free to go. That is, if your girlfriend hasn't already tried to activate the code."

"My girlfriend? She was your wife first, vampire. You think I didn't know that? I could smell you on her. Wasn't sure what it was when I first fucked her, but since I've been in your presence?" The demon shuddered. "You are a part of her. Did you know about her weird and wicked obsession?"

"It's why she's no longer my wife. She's...troubled. And she needs to be contained."

Gazariel lifted an eyebrow. "Well then, it seems you've caged the wrong person. But isn't it like a man to want to imprison those females he can't understand?"

"You're a man, too."

"You think so? When I Fell I was neither one nor the other sex. Not much changed after becoming demon. And by giving Tuesday that hideous curse I found I could be either or. It's cute, the trick. Though I do prefer a dick to a clit. It's much more powerful, don't you think?"

"Apparently, you've never met Tuesday Knightsbridge. That's the most powerful clit I've ever met."

"Yes." Gazariel dragged his gaze up and down Ethan assessingly. "You love her. Poor fellow. You certainly won't survive through the night."

"You're an idiot. I've known her less than a week."

"Doesn't take more than a wink and a kiss to lose one's heart."

"You and I have chatted enough. The dark witches will be returning to bespell you. You'll lead us to Anyx."

The demon rolled his eyes. "I gave you her address."

"My team reports she's gone. The place was a shambles, as if she had no intention of returning."

"Bitch." The demon spat out a few words that Ethan assumed were demonic oaths. "She's really going to do it."

"Seems so."

"I need to get underground."

"We're all going underground in search of Anyx. But you have to do something for me."

"Something even more than being led around on

a leash for the shits and giggles of your merry men? What, pray tell, is that?"

"Promise me you'll take the curse from Tuesday. Give her the freedom to love that she deserves."

Gazariel lifted his hands and shrugged. "You really want me to rip out your girlfriend's heart? Okay, then."

"There's another way," Ethan insisted.

The demon approached the bars, and this time when he gripped them the electricity did not seem to bother him at all. Ethan again checked the steady LEDs to confirm the wards were activated.

"I've become conditioned to the pain," Gazariel said as he curled his fingers tightly about the bars and moved his face closer to Ethan's. His jaw was tense, but his expression remained calm. "You don't know what it is that will set my witch free from the curse, do you?"

"No."

"She wouldn't tell you? Because you did ask her about it. I know that much."

Much as he didn't want to admit his lacking trust with Tuesday to the demon, Ethan shook his head.

"It's not something I can give her, or even do for her," Gazariel said on a steady, deep tone. "You see, it's—"

"Ready to rock!" Savin and CJ wandered into the clean room. The reckoner punched a fight-ready fist into his palm. "Where's Tuesday?"

"I'm here!" The witch walked in and patted a leather bag she'd strapped across her chest. "Got all the accoutrements I'll need for a descent into the bowels of Paris to find a mad vampiress intent on destroying the world. And CJ has a bag of tricks as well." The dark witch patted his hip bag in proof. "Let's get the demon shackled and get on with this, yeah?"

Ethan glanced at Gazariel, who smirked at him as if to say "oh, well, now you'll never know the secret to freeing the witch from the curse."

"All right." Ethan stepped down from the platform. He'd learn the answer later, after they'd found Anyx. He would not set Gazariel free until he knew how to help Tuesday find love. "Can you bespell the demon without opening the cage doors and taking down the wards?"

"Of course." Certainly stepped forward, and with a hand held out for Tuesday, she clasped it and together the twosome began to work their magic.

Chapter 23

A witch generally avoided entering churches and cathedrals—for good reason—yet Tuesday was fascinated as she followed Ethan and CJ as they descended below Notre Dame two stories. Savin's contact had led them through the church basement, underground to a cold dark storage area, then had unlocked a vaulted door that had led into a cavernous blackness.

They'd quickly found a path. The walls were initially paneled with rotting wide boards, along which had been strung electrical cords—probably a good century old judging by the frayed cloth covering. As their footsteps tilted downward, the walls changed to limestone and the floors graduated from hard limestone to dirt.

Behind her, Savin and Gazariel brought up the tail. She didn't argue having the hulkingly handsome reckoner guarding her back. But the demon's presence tugged in her sigil.

By the seven sacred witches, why could she not simply tell Ethan how to break the curse? Revealing the truth wouldn't matter. It was not something he could do for her. And the way to break the curse was not something she could ever ask of another person. It simply wasn't done.

But giving him her truth suddenly felt important. If she told him, then she could move forward. Yeah?

"Bring Gazariel up front," Ethan called back.

As Savin shoved Gazariel past Tuesday, the demon waggled his tongue at her. The magic she and CJ had put on him kept him docile, and the blood compass they'd drawn on his chest would react to Anyx's presence. The demon didn't have to do a thing. They could read directions from the glowing diagram drawn in his own sticky black blood on his chest.

The crew waited, staring at Gazariel's chest, and were rewarded almost immediately with a flash of blue light.

"South," Ethan said, and he turned to lead them down a narrow aisle carved from limestone. Here and there an old section of wooden paneling and some ancient electrical wires were nailed to the wall. Chalk symbols marked by previous explorers were either signs of direction or made-up nonsense, maybe even cataphile gang symbols as Ethan suggested.

Parisian cataphiles were a fascinating subculture. Tuesday knew the crazy compulsion to explore the underside of Paris had existed for centuries. Actually, for as long as the city had existed. Daring cave spelunkers held underground parties and challenged themselves to find new, unexplored and extremely dangerous sections of the labyrinths. The catacombs spread all under Paris and in some areas as far down as seven stories.

When they'd been waiting for Savin's contact to find the right keys, Ethan had mentioned the legend of the vampiress who had been cursed by an angry lover in the eighteenth century. The lover had a witch bespell the vampiress frozen and put her in a glass coffin. She couldn't move her body, but she had remained conscious, always aware of what was going on around her. They placed the coffin somewhere in these very labyrinths. She had been found by a man who truly loved her decades ago. Needless to say, she'd gone mad during those centuries of suspended animation, and still struggled with sanity. It was a long and interesting story that Tuesday would have loved to hear more about.

While she wasn't much for spelunking, she wasn't afraid of the closed confines or the darkness. She had pulled on a white light upon entering and now vacillated whether or not to expend some magic to light up the ground with an illumination spell. There were patches of wet on the uneven limestone and dirt surface and she'd not worn shoes for hiking. Her boots had three-inch heels, and she could run in them, but forget navigating the bumpy surface with any skill. But she didn't know if they would find Anyx, and if so, how much magic she would require to stop the woman if she intended to activate the spell, so she holstered any nervous desire to use the magic for the time being and wobbled onward.

Gazariel walked ahead of them all, turning on occasion so Ethan could view the glowing map on his chest. The demon wasn't tied up, but CJ and Tuesday had put a heavy shackle on him. He was connected to her through the sigil, and much like the bonding spell CJ had cast on she and Ethan, Gazariel had to stay close, within the magic's range. And they'd wrangled as much of his demonic magic as possible. He was pouting, and every so often Tuesday felt the tug when she lollygagged behind.

If it wasn't a vampire leading her around Paris, it was a pouting demon tugging her deeper into the underground.

Gazariel actually deserved a good pout. Poor spoiled prince of vanity. Couldn't get the vampiress to love him so he had risked sacrificing the world to win that love?

Tuesday was able to stop herself from giving him a comforting hug, though.

They may need Gazariel to talk to Anyx. They may also have to use blood magic should the code already be activated. And that may require a lot of blood. From the same source. And they hadn't discussed exactly who that source would be.

By the blessed goddess, she prayed the vampiress had not the smarts to figure out the code from that book. A notebook in which some muse had scribbled down angel names and sigils? How irresponsible to put such to paper. On the other hand, that book had been in the care of an archangel. And now it was not. Superirresponsible. Didn't angels have their shit together enough to keep an eye on one very dangerous book?

Tuesday would give the asshole Raphael a piece of her mind. This whole experience was one big clusterfuck.

On the other hand, this adventure had introduced her to Ethan Pierce. And she wasn't going to begrudge that happy side effect.

The men leading their merry gang stopped walking.

Ethan turned and looked to her and Savin, cupping a hand around his ear as a signal that they listen.

Gazariel stretched out an arm to indicate they should continue walking. "What are we—?" Savin hushed him.

Ethan glanced at the glowing sigil on the demon's chest and then nodded toward the end of the pathway, where the faintest glimmer of golden light flickered. The scent of flame mingled with the dusty dry limestone.

"Is it her?" Tuesday asked the demon.

Gazariel listened, swore, then nodded. He strode away from the front of the line.

"Onward," Ethan announced and took up the pace.

When he reached a T-turn, he stopped without going around the corner toward the light. Tuesday walked up to him and he slipped his hand into hers. "Listen," he said. They both listened to what the vampiress was saying just around the corner.

Tuesday didn't have to eavesdrop for long, or even understand the meaning of the words. The vampiress's tone and cadence made her heart drop in her chest. "She's chanting an invocation. She's cracked the code, Ethan. She's begun the spell."

"We need to move now." Ethan pulled a stake from his thigh holster, surprising Tuesday that he would wield such a thing. He nodded to CJ, who confirmed the command to move. "Get the demon up here."

Savin shoved Gazariel up toward the turn.

"What the hell do you want me to do?" Gazariel said in a tight whisper. "Did you see the scratches on my face? I'm not her favorite person at the moment."

"Talk her down. Get her to stop speaking the spell," Ethan said. "Or she dies."

"With that?" The demon snapped a finger against the stake Ethan held. "That's not going to scare her. She's been staked once before. Survived."

Savin gaped. Tuesday knew it was possible for a vampire to survive a staking if he left the stake in and allowed it to slowly work its way out of the body while it healed. Not a fast process, or, she imagined, painless.

"Then we'll use magic," CJ offered. "Get in there now, Gazariel. She's speaking the spell. We can't let her advance to a final declaration to open the very heavens Above."

The demon stood firm.

So Ethan tugged out a blade from a holster at his back hip and flashed it before Gazariel's face.

"Is that...?" Gazariel swallowed. "A Sinistari blade? Are you kidding me?"

"Does it look like I'm kidding?" Ethan asked.

With a sigh of resignation, the demon led the way into a vast chamber that was lit with dozens of black candles. Flames flickered wild crimson flashes on the stone floor and walls. A dais toward the back of the limestone chamber revealed Anyx standing with her back to them, her arms spread wide. Silver jewelry glinted in her hair and at her wrists and waist. She wore a black sheath and no shoes. All around her a circle of candles flickered. And a dark liquid glinted in the pentacle drawn within that circle.

"Blood," Tuesday said as she recognized the ceremony. Where she'd gotten so much blood—the chick was a vampire. Stupid to even wonder.

Ethan joined Gazariel, who stood stymied by the scene. They didn't walk up to Anyx because a shallow trench about three feet wide and flowing with water dissected them from her.

Tuesday gestured to the flames flickering on the water. "A repulsion spell," she said to the men. "If you cross the water, even try to leap over it, you'll go up in flames."

"Defeat it," Ethan commanded her.

Not at all miffed that he'd sharply ordered her to do something, Tuesday spread her arms wide and chanted a suppression spell. There was no spell a vampiress could enact that she, a witch, could not counter.

Meanwhile Gazariel, nudged on by the threat of Ethan's blade, called, "Anyx! Come on, sweetie, let's not destroy the world today. I really like having humans around. Who's going to make my favorite filet mignon if they are all dead? And who's going to feed you, huh? Have you thought about that? You'll starve, bitch!"

The vampiress paused in her chanting, tilted her head, but did not turn to them. She was smart. If she paused the spell too long, it would dissipate.

A sweep of Tuesday's hand and the utterance *"Deflagro!"* snuffed the flames on the water. With an all-clear nod from her, Ethan jumped across, followed by Savin. Gazariel stayed put.

"So much power," Anyx called. "I must own it!" Now she turned, and with an elegant spread of her arms out from her sides and a curl of her fingers, she announced, *"Sarax conti expulsius!"*

The stone walls shuddered. Dust spumed from cracks, increasing the dry perfumed air. Ethan looked to Tuesday. She wasn't positive, but those could have been the final words to activate the spell. When the blood surrounding the vampiress began to bubble, then she was sure.

"That was it," she said.

"The code?" Ethan asked.

"Yeah, I'm not one-hundred-percent sure of the words, but I'm pretty sure they can be interpreted as 'open sesame, let the angels all fall down.' Get her out of that circle!" Tuesday turned and CJ already stood beside her. "We've got to penetrate her casting circle and strangle the spell."

Anyx shouted over her shoulder at Gazariel, "You were nothing more than a tool, you idiot demon!" And then she turned around completely. Elegant black hair, heavy like oil, spilled down her back. Eyes decorated with kohl glimmered with red. A visible red aura, much thicker than a vampire's usual aura, floated about her body. She was a part of the spell. It was her blood flowing in the water. Her scanning gaze stopped on the approaching vampire. "Ethan?"

Tuesday felt the intensity of the spell falter. The vampiress had to hold her focus to keep it going. If she was suddenly reunited with her ex? Fuck, she really didn't want to do this, but— "Go to her, Ethan!"

Stake held at the ready, Ethan approached the circle.

"It's really you? I've missed you, Ethan." Anyx took a step forward. Then, realizing she neared the edge of the circle, she stopped. Arms stretched out, she unfolded her fingers toward him. "Come to me. We can be together in the new world I am creating."

"Really?" Tuesday heard Gazariel mutter behind her.

"Anyx, you can't do this," Ethan said.

Tuesday and CJ quickly drew a circle on the limestone floor with black chalk before the flowing stream.

A channel cut through the rock from the stream to the dais, which was exactly what they needed. CJ flung out herbs and crushed troll hearts and recited a powerful cleansing spell.

Tuesday drew out the athame and looked at her wrist. Blood was needed.

"A whole freakin' lot of it," she muttered, feeling her heart fall to her gut. They needed as much blood as had already been spilled to counteract the spell.

This had become a no-return mission, and she was not happy about that. Because hey, she'd kind of thought that finding love would be a good thing. Like it was time to give it a go. And she'd found a man she wanted to risk that chance on.

Too late for regrets now. She wouldn't ask anyone else to do this. The magic in her veins was powerful and dark. Strong enough to subdue a spell a mere vampiress had cast.

Tuesday closed her eyes. "Fuck. Really?" The cut of the blade against her wrist did not yet pain her because she hadn't pressed deeply. If there was any other option, she wanted to hear it. Right now.

Five feet away from her, Anyx and Ethan had taken to arguing. He was trying to move her out of the casting circle but it continued to repulse him every time he tried to breach it with a stab of the wood stake.

"Gazariel!" Tuesday snapped her fingers. "Help him!"

With a heavy sigh, the demon leaped across the stream and started an argument with Anyx over her fickle ways. But when he mentioned her inability to come because she was a frigid bitch, she snarled and turned to face the dais again. One shout from the angered vampiress again ignited the flames in the stream.

CJ hissed, as he was nearly burned, and then jumped inside the circle with Tuesday.

"We ready?" he asked her.

"I'll provide the blood," she said.

He looked at her then, knowing what the sacrifice would mean. They'd not discussed who would do this. Because it wasn't something a witch on a suicide mission would discuss. They'd wait until the last minute and hope upon hope it wouldn't be necessary.

"You sure?" CJ asked. "Maybe we should give Ethan a moment to see if he can get her out of the circle."

"Not going to happen. And we're all out of moments. We have to do this now." And as if on cue, the stone walls rumbled and the stream spat up fire. Tuesday pressed the athame tight over her wrist. "It's going to take a while to bleed out."

"No!"

Tuesday ignored Ethan's sudden shout. Bits of limestone began to rain from the cavern ceiling. It was now or never.

Tuesday drew the blade over her skin, but it didn't cut deeply because Ethan grabbed her by the shoulder and shoved her out of the circle. The vampire caught the athame as she dropped it. Tuesday landed hard on the stone floor. And she looked up to see Ethan draw the blade across his carotid. Blood spurted and he bowed over the circle as CJ directed.

"No!" she cried.

It was too late. She had been pushed outside the circle and Ethan's blood had conjured up a seal. She couldn't enter it if she tried.

Her lover dropped to the floor and stretched out his

hand to her. She could not touch him. What the hell was he doing?

She crawled up to the circle. "I wish you hadn't done this. I won't let you bleed out. I can't. There's enough blood, yes, Certainly?"

The dark witch shook his head. "We need so much."

Tuesday bowed her head. She would lose the one person she had just realized she cared about most. It wasn't fair. Ethan was already growing weak from blood loss. His eyelids shuttered. The hand he held extended, dropped limply onto the stone floor.

"Help me!" CJ called as he began the chant that would shut off the Final Days spell.

Though her heart had just broken and shattered, Tuesday nodded and crawled forward. Compelled to stop an evil that could harm so many more, she spread out her palms, embracing the circle and sending energy through her being. She matched CJ's tone with her own rhythmic chants.

Out the corner of her eye she saw the vampiress dash toward the entrance. Gazariel called to the reckoner to go after her and Savin did so.

And from behind her Gazariel suddenly let out an ear-shattering cry that harkened to the angels, who spoke in myriad tongues to mimic all the beasts on the planet.

Tuesday's chest suddenly burned as if the fire had leaped from the nearby stream to singe her. She struggled to concentrate, to focus her vibrations toward the circle and her dying lover. Ethan now barely supported himself. His blood streamed toward the fire. When it touched the flames, they flashed brilliant white and danced up the channel toward the dais.

The fire in her chest was unbearable. Tuesday screamed. The magic she put out suddenly left her in one final gushing effort. In the circle, CJ managed to capture that magic and directed it toward the dais, where the magic ball splashed into violet flames.

The limestone walls ceased shuddering.

CJ dropped to his knees over Ethan.

And Tuesday fell backward, yet landed in Gazariel's arms.

Chapter 24

The demon bowed over Tuesday, inspected her face and smoothed the hair away from her eyes. "The vampire did it," he said in amazement. "He broke the curse."

"The Final Days?" she murmured weakly.

"Well, that, too. I think. We won't know until we go topside and see if all the tourists are flambéed, eh? But, Tuesday, the curse you've carried for centuries—it's gone. Didn't you feel it? I certainly did."

She slapped a palm to her chest, where the sigil had burned so viciously she'd felt as though her insides would sizzle. "But…"

"A true love willing to die for you." Gazariel spoke the means to breaking the spell. "He sacrificed for you, witch. And I am also clean now. That damn curse is completely erased!"

"But that means… Ethan!" She shoved out of Gazariel's arms and scrambled toward the circle, where CJ now stood over the fallen vampire. The dark witch stepped out and jumped across the stream to inspect the dais.

The vampire was lying on his back, arms splayed, eyes wide, his mouth open and the blood continuing to pour from his carotid. Tuesday slapped her palm to the open wound. Blood spurted. She summoned a healing incantation, but it sputtered and merely sprinkled over Ethan's neck. She'd depleted her magic to stop the Final Days.

"CJ, help me! I have to stop the bleeding or he'll die."

The dark witch returned to the circle, which was no longer necessary to keep closed, and kneeled beside her. "I think he's already dead."

"No!" She took the dark witch's hand and pressed it over the wound on Ethan's neck. "Recite the blessing for a vampire's everlasting life."

They did so together while the demon stalked around them, observing. Such a blessing was a powerful invocation that a witch could perform for a vampire, granting him immortality that even a stake or beheading would find difficult to overcome. It was rarely used. And only the most powerful witches could summon such a thing.

After minutes of desperate chanting CJ tugged his hand away from Ethan's neck. "It's not working. We've both depleted our magic. If anything might work—he needs blood. That's a vampire's best hope for survival."

"Then he'll have it." Tuesday searched for the athame and found it tucked under Ethan's leg. Without a second thought, she drew it across her wrist and pressed it to Ethan's mouth. "Come on, Ethan! Don't leave me now!"

He didn't move, so she had to press her wrist tight against his mouth. He didn't swallow.

"Sit him upright," CJ directed Gazariel. "Help me!"

"I'm rather of the mind to get the hell out of here," the demon said.

Tuesday hissed at the demon. "I saved you from being consigned to Daemonia. You will help. Now!"

Begrudgingly, Gazariel helped CJ set Ethan upright so the blood would flow down his throat. It took a while, but after a few minutes Tuesday saw his Adam's apple pulse. He had swallowed. And she was growing distinctly weaker. She'd expelled so much magic that even a little blood loss was not going to keep her upright for long.

Her eyelids fluttered.

"You can't do this," CJ said. "We need another donor."

"You," Gazariel said to the dark witch.

CJ tapped a tattoo on his neck. "Can't. I'm warded against vamps. If he drinks my blood it'll kill him for sure."

"He's warded against demons, too," Gazariel said with a nod toward Ethan's throat.

"We need the vampiress. Go get her!" Tuesday commanded the demon.

"Seriously?"

Tuesday wanted to argue with the obstinate demon, but it was all she could do to keep her eyelids open and her focus on Ethan. He was swallowing now, and that was a good sign.

But with a flutter of her eyelids, she passed out.

Tuesday came to and the first thing she saw was her vampire lover embracing his ex-wife. He held Anyx's slender body to his chest and gripped her head to hold it aside as he supped at her neck. His hand caressed her breast where the thin black sheath had slid aside to expose the nipple, and she moaned in ecstasy. And Ethan increased his efforts, drinking from her. Taking from her. Enjoying her. Rubbing her nipple to give her pleasure.

That was not a life-saving moment. It was a graphic display of sexual desire.

Backing away on the limestone floor, Tuesday's back hit a wall. Someone grasped her hand and helped her to stand. "You okay?"

"No," she said to CJ. And she wasn't. Her head felt as if someone was stirring her brains with a spatula. And her chest might explode if she did not— "I need air. I have to get out of here. Now."

Turning, she crept out of the chamber in the direction they had come. No one followed her blood-drained wobbling pace. CJ would stay behind and keep an eye on Ethan. She hadn't recalled seeing either Gazariel or Savin in the chamber. Only the two ex-lovers entwined in a disgustingly sensual embrace.

Vampires did not have to hold their donors so... intimately. Taking blood could be functional and discreet. They couldn't have been closer if they had climbed inside one another. She didn't want to think about it. She wanted to erase that image from her brain.

Stumbling blindly forth, Tuesday entered a dark tunnel and summoned a glow of light on her palm. It sputtered. She was weak. She needed rest and to heal. To restore after the tremendous expulsion of magic and blood. She'd given Ethan her blood to save him.

But what had she saved him for? A grand reunion with his former wife.

Noticing the strong coppery smell from the old electrical wires that had greeted her upon descent into the catacombs, she knew the surface must be close and raced forward. And there by the old wood door that led into the bowels of the church above, stood Gazariel.

"I need to get out of here." She pushed past the demon, but he gripped her wrists. She did not bleed anymore and stopping movement now brought the woozy dizziness up again. Standing still was impossible. Her world wobbled. Or did she?

"You're weak, witch. You need rest."

"I will. But I need air now!" She faltered.

Gazariel lifted her into his arms and carried her up and through the ancient church basement. It was well into the morning hours, so the church was closed to tourists and their exit was not observed.

Finally, fresh cold air smacked Tuesday's face. It was still dark, yet the moon beamed across her face. As if blinded by a desert sun, Tuesday closed her eyes.

"Where should I take you?"

"Away from here," she murmured, then passed out.

Ethan emerged from below Notre Dame and staggered across the street from the church to sit on the sidewalk before a closed souvenir shop. Behind him CJ filed out and stretched his arms. The book containing the Final Days code was tucked in his waistband. Savin was carrying up Anyx—whom CJ had bound with magic, though she was nearly drained of blood not only from him but from the spell. She may or may not survive. He didn't care.

Tuesday and Gazariel had not been below when Ethan had finally ceased drinking from Anyx. He'd pulled away from her neck, swallowed the last hot gulp and had felt himself again. He'd touched death while lying in the circle. Hell, he must have briefly died. But Tuesday's blood had lifted him from that abyss. He'd felt it trickle down his throat as if a cool, clean elixir. And yet, he'd held back from taking too much from her. He hadn't been willing to take her life to save his own. Better to die than to take Tuesday along with him. She'd done nothing to deserve death. It had been he who had forced her into this nightmare.

When someone had dropped an unconscious Anyx before him, he'd dove in, knowing he could take enough blood from her—and not caring for the outcome. He'd fed on her viciously, yet the blood lust had spurred his desires. He hated that feeling, yet it had saved his life.

A heavy sweep of wings preceded the sudden appearance of Gazariel by his side. The demon kneeled beside Ethan, and gazed skyward. "Morning soon."

"Where is she?" Ethan could only manage to whisper the question. He was exhausted. He needed rest to fully recover.

"She wanted to get away from you."

Why would she…? And then he remembered seeing Tuesday shuffle across the chamber floor. The look in her eyes had not been of horror, but rather…betrayal. She'd watched him drink from Anyx. But she couldn't have believed that meant anything to him beyond sustenance.

Of course she had. He had seen it plainly in her tearing blue gaze.

"I took her to the airport," Gazariel said. "My witch is free of the curse. You broke the spell."

"I—I did?"

Gazariel chuckled. "She never did tell you what would do it, did she?"

He shook his head.

"It's something she has known since the day I placed the curse in her. A true love had to be willing to sacrifice his life for her. And...her true love did." The demon winked.

"True love? But I thought..." Ethan blinked, sorting out the few details he'd learned about Tuesday's dark curse. "If she couldn't have love, then how...?"

"Oh, someone could fall in love with her. Just, the moment the guy realized it, or she did, then all goes to Beneath. Apparently, her true love realized how much he did love her only in that moment before it would have went to hell. You pulled through by the skin of your teeth. Good going, vampire."

Gazariel stood. With a sweep of wings, he misted into black smoke and was gone.

Ethan closed his eyes. He was thankful Tuesday had been freed of the curse. And because of love?

"Yes." He did love her. And perhaps he had only realized it that moment he'd dove to push her out of the circle so she would not die to stop the curse.

And now?

"I need to get to the airport."

Chapter 25

CJ directed Savin to bring the vampiress to head-quarters, where she would be contained. The Council would decide what to do with a vampiress who would see fit to bring an end to the world.

He told the reckoner he'd be close behind, but needed to do something first. Rather, he needed to follow the whisper that had not ceased since he'd stepped out of the church. It was a disembodied voice that he suspected only he could hear. And it was close.

Wandering across the street and toward the gated garden behind the grand church, CJ slipped through the thick shrubbery and into the quiet privacy of a small yet groomed garden that saw many tourists during the day. Now he was alone. The whisper lured him toward a bench that faced the back of the church, before a view of the flying buttresses and the massive iron cross that tipped the church.

CJ did not recognize the man who sat on the bench. He was tall, appeared slender and was dressed in a smart brown-and-black pinstriped suit. His palm was propped on the top of a straight black cane, which looked more accessory than necessity. He didn't look at CJ; his stare seemed fixed on the cross atop the church.

"Give me the book," the stranger said.

And hearing the voice, which sounded like a mix of all the accents of the world, yet was clear and precise, and so *ethereal*, CJ knew who the creature was on the bench. Ethan had mentioned who had sent him on this mission.

CJ tugged the book from his waistband and clutched it tightly to his chest. "You didn't do such a good job holding onto it the first time."

"Give it."

"No."

The book flew into the angel Raphael's hands. And now he met CJ's gaze with eyes that were all colors and glowed with a depth that CJ thought surely he could fall into and never land. And that wasn't a romantic notion; it was a deep and abiding fear that tightened the skin all over his body and closed up his throat.

"I was having a little fun," the angel admitted. "We do things like that every now and a thousand years or so. Ta."

And with a massive swoop of wings that lifted the hair around CJ's face, the angel disappeared.

And CJ dropped to his knees, utterly relieved, pissed, and thankful to be alive.

This time, Tuesday crossed through security without once looking back. Determination held her head high. Her flight left in forty-five minutes. As she waited for a little boy ahead of her to put on his tennis shoes, she grabbed her coat from the conveyor belt and pulled it on. Slipping into her ankle boots, she frowned at the dusty dried mud from the catacombs on them. It was time to get the hell out of Paris.

With a toss of her hair over a shoulder, she wandered forward. Her gate was to the left, and she— All of a sudden, she stopped at the junction of the turn and stood there, allowing the world to swish by her on all sides as if sped up on a security tape.

Time seemed to stop and voices were muffled. Clothing brushed past her. The stifling inner air ceased to bother. Her heartbeats thudded to recall what Gazariel had said to her.

True love had broken the curse.

But if so, then how had he been capable of holding his ex-wife like that? Was she wrong to think that moment in the catacombs had meant something to Ethan? His love for her *had to* be true to break the spell. Or had it dissolved as quickly as his ex-wife's blood had entered his system?

She'd been starting to have fun with Ethan Pierce. And yes, she may have even begun to love him. Or at least, leave a hopeful door open that she'd recognize it if it was love.

But all for nothing, apparently.

And yet… "I really did fall in love." Her throat tightened. Tears threatened.

So when someone turned her around and pulled her into an embrace to kiss her, Tuesday beat at the man's shoulder and kicked him on the shin in defense. When she saw it was Ethan, wincing as he bent up his injured leg, she gasped.

"Sorry," he said. "I shouldn't have surprised you like that. That was a Richard move. But I love you, Tuesday. You can't leave me. Not like this."

She slammed her arms across her chest and lifted her chin. "What about your wife?"

"You mean my ex-wife, who has been taken into custody to stand trial for reckless acts against humankind?"

"But I saw you." She squeezed a fist, hoping to staunch the tears, but they dropped down her cheeks. "You were holding her so tightly. Caressing her. I saw you stroke her…" She couldn't say it. It hurt too much to think of right now.

"I was taking her blood, Tuesday. And yes, I experienced a moment of sexual satisfaction. I'm a vampire. Drinking blood turns me on. But ultimately drinking Anyx's blood was a means to stay alive. Tuesday, please." He took her hands. "She means nothing to me."

"She's the one who saved your life."

"Not without your help. And your curse." He pressed his palm to her chest, right over her heart.

Tears spilled down Tuesday's cheeks as she struggled against throwing herself into his arms. "You've taken the curse from me. The sigil is gone."

"Gazariel said as much. It's true." He bowed his head to hers and tilted up her chin with a finger. "I love you, Tuesday. Truly. Deeply. Insanely. Not like the false, surface love you accused Gazariel of experiencing. I love you on a soul level. I can feel it in my blood, my bones and my spirit."

She gasped.

"And if you get on that plane and leave me I'm not sure what I'll do."

"You'd survive," she said simply. "We all do."

"But I don't want to survive without you. I know it's a lot to ask. And you have a home in Boston. But would you stay with me? Just a while longer? Please, Tuesday." His breath hushed against her ear. "I love you. I need you to believe me. I. Love. You."

The words felt true. They *were* true. Because if they were not, she would not recognize that right now. She'd still bear the curse and they might be standing in a desolate wasteland covered with the ashes of humans and angels alike.

The curse was gone. She could be loved. And…she was.

By the seven sacred witches, she really was.

"This is the second time I've come back to this airport intent on leaving."

"I don't think you're meant to leave." He smiled against her cheek then kissed it. "Not yet, anyway. Not until we've talked about us. You helped me to stop the Final Days. We've been through a lot. We've both literally walked through fire. Don't walk away from us now."

Us. Yeah, the word felt right. For now? For maybe a little longer. Together. Sharing their lives. She wanted to embrace that, to own it.

"I love you, too," she said. "I think I've known it for days."

She hugged him and tilted her head against his shoulder. She was tired and weak and, hell yes, she loved this man. Of course, he'd only been taking blood from Anyx to survive. And his honesty about how it had felt meant a lot to her.

"Take me home," she said to him. "Your home."

Epilogue

A year later...

Tuesday dusted a long rosewood shelf lined with sea-shells of all shapes, sizes and colors. She could hear the ocean echo out at her, and wasn't at all surprised when a tiny giggle sounded from within the spiral of a nautilus shell. With a bounce to her step, she moved on to the next shelf, where a triton fashioned of more shells and some kind of metal that gleamed green was kept under glass.

This was the mermaid room in the Archives, and she'd been assigned to tidy it up today. And tomorrow. And for however long it took to clean the small and crowded room.

Certainly Jones had offered her the job after she'd decided to stay in Paris with Ethan a year ago. They'd gone back to his place from the airport, talked and... had a lot of hex. Blood-bone-spirit sex. Soul-deep stuff. They were really in love. And that was something neither of them had felt in a long time.

They'd wanted to ride that feeling and follow it wherever it would lead them, so she'd made a quick trip home to Boston, had rented out her property for an indefinite period of time and packed up her clothes and magical accoutrements. Now Ethan's place was a bit more untidy and he'd had to relegate three quarters of his closet to her wardrobe. And Stuart now answered to her commands, as well as Ethan's.

And every morning Ethan either woke her with croissants and orange juice, or left them on the counter because he'd gone in to work and hadn't wanted to wake her. She'd never felt happier.

With the curse completely gone it was now easy to recognize love. Small things, such as the sun shining on this snowy February morning, had lifted her smile and given her a bounce to her step as she walked to work. She had a purpose now, and a fantastic lover.

Life was about as fabulous as it could get.

Bending to inspect a glass container filled with some kind of sparkling jewels, Tuesday realized the thin diamond-shaped items with one curved edge were possibly mermaid scales. Cool. She'd never in her lifetime met a mermaid, and wasn't sure she wanted to. They were supposed to be vicious.

When a man's hands suddenly covered her eyes from behind, she sprang upright. She hadn't heard anyone come in. And Certainly Jones, her boss, would never do such a thing. So...

"Is it lunchtime already?" she asked with hope.

"I'm a little late." Ethan leaned in and kissed the side of her neck, sending a visceral shiver over her skin. "Had some business to deal with. Can we have a quickie?"

"Did you lock the door?"

"Always." His hand slipped around her waist and glided under her gray T-shirt that snarkily declared in block letters Don't Be A Richard.

Lunchtime sex had become a norm, and they were pretty sure no one was aware of their stolen liaisons. CJ would say something if he knew. That witch was a stickler about work ethic and protocol. So they were careful, but never quiet.

"I missed you," he said, turning her around to face him.

"It's been three hours since we drove here together from home."

"Three hours too long. I'm going to have to bite you again, and soon."

Their blood connection lasted about twenty-four to forty-eight hours. The shared sexual gratification that developed with a bite gave them the ability to hear one another's thoughts and to feel their emotions and sexual sensations. Love was a wondrous emotion that shimmered off Ethan like a warm summer sun. And yes, when they argued they could feel one another's anger, even fear, but that made the need to make up quicker. And they never quarreled much.

Tuesday tapped her neck. "Right here, big boy."

The vampire pierced her neck with his fangs, and while he did so, he slid down her leggings and she unzipped his fly. Behind her rose a nineteenth-century desk that he set her on as he licked at her blood.

Tuesday moaned as he slid his erection inside her and

pumped slowly yet deeply. She enjoyed when they went at it fast and furious, but even more so when he prolonged every move, seeming to luxuriate in the depths of her.

"I've got another job you might be interested in," he said.

"For Acquisitions?" She had helped him with one case regarding retrieving a grimoire from a crone a few months ago. All it had required was some sweet talk and a commitment to drinking the bitch under the table. Tuesday would never touch moss liqueur again. Oh, the hangover! "Does it involve another washed-up crone?"

"Faeries."

"Why me?"

He shrugged and licked her neck to seal the wound. He thrust inside her still. "It's a magic thing. Faeries are trafficking in humans, accept without the usual changeling to replace the stolen baby."

"And why, exactly, does Acquisitions need to get involved? What do you need to acquire, Monsieur Director? And would you tell me if an angel were using us as pawns in his stupid game of playing with the inhabitants of the mortal realm again?"

"I would tell you, and Raphael has not been seen or heard of since his selfish ploy. Did I tell you the book with the Final Days code suddenly appeared on a shelf in the angel room a few weeks after our adventure?"

She gripped his ass, pulling him deep into her. "You did not. But good to know. I hope it's chained, warded and bespelled to Kingdom Come. Mmm, lover, pull out and slip your cock over my clit. Yes. Like that." She bowed forward, putting her forehead to his shoulder.

"The faery thing will be fun for us," he said. "Maybe?"

She knew that tone. He was diving in to adventure once again. For a man who had worked a desk job for so long, he'd been taking on more jobs himself. And fieldwork suited him. As it did her.

"I do like trying new things," she said. Grinding her body against his erection, she mined the humming orgasm that whispered up to her core. "You think we'll ever get back to America?"

"Do you want to return?"

"It does carry memory of a lot of good times."

"Like witch hunts and torture?"

"Yes, Richard, just like that. You know me too well."

He hilted himself inside her, and that was all it took to fly. Tuesday's head fell back and she pulled her lover down to bite through her shirt at her breast. He didn't break skin. They'd save that for later.

"I'd like to keep the witch in Paris for a while," he said as he watched her face move through the joy and elation of orgasm. "Deal?"

She pulled herself back up to stare into his eyes. "You do have a lot to offer a witch who has been without love for centuries. Deal."

* * * * *

Author's Note

I hope you enjoyed Ethan and Tuesday's story. Ethan had brief appearances in *HER WEREWOLF HERO*, and *THE VAMPIRE'S PROTECTOR*. If you're interested in learning about some of the secondary characters mentioned in this story, you can find them at your favorite online retailer.

Cinder's story is *PLAYING WITH FIRE*.

CJ's story is *THIS WICKED MAGIC*.

Ed and Tamatha's story is *CAPTIVATING THE WITCH*.

Thomas briefly appeared in *BEYOND THE MOON*.

And if you're curious about the vampiress imprisoned in the glass coffin that story is *SEDUCING THE VAMPIRE*.

Watch for *THE BILLIONAIRE WEREWOLF'S PRINCESS* coming soon! And Savin Thorne's story will be out in the fall of 2018.

LET'S TALK
Romance

For exclusive extracts, competitions
and special offers, find us online:

f facebook.com/millsandboon

◉ @millsandboonuk

𝕏 @millsandboon

Or get in touch on 0844 844 1351*

For all the latest titles coming soon, visit
millsandboon.co.uk/nextmonth